ECHOES

MARISSA LETE

Echoes
Book 1 of the Echoes Trilogy

Copyright © 2021 by Marissa Lete
All rights reserved.

No part of this publication may be reproduced, distributed, or transmitted in any form or by any means, including photocopying, recording, or other electronic or mechanical methods, without the prior written permission of the publisher, except in the case of brief quotations embodied in critical reviews and certain other noncommercial uses permitted by copyright law.

This is a work of fiction. Names, characters, businesses, places, events, locales, and incidents are either the products of the author's imagination or used in a fictitious manner. Any resemblance to actual persons, living or dead, or actual events is purely coincidental.

ISBN: 978-1-957204-00-0 (paperback)
ISBN: 978-1-957204-01-7 (hardcover)
ISBN: 978-1-957204-02-4 (e-book)

Cover art by Donn Marlou Ramirez
Cover Copy created by BlurbWriter.com

www.MarissaLete.com

For Briana,

The first one to believe in me and my writing

BOOK ONE

CHAPTER 1

WHEN THE BELL RINGS to let the students of St. Martin High School know that it's time to head to class, I sigh in relief. Within seconds, the noise around me dulls. Students say goodbye to each other, then head in different directions to their classrooms, and as they leave, the once stifling, endless stream of sound fades. The sounds of this year, last year, and the years before that, all piled up in one room where teenagers are constantly talking over each other can get *really* loud.

I would know because I can hear it all.

And that's why, when the last bell rings to indicate the start of class and the first thing I hear is Mrs. Andrews telling everyone to turn in their research papers at her desk, I start to panic.

Research paper? The one I hadn't even started working on yet because the due date—I'd thought—was still two weeks away? Did I accidentally get the date mixed up with something else?

My head shoots up from where I'd been resting it on the desk, and I glance around the room in a moment of confusion as the sound of papers shuffling fills the air. But, I realize with a sigh of relief, no one in the classroom has moved. In fact, Mrs. Andrews is still sitting at her desk, pulling up today's presentation on the projector.

I'd misheard. The research paper in question isn't from today's class, it's from last year's. What I'd heard was just an echo—a sound from the past—and I hadn't been paying enough attention to recognize the distinction.

Mrs. Andrews gets up from her desk. "Good morning, everyone!" Her voice is just as cheery as last year's, but this one, I can assure, is definitely from the present. Her past voice continues speaking, too, but I try to ignore it, focusing on the present version of her as she introduces the lesson. At least, until my best friend distracts me.

"I went to a party," Grace whispers to me from the seat on my left, a look on her face that tells me all I need to know about this supposed "party": it wasn't good.

I raise an eyebrow, questioning. "You did?"

"Well, *Andy* went to the party, without telling me, and got drunk and ended up fracturing his wrist. I had to go get him." Her lips purse in frustration.

I scowl. "What do you mean, you had to go get him?"

"It was—"

"Laura and Grace? Do you have something to add?" We both turn our heads towards Mrs. Andrews, who is glaring at us in annoyance. As the room quiets, I hear her voice from last year explaining the lab the class was going to do that day, and behind it, barely audible is the low timbre of the male teacher from two years ago mumbling something to his class. I'm pretty sure the guy never took a public speaking class because no matter how hard I try to listen to his lessons, I can never make out any of the words. Which, in retrospect, is kind of nice, because it means I have less noise to ignore when I need to focus on the present.

"No, sorry," Grace says, looking down at our shared desk a little sheepishly. Mrs. Andrews gives us a stern look before going back to teaching, and an awkward feeling spreads through the room as our classmates share glances at one another, then look back at us.

When Mrs. Andrews isn't looking, I roll my eyes in Grace's direction; it's not like we were being *that* loud. Mrs. Andrews just has it in for Grace, most likely because Grace is well known for being one of the chattiest students in the school. She might have tried to separate us, except early on, Mrs. Andrews learned that it doesn't matter who Grace sits next to—she'll talk to anyone. Putting Grace next to me was her last, exasperated effort to quiet the unruly student. Which, in theory, was a nice plan, since my reputation of being "the quiet one" usually meant that anyone around me stayed pretty quiet, too. Except Mrs. Andrews didn't know that Grace is my best friend, one of the few people in the school I actually *do* talk to.

Surprisingly, for the rest of the period, Grace manages to hold her tongue. While she's busy trying to keep her lips sealed, I just listen to everything. As is the case with any classroom I'm in, there are a lot of echoes: students talking to each other, equipment moving, Mrs. Andrews helping with the lab from last year. Fortunately, the sounds of the past are generally quieter than the present ones, fading like an echo bouncing around in a cave. Every year that passes since the sound happened puts it farther away until it gets lost in the endless, dull ringing of time. But the noise still piles up, and I have to constantly focus on tuning it out for the rest of the period.

"Chemistry is going to be the death of me," Grace groans as we make our way into the hallway after class. The moment I pass through the threshold of the doorway, a wall of sound hits me from all angles. Even without the echoes, it would be hard to hear out here because of the loud chatting of students in the hallway, voices bouncing off the metal lockers and concrete walls. But *with* the echoes, it's so much worse.

Luckily, years of practice have taught me how to focus on the voices I actually want to hear. "That and your crappy boyfriend," I reply to Grace. I know she'll bring the subject back up eventually, so I might as well get it over with.

She rolls her eyes, not even attempting to defend her less-than-stable relationship, and flips her jet-black hair over one shoulder. "Speak of the devil," she says, glancing across the hallway. My eyes follow hers and I spot Andy walking toward us, his left wrist in a cast and his right arm waving, trying to catch Grace's attention.

"Grace!" he calls, the sound barely making it into earshot as he shoves his way past students and bulging backpacks towards her. She ignores him, turning her back and shuffling stuff from her locker into her bag. When he finally reaches her, he pauses a few feet away, a desperate look on his face. "I tried calling you four times last night. I can't apologize if you don't let me."

She closes her locker a little forcefully and turns to him, a hand on her hip and fire in her eyes. "Apologize? Go ahead. Spit it out."

"I'm sorry. I am. I didn't mean to—"

"Didn't mean to what? Put your hands all over Dana?" Grace's voice rises, making it easier for me to hear over the thunder of voices around us. I blink in surprise. Grace *can't stand* Dana Stevens, mostly because of a certain history between her and Andy. I suck in a breath, realizing that this encounter might end up being more than just the usual small fight the couple often experiences.

"I—I was drunk!" Andy stammers, the frustration in his voice growing. I exhale slowly, mentally preparing myself for the inevitable.

"Exactly!" Grace half-yells, cutting her hands through the air in exasperation. A few heads turn towards us. "You didn't even tell me you were going to her party. You know how I feel about her! You went behind my back and screwed everything up. Again." Then, Grace's tone turns from borderline hysterical to menacingly calm. "Let me spell something out for you, Andy."

"Grace, please—"

"We. Are. Done."

Once the words are out of her mouth, she grabs my arm and shoves past him down the hallway. Andy tries to follow, pushing people out of the way as he reaches for her. "Babe, please—"

"Stop," I say from Grace's side, turning to glare at him. "Just stop." He meets my eyes for a long, tense moment, then finally drops his hand. I tug on Grace to keep moving.

"I can't believe he has the nerve!" Her voice rises as we move through the hall, snaking our way through the sea of people. I breathe deeply through my nose, almost wanting to roll my eyes at the situation. Grace and Andy have been on-and-off since, well, before I even met Grace a year ago. Grace has told me the story a thousand times— he was the swoon-worthy quarterback with girls falling at his feet, and Grace was the new girl from a small town back in sophomore year. They, as Grace often put it, were from two different worlds, but had been brought together by fate. Andy fell in love with her, and despite his reputation, committed himself to a serious relationship. Grace, after realizing he (supposedly) wasn't the jerk she thought he was and that he really, truly was a good person on the inside, fell for him too.

At least, that's the way Grace tells the story. My version recognizes their "love" as the dysfunctional relationship it is and includes me, the best friend that often has to deal with the aftermath.

It takes all of my effort not to sigh in disdain. "You really shouldn't put up with him," I tell Grace in as gentle of a tone as I can muster. I've told her this before, of course, but normally she gets defensive about the subject. This time, however, she sighs in defeat.

"I shouldn't," she admits. "Which is why it's officially over. I'm done with him."

She's said this before, of course. And both of those times, they ended up getting back together. But one can hope. "Are you going to be okay?"

We reach the bathroom and Grace pauses, her hand on the door and her eyes slightly damp. "Yeah, I will be. I've got you, at least."

"And you always will," I punch her lightly on the arm, smiling as wide as I can for her. She laughs softly, then pushes the door open.

"What exactly did he do with Dana?" I ask once we're in the bathroom. Since the whole school hasn't been through here in the past few years, the echoes that were screaming in my ears in the hallway dull, and I feel like a weight has been lifted off of my body. I grab a wad of tissue for her to dry her eyes, and she sniffles before answering.

"I don't know. I walked in and they were sitting on the couch together, his arm around her. He was—"

Behind me, in the far corner of the bathroom, a chorus of laughter fills the air. I turn my head around, ready to snap at whoever might be making fun of Grace's distress, but realize that no one is there. It's only an echo, probably some girls from last year laughing over a text message or something one of them said.

"Did you see the other one yet?" a girl's voice says amidst the laughter. I pull my focus away from the echo as another voice responds, turning my attention back to Grace.

"—called me about him falling down the stairs. 'Here to clean up your mess?' she said." Her voice turns obnoxious as she mimics Dana, and she's oblivious to the small interruption I'd just experienced.

"Are you serious?" I ask in disbelief as I try to fill in the gaps of the conversation.

She dabs her eye before answering, mascara staining the white tissue paper. "Yeah, it's ridiculous. She clearly set the whole thing up. Maybe he didn't mean to, maybe he—"

"Whoa," I put a hand up, "hold on. Andy went to that party without telling you— and he knows you don't trust Dana. He was not thinking about your feelings at all."

"When has he ever?" A sob wracks through her body.

I pull her into a hug. "My point exactly."

"I'm so done."

"I know." I hold her there for a minute, soothing her. When she finally pulls away, the second-period bell rings.

"You know what, I'm not even going to cry anymore," Grace says, drying her eyes. "And instead of boohooing and eating ice cream from the tub all day, we should celebrate."

This is a surprise, but I'm all for it. "What do you want to do?"

"Let's skip the rest of school. Go explore, or something." I watch her face brighten as the idea solidifies in her mind.

My eyes widen. "Skip school? But I've never—"

Her mouth spreads into a grin, and she takes my hand. "Come on!"

✳✱✳

TWO HOURS LATER, we're sitting in my car in front of my house, the brisk October air quickly sapping any remnants of heat from the inside.

"That," I say, "has got to be the *best* cookie dough ice cream I've ever had."

Grace shoves the last bite of her ice cream cone into her mouth. "It was, in fact, very delicious," she replies, chewing through each word.

I laugh, shaking my head. Skipping school wasn't exactly as hard as I'd imagined it to be. A trip to the nurse's office and a call to my mom saying I wasn't feeling well—including several reassurances that yes, I was well enough to drive myself home and that no, I didn't need her to come home from work to take care of me—was all it took, and then Grace and I were free to go. Both of our parents would be at work until later in the evening, so we had plenty of time to roam downtown Shorewick before stopping for food. Grace had still wanted ice cream, but we got it in cone-form, which is much less depressing than right-from-the-tub form. Then we drove back to my house, where we sat in the car, finishing up those ice cream cones.

Grace reaches out to turn the volume of the radio up. A pop song I've never heard before blasts through the speakers. "I love this song!" she says, excited.

I shrug in response. "Never heard it before."

Grace gapes at me. "Are you serious? This is, like, in the top ten right now. All the radio stations play it!"

I shrug again. Truthfully, I don't think I've ever turned the radio on in my car before. Cars are one of the only places that I never hear the echoes, so when I'm in one, I like to relish in the silence, something I rarely get to do. At least, I used to rarely get to do. Things are a lot better now than they had been when I was younger.

Growing up, the echoes weren't exactly something that made sense to my parents. When I was little, they chalked it up to me just having a lot of imaginary friends, but when I started to get older, and I was still commenting about all of the noise I was hearing, they started to worry. Eventually, they started taking me to a stream of mental health experts, all of whom came to the conclusion that I had schizophrenia, bipolar, or some other personality disorder. For a while, I even believed it myself. I was hearing things that no one else was, which was strange. I had to be hallucinating.

At least, that's what I thought until I started remembering the things I was hearing. My parents singing happy birthday from last year, Dad watching the football game that aired exactly two years ago. And then it all made sense: it was all sound from the past, not just a bunch of random concoctions of my brain. Everything I could hear was something that had *actually happened.*

After I realized that, it didn't take long to figure out how to prove it to my parents and my psychologist—all I did was listen for the name of the patient who had been in my psychologist's office on the same day the previous year and convince her to check her records. When the same name was right there in the file, things slowly began to change. My parents spent a lot of time in denial about it, but I can't really blame them because it isn't really something that seems possible. I had to answer a lot more questions about past things to fully convince them, but when I did, they were baffled by the situation.

Turns out, I just have this strange ability to hear the past, and it isn't something anyone understands. My psychologist wanted to get some doctors involved and do a bunch of tests, but my parents quickly stopped that before I could be turned into a science experiment. It took them a while to come to terms with this new reality, but eventually we decided to move, partially because the echoes of the past had piled up over the years in our old house and partially because it would give me a fresh start to try and be a normal teenager and make friends, something I'd failed to do up to that point.

We had a brand new house built here in Shorewick—one with no past to echo at me—and we set aside an entire room we call the "office" where no one is allowed to make any noise so that I can go there when I need silence. Now, the office is mine, one of the only places besides cars where I don't have to constantly hear the echoes of the past.

"Alright, let's go watch some sappy rom-coms and complain about how awful boys are," Grace pulls the handle of her door, stopping the music and startling me out of my thoughts.

I take a deep breath, pausing after Grace closes the door. One year ago today was the day we moved here to Shorewick, so today, I will start hearing echoes of the past in my own house again. I remind myself that it's okay, that I've dealt with this before, and that I still have the office if I need a break. But even so, it takes all of my effort to tear myself out of the car and force my feet up the walkway to the front door.

Inside, Mom's voice rings out from the past, though she's not even home yet today. *"No, no, we need to flip it on its side! Jeff—"*

"Hold on, it's almost through—" Dad's echo grunts in reply.

"Wait, stop, you're scratching the wall!"

Then there's a scuffling of something, in fact, scraping against the wall, followed by a *thud*.

"I'm going to get the movie set up in your room, you get the snacks?" Grace tells me after setting her bag down and taking her shoes off. She doesn't wait for my reply before darting up the stairs.

"Sounds like a plan," I call to her, then watch her go, my focus going back to the abundance of echoes in the entranceway.

Dad had apparently believed that he could squeeze the couch through the narrow entranceway into the living room at the back of the house, and had, in the process, left several scratches on the walls. I remember those scratches, which Mom had demanded we paint over not a week after moving in.

Attempting to tune out the noise, I start towards the kitchen, imagining the snacks I can grab. But then the doorbell rings, causing me to pause mid-stride.

"*Laura! Can you get that please?*" Mom's echo calls out from the living room. A moment later, footsteps appear on the staircase, making their way down to the door. I hesitate in the entranceway, trying to decide if I should tune out the noise or follow the echoes. I don't remember who our first visitor at this house was, so my curiosity gets the best of me and I walk over to the door.

I hear it creak open, then the sound of my own voice greeting whoever is at the door. "*Hello?*"

"*Hey there!*" a woman's voice answers jubilantly.

"*Who is it?*" Mom's echo appears in the hallway, her footsteps thudding toward the door.

"Hi! My name is Annie, and this is my son, Maverick. We're your new neighbors!" the woman says, but her voice doesn't sound familiar.

"Oh hello! It's so nice to meet you! Which neighbors are you?" Mom's voice replies.

"Across the street and to the left, the one with the yellow flowers in front," Annie's echo answers, and I furrow my brows at the statement. Hadn't that house been abandoned since before we moved in? I rack my brain, trying to remember. Our neighbor Kate and her two poodles live directly across from us, and an old man named Riko lives to the right of her. But I don't remember anyone living to the left.

"Well, it's so nice to meet you! You can come on in if you'd like, but it's a little messy still. We're just barely getting our furniture moved in," Mom's echo tells the new neighbors.

"Oh, no, we don't want to intrude! But we did want to bring you this," Annie replies, and then I hear the shuffling of something across hands.

"Wow, thank you so much! This vase is gorgeous." Flowers, then. I don't remember our neighbors bringing us flowers when we moved in—or anyone bringing us anything, for that matter. But maybe I'd just forgotten about it?

"Don't be fooled, it's only some fancy paint, not real stained glass," Annie laughs.

"Well, it's beautiful all the same!"

"I'm glad—" Annie begins, but gets cut off by the sound of Dad yelping loudly from the living room across the house, followed by an assurance that he was, in fact, okay.

"*Oh no! I'm so sorry, Annie. That's my husband, Jeff. We're having some... trouble getting our furniture moved into the house.*" Mom tells her with a laugh.

"*Don't worry about it! Is it just the three of you? Could you use any help?*"

"*No, I couldn't ask that of you!*"

"*Nonsense!*" Annie insists. "*I might not be able to help with the heavy lifting, but I can bring in some smaller boxes and things. And I've got a very capable seventeen-year-old boy here who'd be glad to help move some of the heavier stuff, right Maverick?*"

"*Sure, what do you need?*" a male voice replies from next to Annie's on the porch.

Mom, sounding like she doesn't want to ask so much of a couple of strangers but also like she's frazzled enough to do it anyways, replies, "*Alright, then. Come on in, I need to go check on Jeff to make sure he didn't seriously injure himself.*"

Mom's footsteps clatter down the entranceway towards the living room, followed by another, softer set of footsteps. Two pairs, however, linger by the door, trailing slowly behind.

"*I'm Maverick,*" the guy's echo says, and though I still don't remember who he is or what he might look like, I can distinctly hear the smile in it.

"*I heard,*" comes the sound of my voice, then a bit of an awkward pause. "*I'm Laura.*"

"*Laura,*" Maverick's echo repeats softly, like he's tasting the name in his mouth for the first time, trying to decide if he likes it. "*It's nice to meet you—*"

"Laura?" Grace's voice rings out from the top of the stairs, dragging my focus from the echoes. "Are you coming with those snacks, or what?"

My thoughts scatter, flashes of questions and confusion. Who were these people, claiming to be our neighbors in an echo of the past that I don't remember? Sure, I might not remember every moment of the day we moved in *exactly*, but wouldn't I have recalled something about our neighbors stopping by and offering to help us move our stuff in?

"Laura, are you alive?" Grace's voice grows louder, halting any further thoughts in my mind.

"Sorry, I just forgot something in the car!" I call back to Grace.

Apparently, what I really forgot about was meeting Annie and Maverick from across the street last year.

CHAPTER 2

AT THE SAME TIME THE popcorn starts popping in the microwave, the sound of the intro music to a movie floats down the stairs from my room. Strangely, though, I find myself attempting to tune out the present noise and focus on the past. Normally, it's the other way around.

But even as I stand in the kitchen, listening to the echoes happening in the adjacent living room, I don't catch anything that gives away more information about the neighbors I don't remember meeting. It's just Mom explaining where she wanted the couch moved, and then the sounds of people moving it. The front door opens and closes a few times, too, but I don't hear any more talking.

By the time the popcorn is done, I'm getting antsy. These neighbors—the ones who claimed to live in the house that no one lives in—had helped my family move our stuff in, and yet, I can't seem to picture their faces, or recall meeting them at all. Would I have remembered them, though? Maybe because I never saw them again, I just forgot about them.

But still, I find myself wanting to listen to the echoes downstairs, wanting to know more about Annie and Maverick.

"Grace?" I call up the stairs.

The movie pauses. "I'll take some kettle corn if you have it," she calls back to me.

"Actually, I…" I hesitate, wondering if Grace will think it's weird for me to ask this, but then I do it anyway. "I was wondering if you wanted to watch the movie downstairs instead?"

There's a pause, and then, "I guess so. If you want to?"

Sighing in relief, I reply, "It's a bigger screen, so it might be better."

"I'll bring the movie down, then!"

Grateful, I head back to the kitchen, where the popcorn has finished popping in the microwave.

"So where are y'all from? What brings you to Shorewick?" Annie's voice from behind me almost startles me; I hadn't heard her echo come into the kitchen.

"Pendleton! We just needed a change, I guess. Got tired of the big city," Mom's echo responds from the dining room.

"Well, you certainly got one! That is quite the change in scenery, I bet!"

"It really is. Have you—" Mom's voice begins, but then Grace enters the room and I force myself to snap back into the present.

"This is what I chose," Grace holds up a DVD case of the movie she chose, and I half-heartedly pretend to look at it while focusing back on the echoes.

"We moved from another small town not too far from here, right after Maverick turned eleven, and we've been here ever since." Annie's echo answers.

But then there's a scoff from across the living room. *"Which is far too long, if you ask me,"* Maverick adds.

"Why is that? Are the schools okay?" Mom's voice becomes instantly etched with concern.

"Excuse me?" Grace says, slightly annoyed. I snap my head around to where she's standing by the microwave. "I thought I asked for kettle corn."

"Oh, sorry," I hurry towards her, reaching for the bag, but she pulls it just out of reach, grinning.

"I'm just kidding, this is fine, honestly." Grace snatches the movie from my hands and goes over to the living room, turning on the TV. "But you better pop another, because I'm definitely going to eat this entire bag."

I roll my eyes and sigh, glad that she's preoccupied for a minute so I can keep listening to the echoes. I grab another bag of popcorn from the cupboard and put it in the microwave, using the two and a half minutes I have to stand there, listening.

"—though Maverick only went there for two years before he started the early college program. But, I assure you, St. Martin is a great school, and Laura will be just fine," Annie finishes saying. I try to fill in the gaps of the conversation, hating the fact that I keep getting distracted from it, but hating that I don't remember any of it even more.

"Well, that's good to hear. What's wrong with Shorewick, then?" Mom's echo is clearly relieved, but still contains a bit of hesitancy.

"Nothing—" Annie begins.

"It's just—" Maverick starts at the same time. *"It's boring,"* he continues when his mom pauses, *"Small. Too quiet."*

Mom's laughter fills the air. *"I think quiet is exactly what we were looking for."*

Annie chuckles, too. *"Then you'll love it here. Don't mind Maverick, he's just tired of living in this town where everybody knows everybody. We're grateful for some fresh faces when we see them!"*

In the living room, the movie starts up again.

"I know we've seen this one a thousand times, but I still love watching Marcy and Dante's playful banter every time," Grace comments, shoving a handful of popcorn into her mouth.

"So Laura, you're a senior, then?" Annie's echo asks.

"Junior, actually," my echo replies.

"My condolences," Maverick's smooth voice says, halfway into the kitchen now. The smile I'd heard before is back, seeping between the words. *"I can't imagine the torture of having almost two years left of high school."*

"Don't remind me," comes my reply. It's a strange feeling, hearing myself take part in a conversation that I don't remember having. As if I'm listening to an entirely different person in an entirely different life, and yet, we share the same voice and house and family. Like a parallel universe, shifting into mine for a small moment.

"Are you okay?" Grace's fingers snap in front of my face, causing me to jump.

I shake my head, feeling heat blooming across my cheeks. "Yeah, I'm fine. Sorry."

"You've just been standing there, staring at the bag of popcorn in your hands as if it was a long-lost lover you've finally been reunited with," she chuckles.

"Sorry, I just got lost in thought," I tell her, turning to the empty bowl on the counter.

Grace snatches the bag of popcorn out of my hands, then opens the microwave. "I guarantee that the reunion with this lover of yours will be much better *after* the bag has been popped."

I let out a nervous laugh, closing my eyes for a few seconds to regain my bearings. I can't keep doing this—getting so lost in the noise of the past that I forget the present. It's already hard enough to act like a normal teenager while the echoes are always surrounding me. I've used every excuse in the book to get out of going to concerts, movies, dances, and other loud places with Grace. If I can't even act normal with her in my own house, then I'll never be able to carry out a normal life and go to college and fit in with society. I have to act normal if I want to *be* normal.

So when the microwave beeps, I pour my popcorn into a bowl, join Grace on the couch, and try my best to ignore the echoes for the rest of the movie.

* ***** *

AFTER GRACE LEAVES, I spend most of the afternoon attempting to start writing the Mrs. Andrews-assigned research paper I'd almost thought was due today. It isn't actually due for another two weeks, but the echo from this morning served as a good reminder that I should at least *start* working on it.

I don't get very far.

Apparently, last year when we were moving into the house, I had chosen this exact time frame to start bringing things up to my room and unpacking it all. I can hear the past version of myself pacing the floor of my room, cutting open boxes, and shuffling things around. Hearing echoes like this isn't new to me because I hear things like this all the time outside of the house. But it's been an entire year since I've heard echoes in my own home, and I realize very quickly how much I've taken the silence for granted.

I know that, theoretically, I could cross the hall and work on my paper in the office we've set aside as a quiet room for me, but I imagine that even there won't be very quiet either, since we still had to move things into it on this day.

So, by the time my parents get home from work and Mom gently taps on my bedroom door, I've only read through one chapter of the book about acid rain I'm supposed to use as a source.

The door swishes open, and Mom's soft smile emerges from behind it. "Hey, Laura."

"Hey, Mom," I greet her with a smile.

She crosses the room in three strides, her eyebrows creased in concern, and then presses a hand to my forehead. "How are you feeling?"

A beat of confusion passes over me until I remember that I'd left school earlier because I'd been "feeling sick." I feign a sniffle. "I'm okay. I think it's just a cold."

Mom keeps her hand on my face, unconvinced. "You feel kind of warm. Maybe we should take you to the doctor. I can—"

I pull her hand off my forehead, cupping it in my own. "No, Mom. I'm okay. I promise. I might have just been feeling anxious," I tell her, trying to stop the worry-hole she's about to spiral down. Except, a beat after the words are out of my mouth, I realize I might be digging that hole deeper.

Mom's brows crease, and she looks even more worried than before. "Anxious? Is it because…" she hesitates. "Well, I know that today is… you know…"

Fighting the urge to roll my eyes, I say, "The one-year anniversary of living in this house? The day I can start hearing echoes in my own home again?"

She bites her lip. "Yeah. That."

"It's okay, Mom. I was a little anxious, but I've been here all day and I'm fine."

She tucks a strand of hair behind my ear, sitting on the bed across from me. "Are you sure? Have you been…" she trails off again.

"Hearing echoes of the past?" I flash a grim smile. "Always." Then a memory tugs at me. *Annie and Maverick.* The neighbors I don't remember.

Clearing my throat, I try to build the courage to ask my mom if she remembers them. I don't want her to worry even more than she already does, so I have to be careful about how I phrase it.

"Do you remember the day we moved in last year?" I ask nonchalantly as if I'm just bringing up a pleasant memory.

Mom smiles brightly. "Of course I do. You were so excited."

I smile back. "I was. This house was so great. It still is. I love living here."

"I'm so glad to hear that," she replies, a shine glossing over her eyes.

"And it's such a great neighborhood, too. With friendly neighbors. Didn't some of them drop by to welcome us?"

Mom nods. "They did, didn't they? Riko dropped by a few days after we moved in, I think. He's such a nice man. And then I think Kate stopped to chat with Dad once while she was walking her dogs."

"Oh yeah, that's right," I chime in, remembering. "And then, wasn't there another family that stopped by? A woman and her son?"

Mom pauses, thinking. "You must be thinking about Lily and her daughter—I can't remember her name. They live next door, and they've always waved, but I don't think we've ever spoken to them."

My stomach drops. Mom doesn't remember Annie and Maverick either. How could that be?

"Yeah, that must be who I'm thinking of," I add softly.

"Well, anyway," Mom stands up from the bed suddenly. "I was thinking we should do something special for dinner tonight, to celebrate a year in our new life. What would you like to have?"

"Didn't you prep a casserole yesterday?"

"I did," she drawls. "But I was thinking, maybe we can go out to eat, or something?"

"You know I hate restaurants," I say, realizing where this is going. Mom's trying to get me out of the house because she's worried that I'm going to be anxious about hearing the echoes.

"We could eat in the car, of course," she quickly adds.

"Mom, it's fine. We can eat here," I say firmly.

"I know. I just don't want you to—"

"To hear the echoes? The ones I hear all the time? You can't protect me from those. They're not going to magically disappear," I tell her. It isn't until I see the hurt look on her face that I realize I might have been a little too firm. I quickly pull her into a hug. "I'm used to them anyway. Sometimes I like listening to them. It's totally fine, Mom. You don't have to worry about me."

She squeezes me tight. "That's the thing, though. I will never stop worrying about you."

I bury my face into her shoulder, trying to ignore the tug of guilt that flashes through me. I know how long Mom and Dad waited to have a child. And I know that they wanted to give me a sibling or two as well, but couldn't. They got one kid, and that one kid came with an inexplicable ability that makes living a normal life ridiculously hard.

I can't let myself be more of a burden for them. All I want is for them to be happy, to enjoy their only child and the life they always dreamed about. I want to make them feel like normal parents, raising a normal teenager that does normal things. And for putting up with me the past seventeen years, they at least deserve that much.

CHAPTER 3

THE NEXT MORNING before school, I get a call from Grace.

"The Beast won't start," she says. There's a click, then a low, stuttering sound somewhere in the background. "I think he's gone."

"Like, really gone?"

"Yes!" she exclaims. I can feel her excitement through the phone.

"Finally! I'll be over in a few." I hang up and call goodbye to my parents, shuffling out the door. The Beast is Grace's car. Her parents, though they were definitely not short of money, bought it straight out of the nineties thinking it would help their daughter "build character." The only thing it really built was a never-ending list of problems. Grace has been waiting for the thing to die for months now, hoping her parents would get her a new car when it did. This is her chance.

"I was beginning to think that old piece of crap was immortal. Thank goodness I was wrong," I say when Grace gets into the car.

"They're taking it to the shop tomorrow. Keep your fingers crossed."

"Trust me, I will."

When we get to school, our friend Leo is standing next to our lockers in sweatpants and a plain white t-shirt, his eyes bloodshot and his shaggy red hair untamed. He waves, calling something out to us that looks like a simple, "hey," but with the hallway noise from this year, last year, and the year before echoing all around us, I can't hear him.

When we reach where he's standing, Grace looks him over, barely trying to hide the disgust on her face. "Where have you been, it looks like you haven't slept in weeks!"

"I had the flu, thanks a lot for checking up on me," he deadpans. We're close enough now that I can hear him a little bit better, but he's always had a quiet voice, so even standing next to him I have to listen carefully.

"Gross!" Grace screeches, taking two big steps back, then using me as a shield between her and Leo.

"Hey!" I protest, backing up, too. "I don't want to get sick, either."

Leo throws his hands up like a peace offering. "I'm not contagious anymore! Promise. The doctor said I can come back to school today."

Grace doesn't look convinced, but she relaxes slightly, allowing herself to stand a few inches closer to him.

"Sorry we didn't check in when you were absent yesterday," I tell Leo, shooting a glance at Grace. "We were a little bit… preoccupied."

"Brace yourself, Leonardo. I have big news," she says, pausing to make sure his attention is completely on her.

He lifts an eyebrow, folding his arms across his chest.

"Andy and I broke up."

"That's *big news*?" Leo scoffs. "Okay, sorry, wait. Let me pretend to be shocked."

"Come on, Leo! We're not getting back together this time. Seriously."

Leo rolls his eyes. "Okay, Grace, whatever you say."

"I thought that at least *you* would be happy," she says, turning to her locker to offload a few books from her backpack. It's no secret that Leo despises Andy with a passion. The rumors tell me that sometime in middle school, Andy got a bunch of the other kids in our grade to start calling Leo names, and at some point, they poured chocolate milk down the front of his shirt. Leo's been sort of a social outcast ever since. Grace befriended him in freshman year when she moved here, and I was the most recent addition to the group.

We're kind of misfits, but I love our little trio regardless. Because of the echoes and the slew of mental health experts I had to see throughout my life, I'd been homeschooled for most of middle and high school, and I hadn't been able to make many friends since I was a little kid. When Grace and Leo sat down next to me at lunch on my first day of school, it had felt strange to be talking to people my own age, who didn't think I was mentally ill or knew anything about my history. I'd been shy at first, but soon enough, I found myself joining in on their banter and hanging out with them after school.

And it was nice. Nice to have friends to talk to and spend time with, who accepted me even though I usually turned down their invites to movies and festivals and other loud places. It helped me to feel like an actual teenager rather than a girl with a scientifically unexplainable ability. Normal. Or at least, *almost* normal.

The bell rings, interrupting whatever rebuttal Leo had most likely been forming, and we wave to him as Grace and I head to our first class.

AFTER SCHOOL, TROUBLE awaits Grace and me in the parking lot. As we walk, I spot Andy parked three spaces down from my car, leaning against his Jeep as he searches the crowd of students pouring out of the school. He notices us moving in his direction and waves his casted wrist in the air, calling out to Grace.

I try to veer Grace away before she notices him, but at that exact moment, she lifts her head from her phone and spots him. Her steps slow to a stop.

"Here we go again," she sighs, putting on her best neutral look as Andy begins to walk toward us.

"We should just lea—" I begin, but pause when I notice someone walking up to Andy. It's Dana Stevens. She tosses her arms around his neck, throwing her weight into him as she plants a kiss on his left cheek. To his credit, Andy looks surprised, but before he can push her away and go back to waving Grace over, I grab her by the arm and tug her to my car.

"He makes me so sick!" Grace exclaims as I slide into the driver's seat. "And who does she think she is?" She cranes her neck to look outside at him, but I just focus on turning the key and shifting the car into drive. Better to make a quick getaway than get stuck in the drama.

"Not someone worth getting worked up about," I reply as we roll out of the parking space.

"You don't understand how *done* I am," she says.

"Oh, I think I do."

"I just can't—" she begins to say, but her phone starts buzzing in her pocket. "It's him."

"Are you going to answer?" I ask, making a left turn.

She hesitates, then, "No."

"Good."

Except, a minute after the phone stops ringing, Grace exclaims, "He left a voicemail!" I glance at her, noticing the eager look on her face as she opens it up.

"Put it on speaker."

Grace places the phone on the center console for both of us to hear. "Grace, please stop shutting me out," Andy's voice crackles through the phone. "Look, I've been trying to get rid of Dana for years. I don't want anything to do with her. I promise. It's *you* that I want. Grace, I-I love you. I can't let us go like this. I'm sorry for what I did. I really am. It was a stupid mistake. Please call me." The line goes dead. I shoot a look over at Grace to gauge her reaction, but she's distracted by something she sees in the side mirror. I hear the blasting of a horn a second later.

"Oh my gosh, did you see that?" she flips around in her seat to look behind the car.

"What is it?" I ask, startled. I look in the rearview mirror as the sound of tires screeching fills the air, but all I can see is the shiny front grill of a black Suburban following too closely behind me.

"That Suburban just cut off the blue car that was behind you, big time. I thought they were going to collide!"

"Wow," I glance at the Suburban again. The front windows are tinted, so I can't see who's driving the car.

"What a jerk. Now he's tailgating you."

"Should I slam on my brakes so he'll hit me and collect some insurance money?" I joke, but Grace shakes her head, serious.

"I wouldn't want to meet whoever's driving that car."

At the next light, when I make a right turn, the Suburban does as well.

"Oh please, don't tell me he's one of my neighbors," Grace says. But when we turn off onto her street, the Suburban's engine revs up and it speeds past us. "Freak," she mutters after him.

When we pull into her driveway a few minutes later, Grace doesn't have to invite me in. It's become pretty standard that whenever one of us has to drive the other home, we're expected to stay and hang out for a while.

When we enter the house, I leave my shoes at the door. At my own house, I wouldn't bother to remove my shoes until plopping onto the couch or heading up to my room, but at Grace's, it feels like a requirement to enter.

The cute downtown house was built in the early 1900s, complete with high ceilings, wide and spacious rooms, and massive paned windows. Even though it's old, Grace's parents have done a good job at modernizing the inside. The kitchen features sleek black countertops and stainless steel appliances, the living room includes a wall-mounted seventy-five-inch TV, and all of the windows are fixed with motorized drapes that open and close at preset times of the day. And because of a housekeeper that comes twice a week, the place is usually spic and span. It's the kind of place that demands the respect of bare feet when you step inside.

The first time I'd come to Grace's house and seen how old it was, I'd worried that the echoes inside would be unbearable. But apparently, the house had sat empty for a long time before Grace and her family moved in a few years ago, and despite them living there for that time, the place is usually eerily quiet. Grace's parents work long hours, and Grace and her younger sister often spent most of their time out of the house. So only occasionally do I overhear a family conversation at dinner from last year, or a short conversation from two years ago, which is nice.

When we walk into the dining room, a note and two twenty-dollar bills are lying on the table.

Grace,

Dad and I have to work late tonight. Big project this week. We won't be back until 8 or 9. Order some dinner with this and keep an eye on Briana for me. Love you,

—Mom

"Pizza?" Grace asks when we both finish reading the note.

"Do you have to ask?" I reply with a grin.

"Now, or later?"

"Do you have to ask?" I ask, and she responds by picking up her phone.

We spend the rest of the afternoon doing bits of our homework while flipping through TV channels and munching on cheesy breadsticks. Grace's younger sister Briana gets dropped off by the bus about an hour after we get home, but she gets busy with her own homework and isn't much of a bother.

Grace seems to have either forgotten about or completely ignored Andy's voicemail from earlier, which is strange for her. I start to wonder if maybe she finally sees that he's no good for her and has decided to let go. I can only hope.

WHEN I STEP OUTSIDE later in the evening to head home, the air has cooled down quite a bit, and I crank up the heater in the car. Almost all traces of daylight have faded except for a soft glow around the horizon as I pull out and drive down the street. When I round the first corner, I notice a black Suburban that looks eerily similar to the one from earlier parked on the side of the street between a couple of houses. After passing it, I check my rearview mirror to get a better look, and as I do, I see the headlights pop on.

I try to shrug off the twitch of unease running through me, hoping that it's all just a weird coincidence, but when I turn left onto the main road, the Suburban does as well. Except, this time it hangs back between a few cars, keeping its distance instead of driving right up behind me like before.

My heart rate quickens, and I keep an eye on the car as I drive. When it follows me at the next turn, I start to get anxious. Are they following me? Who could it be? And why? I can't think of anyone or any reason, so I decide to test something just to be sure. I turn off onto the next road I see, one I've never been on in my life. I keep a tight watch on the rearview mirror and follow the movements of the Suburban as it turns down the road ten seconds later. When I look back forward, I catch a glimpse of a "Dead End" sign right as I pass it.

"Shoot," I mutter under my breath.

Looking ahead at where the road curves, I think fast, pulling into a random driveway next to an old red truck just after rounding the curve, hoping the house's occupants won't come out to question me. I turn the car off and slouch down in my seat so I won't be seen. Seconds later, the sound of the Suburban's engine reaches earshot, and the headlights pass by my car. I wait in dead silence as the Suburban goes to the end of the street and turns around. When it comes back, it slows for a moment behind my car, the brakes squealing as it rolls to a complete stop. I hold my breath.

Eight, nine, ten seconds pass. Then, finally, the driver hits the gas and the Suburban speeds off into the distance.

I wait for several minutes before shakily starting my car back up and pulling out of the stranger's driveway. I don't know who was in that Suburban, or why they were there, but one thing is undeniably clear: *they were following me.*

As I drive home, a million scenarios are blazing through my head. None of them are good. I circle the block three times before pulling up in the driveway, just to make sure. I arrive twenty minutes after curfew, so Dad asks why I'm late, but I brush it off by saying that Grace and I got carried away with our homework. My parents trust me enough to let it go, and I quickly go to my room, my hands shaking.

Why me? *Who would be following me?* If they were going to hurt me, wouldn't they have done it? But all they did was follow, then drive off. Maybe they were going to spy on me? But how would they know it was *me*? They aggressively pulled out behind me earlier, so did they know my car? If so, would they find out where I actually live eventually? What would happen when they did?

I think that maybe I should tell my parents. I've always tried my best to be honest with them. But it took them years to believe me about the echoes, would they really believe that someone in a black Suburban was trying to follow me home? And do I really want to worry them about something that might just be nothing at all?

I decide not to. Maybe the person following me thought I was someone else and will realize it soon. Plus, what real evidence do I have? I didn't get a license plate number or even a description of a person. Even if the police got involved, it would be impossible for them to do anything about it.

So instead, I calm myself down, take a long hot shower, and go to bed.

CHAPTER 4

THE NEXT MORNING, an alarm is going off in my room that is not from today. I check the clock, and it's only six o'clock, an hour earlier than I normally get up for school. I reach for my phone as if to turn it off but realize there's nothing I can do. I groan, pulling a pillow over my head and cursing my past self. Today last year must have been my first day at the new school, so of course I would have gotten up extra early.

By the time my past self turns off the alarm, I am wide awake, so I decide to get up and make myself breakfast.

Halfway through cooking some eggs, I hear footsteps coming down the stairs. It's noise from last year, so probably just my own echo coming down to eat before school, too. I remember leaving extra early that morning to allow time to find my classes.

As I'm sitting there, munching on a piece of toast, my phone starts ringing.

"I'm panicking. My homework is missing. That Chemistry assignment we spent an hour on last night. I can't find it. Do you have it?" Grace starts talking the second I answer the phone.

It takes me a minute to remember what she's talking about. "I think it might be in my backpack, probably got mixed in with all the papers," I tell her.

"You *think* you have it, or you *do* have it? I need confirmation because otherwise I'm screwed," she says.

"Let me check. It's in my car."

"I'm staying on the line until you confirm," she tells me, and I laugh.

"Maybe if you kept better track of things, you wouldn't have to deal with situations like this," I tease, standing up from the table and reaching for my keys on the key rack.

"I don't need a Laura lecture right now. I need my homework," she replies, serious.

"Okay, chill. Give me one second." I walk to the front door, and just before I touch the handle, I hear the sound of it opening up from last year. Twenty minutes early, just as I remembered.

However, something I don't remember happens just as I'm about to open my car's door. A voice calls from across the street.

"*Hey! Laura, right?*" It's an echo of the same boy I heard two nights ago, coming from the direction of the abandoned house across the street. His voice is unmistakable. I look over as if to see someone there, but the street is empty. I freeze, one hand on the car door handle, the other hand with the phone in it dropping to my side.

"Yeah! Mark?" My past voice calls back from the driveway. *Maverick,* I correct myself now, though I still don't remember any of this. I turn around to face the abandoned house, feeling a strong urge to hide as if I was eavesdropping on a stranger's conversation. But it's just me, alone.

Footsteps tap across the street, towards where I stand now. *"Close. Maverick,"* he replies with a laugh, probably a few yards away.

"Oh, I'm sorry," I can hear the embarrassment in my voice.

"No worries. First day of school?" he asks.

"Yeah, it is," my echo replies. I find myself at a loss. You'd think I would remember somebody after meeting them twice.

"Don't stress, St. Martin isn't a bad school. Just don't eat the lasagna and you'll live."

My echo laughs. *"Thanks for the tip, I'll avoid it."*

"Is that your schedule?" Maverick's echo asks.

"Oh! Yeah, do you want to see?" I reply. Two sets of footsteps walk towards each other. A paper shuffles between hands.

"Hmm." Maverick's voice is deep but soft. *"Mr. Gleems! I had him last year. Old guy. That class is going to be a breeze. I slept through most of it and still got an A."*

"That's good to know. I was actually worried about Biology," I hear myself say. I remember being worried about Biology, and I remember Mr. Gleems having a surprisingly easy class. But I don't remember Maverick telling me this.

"Ms. Harding is a good English teacher, but you can't get away with sleeping in hers. Pay attention and you'll be fine," Maverick tells my past self. She was a good teacher but made me

work for my A. *"I don't think I ever had the other teachers you have, so I'm gonna have to say good luck with those."*

I hear my own laughter, then, *"Any recommendations for extracurriculars?"*

"Anything you want, but definitely not *softball. That's what all the snobby, cool people do."* I can almost hear him making air quotations around the word "cool."

"So are you implying that you're not *cool?"* I hear my echo say.

He laughs. "Definitely *cool.* Not *snobby."*

"Don't worry, I can definitely tell by the skirt you're wearing." Was I… *flirting?*

"Excuse me, but this is, in fact, an apron, *thank you very much."* More laughter.

"Oh, I see now. So you're what, a waiter, or something?"

"Cook, actually. I work at Louise's, a little diner off Main Street."

"Is the food any good, then?"

"Only the best," Maverick replies, that distinct tone of the smile I'd heard the night before still audible in his voice. *"Come by some time and I'll prove it."*

There's a brief pause. Then my own voice, stumbling over words, *"I'll, uhh, have to do that then. Come by. The diner."* Even now, without remembering any of this, I feel a blush rising to my cheeks.

A soft chuckle comes from Maverick, followed by, *"Sweet. I guess I should probably head to work now though, so I'll see you around?"*

"Definitely." I hear my voice say.

Footsteps start to cross the street, towards the house with the yellow flowers. A few seconds later I hear the sound of my car door opening and closing, the engine cranking, and tires rolling out of the driveway.

I stand there in the present, my car sitting still cold in the driveway and my mouth hanging open. In my life, I've never even had the chance to *think* about boys at all, much less *flirted* with one. I have no recollection of this encounter, and I'm sure now that this is *definitely* not something I would forget about. *Right?*

I snap out of my thoughts as I hear Grace's voice, loud, from the phone in my hand. I put it up to my ear, but have to pull it away as she yells, "Are you there?!"

"Yes, sorry, I… f-found something," I stutter out as I quickly open my car door and pull out my backpack. I find a pile of papers and shuffle through them, shaking.

"I need to know, *now*!" Grace says, and I try to go faster, but as I do, half of the stack slides out of my hands onto the ground.

I kneel on the ground, moving papers around and searching frantically for Grace's homework. The second I spot it, I lift the phone to my ear and say in a rush, "Yes, I have it, it's right here, I'll bring it, meet me in the parking lot. I gotta go, bye." I hang up without letting her reply.

And then I'm there, on my knees beside the car with papers scattered around me, all alone, processing what I just heard. Maverick, again. No memory of it, again. I remember leaving extra early, but I don't remember the conversation with Maverick. And it doesn't make any sense.

＊✳＊

FOR THE REST OF THE DAY, I'm on edge, making it hard for me to focus on my classes. I have no idea what to think of the strange events that have happened to me. The Suburban following me down the road, the encounters with Maverick I apparently had a year ago. It makes me wonder if they are connected. But how would they be? How can I be sure that the echoes of Maverick even actually happened?

Maybe something really is wrong with me.

But it can't be true. I won't admit that, not yet.

Then a thought strikes my mind: this morning, the echo of Maverick had mentioned working at Louise's. The little diner on Main Street, about a mile away from St. Martin. I've never been there, but I've driven past it a few times. Maybe the workers would know about Maverick since he supposedly worked there?

I decide, then, that I need to go there. I need to find out for myself what is going on.

At lunch, Grace doesn't take the news very well.

"You want to go *where?*" She asks with a look of disgust.

I hold her gaze firmly.

She blinks. "That place looks like a dumpster. It hasn't had a new coat of paint since it was built—which was probably in 1905. Why in the world would you want to go *there?*"

I struggle to think of an answer. "I heard it's good." It sounds more like a question.

"From *who?*"

"My parents?" I bite my lip. I didn't plan this out very well.

"So you're telling me that you, Laura Jones, actually want to go *out* somewhere for once, and the one time you do you choose *Louise's Diner*, of all the wonderful, delicious places we could have gone?"

I nod, biting my lip. Grace has begged me to go out and do things with her so many times. Half of them I come up with some excuse not to, and the other half I bail extra early. I didn't know she'd been keeping track, though.

Grace shakes her head. "I don't even know anyone who's gone there! What if it's terrible?"

"I've read some mixed reviews about that place, actually. But I'm down to try it out." Leo chimes in.

Grace's eyebrows scrunch upwards, giving me a look of desperation.

"Please go with us? For your best friends?"

She looks between me and Leo, then sighs. "Fine. But you owe me, okay?"

"Done." I smile sympathetically. She rolls her eyes.

"If we get some kind of disease from this place, I demand that you do all of my homework for the next two weeks," Leo says.

"Don't say that! I just got Grace to agree to come!"

"It's okay. If it looks super sketchy, I'm not even going to buy a drink," she replies.

"It can't be *that* bad," I assure them both, though it doesn't do much to assure myself.

* ***** *

WHEN WE WALK THROUGH the doors of Louise's after school, the first thing I hear is a bustle of noise. Chatting, dishes clinking together, music playing in the background. The dull hum of a busy restaurant. The strange part, however, is that none of it is from today. Today, the place is empty except for us. It is, however, surprisingly clean. And even kind of cute, with its homey decor. The white linoleum floors are spotless, and every table is covered in a blue-checkered tablecloth and glass vase with plastic flowers in it. A sign at the entrance reads "Please Seat Yourself," and Leo immediately sits down in one of the bar stools, taking in the menu.

Nothing about this place is familiar to me, meaning either I have never been here before or I've simply forgotten about that, too. I'm afraid that the latter might be the truth.

A short, older woman with the nametag "Penny" comes out of the kitchen as we take in the place, a smile on her face.

"How are you all doing today?" she asks cheerily.

"Pretty go—" I start to say but am cut off.

"Is this a legit jukebox? Like, from the '50s?" Grace calls from the other side of the room.

"It sure is! Been here since the place opened."

"Oh. My. Gosh." she swoons, digging through her pockets for some change.

"What can I get you all to drink?" Penny asks us.

"Cherry Coke," I say.

"Make that two," Leo adds.

"Three!" Grace walks back over, the jukebox starting up a tune behind her. The sound of it mixing with the echoes of the past would normally be a lot to listen to in a place like this, except that there isn't much noise today. When Penny leaves to get our drinks, Grace says, "I immediately take back everything I said about this place earlier. It's so *cute*!"

"I'm not sold yet. I'm going to have to try the food first, then make my judgment. Speaking of which… Grace, do you think you can cover me? I forgot my wallet."

Grace groans. "Fine Leo, but it seems very convenient that you tell me that *after* you've ordered a drink."

"It happened instinctually; I couldn't help it. I'm sorry!"

We all laugh and then look down at the menu. It appears to be typical diner food—burgers, chicken, sandwiches, sides. When Penny comes to take our order, I choose a basic hamburger and fries, hoping that the quality of the food is as much of a surprise as the cleanliness of the restaurant.

"If they cleaned up the outside, they would have so much better business," Grace comments, waving her arm at the empty room.

"You might have a point, but honestly if the food is good enough, people will come anyway," Leo replies.

"Or maybe people care more about the fact that it looks like a *dumpster* from the outside," Grace contends.

"I definitely value quality more than appearances," Leo shoots back.

"And I value appearances. If the food is actually good, then I guess that will decide who wins this argument."

As they are bantering, I notice the wall across from the jukebox is covered in a massive corkboard with various papers tacked to it. I can barely make out a block with the words "Employee of the Month," in the upper right corner, and a photo hanging underneath. I stand up and walk over, hoping it will lead to the information I'm looking for.

My hope dissipates as I get closer. The photo for the Employee of the Month is of a middle-aged woman with dark hair, and the rest of the announcement is just a list of months with slots for employee's names next to them. The names are only listed back to June, and the rest of the slots for the year are empty. None of them say Maverick or anything that could be close to the name.

I remember the echo I heard from the past, of Maverick telling us he was the cook here. Maybe he simply wasn't ever an Employee of the Month? Maybe he doesn't work here anymore— it *has* been a year since I supposedly met him.

I search the board for another minute, looking for any kind of helpful information, but all I see are lost pet announcements and newspaper clippings about things happening in Shorewick.

I return to the bar, where Grace and Leo's debate has taken on a whole new subject.

"No one even sees your socks half of the time!" Grace exclaims. "Why does it even matter?"

"Because when you bought the socks, you bought two of them, not one. They were made to be worn together—you can't just switch it up with different ones. It's not stylish, it's a sign of your inability to keep your socks together," Leo rants.

"But some socks come in a pair with a sock that looks completely different. What about those?" Grace fires back.

"Those are a sin!"

"No, they're not!" Grace says, and just then Penny comes through the door with a tray of plates in her hands, bringing the debate to a halt. When she places our food in front of us—burger and fries for me, club sandwich and chips for Leo, and a chicken sandwich with fries for Grace—we all dig in. The burger is decent, but nothing special. The fries are a little worse. Half of them are burnt or way too crunchy, and the other half are a bit soggy. Leo reaches for my fries to taste them.

After one bite, he nods his head. "Just as I thought, it's not about the appearance. It's the food. Mediocre at best."

"I think the food is just fine," Grace says. I notice, however, that she hasn't touched her fries yet.

"Hard to screw up a chicken sandwich. The fries are the telltale," Leo replies, tapping his finger on the table.

I laugh at their bickering, then push my plate over to Leo. "You can have the rest if you want. They are pretty bad."

Then I remember Maverick's voice.

"Is the food any good, then?" I had asked him.

"Only the best," he'd replied.

If it *was* the best, then it definitely isn't anymore. Maybe he was the only good cook? That would explain why it was so busy on this same day last year, but a ghost town today—they lost their best cook. But why wouldn't his name have been on the Employee of the Month board? It had empty slots back to last October. There could be numerous explanations, but I decide the best way to find out is to ask.

When Grace and Leo are finished with their food, we all get up to leave, and I let Grace pay for their food first. When they finish, I toss her my keys. "Go ahead and start the car, I'll meet you out there."

Grace doesn't bat an eye when she takes the keys and walks out the door. Leo follows, too.

Penny smiles at me. "That'll be eight twenty-three, darling."

I smile back, pulling out my money to hand to her. I try to come up with a discreet way to get the information I want, but all I end up saying is, "Is there someone named Maverick who works here? Or used to work here?"

Penny focuses on counting out my change before she answers. "Not that I can remember. Mostly just Tony and me working these days." She jabs a thumb towards the kitchen. I see an older man in the back through the little window she's pointing at.

I think, quick, trying to process the information. "How long have you been here?" I ask, hoping that maybe she's new and that this Maverick guy worked here before her and that I'm not going crazy.

"Longer than you've been alive, hon. Tony and I bought this place thirty-seven years ago. We've had employees come and go, but I don't think I've ever hired a fella named Maverick." She hands me my change and my receipt.

"Oh, okay," I respond, shooting her a smile. "Thanks anyway."

"Thank you, sweetie."

As I drive Grace and Leo home, I wonder how any of this makes sense. How can I be hearing myself talk to someone I've never met? How can this person exist at all, if there's no evidence that he did? Perhaps it's possible that it did happen, that this Maverick guy was lying to me about working at Louise's, and that my memory isn't as good as I thought.

But maybe it's not my memory screwing up. Maybe it's my ability to hear the past. Maybe it's less of an *ability* and more of an *illness*.

CHAPTER 5

"HELLOOO, EARTH TO Laura, are you in there?" Grace has a finger to my forehead, tapping rapidly across the lunch table.

My eyes snap into focus and I pull away with a jolt. "What are you doing?"

"We've been wondering the same thing about you," Leo says from my left.

"Seriously, are you okay?" Grace puts her hand on my forehead. "You feel a little warm, are you sick? Is that why you've been acting so strange lately?"

"What do you mean, strange?" I snap, pushing her arm away a little too forcefully.

"*That's* what I mean. These past few days you've bounced between Laura the snapping turtle, Laura full of paranoia, and the most annoying, Laura who's on some other planet."

"I'm fine," I tell her. It's a lie, of course, because it's been two days since I heard myself talking to a stranger that morning, and though I've been trying hard to listen to all of the echoes from the past since then, there haven't been any further conversations or clues that would hint to his existence.

"You were just zoned out, staring at the table for like five minutes straight. That doesn't look fine to me," Grace replies.

I sigh. "It's just…" I trail off, pretty sure saying "I think I'm going crazy because I've been hearing things I'm pretty sure never happened and I'm also pretty sure someone is following me" is not the correct plan of action.

"Oooh, is it *that* time of the month?" Grace gives me a sympathetic look.

It's not, but it's a good enough excuse, so I roll with it. "Is it really that obvious?"

"Kind of," she gives me a small smile. "Do you need an aspirin or anything?"

"I'm fine. I just need some rest, I guess."

"Well, you'd better rest up. Because we need to get into serious planning mode this weekend. The Halloween dance is coming up soon, and neither of you are skipping out on me for this one." Grace looks between me and Leo, ensuring that we've heard her statement.

Leo responds first, hands up in defense, "You know I'm always down to party. The only reason I missed the last one was because of that scheduling conflict with the SAT. But this time I'm clear. Promise."

Grace shifts her gaze to me. "That's the kind of attitude I want to hear."

I sigh. Parties, dances, or any kind of place that involves loud music and lots of noise are not my kind of thing. Going out, in general, isn't my kind of thing. I usually prefer to spend my free time somewhere quiet. "I don't know, I don't think I'll be going."

"No, no, no! You're not getting out of this one," Grace presses. "It's our senior year, and since you moved here you've never come with us to a single dance or party. You've got to do it just once. And Halloween is the perfect time because no one even has to know it's you!"

"But—" I try to protest, even though I know it's probably futile.

"No buts! I already paid for your ticket."

"How much was it? I'll pay you back."

"Come on! Laura, please."

"Please?" Leo chimes in. They both give me a puppy dog look.

I look between them, contemplating. I want to go out and enjoy a night with my friends. I want to be a normal teenager and do normal teenager things. And even though I'd much rather be sitting in the office in peaceful silence, I realize that I should try it, at least once. And anyway, I can just leave if it's too much to deal with.

I take a deep breath, knowing I won't be able to take back my decision once I say it. "Fine."

Grace puts a fist up like she just won a trophy. "Yes! This is great, but we really need to start working on your costume, then."

"I'll pick it myself," I say firmly. Not firm enough, though. Grace ignores me, pulls out a notebook, and starts listing off ideas for wild, over-the-top costumes she knows I'll never wear. "I'm just going to wear all black and put on a pair of cat ears. Minimal effort, and still technically a costume," I say.

"But it's the only day of the year where it's okay to go overboard. We have to take advantage of it while we can!"

I sigh.

"So we need to go shopping after school. I bet we could find some good inspiration at the thrift store," Grace tells me.

"Sure. Let's just get it over with," I say.

"You in?" Grace asks Leo.

"Heck yes!"

After school, we spend three hours scouring the clothing racks at the two different thrift stores in downtown Shorewick. By the end of the trip, all of us have at least half-completed costumes, so Grace deems our work a success. When we leave the store, we don't have to discuss our plans for the rest of the night because it's become a tradition that Friday nights are movie nights at my house. My parents have made it abundantly clear that my friends are *always* welcome to come over—probably because it makes them feel more like normal parents—and started making sure they stocked up on all of the best snack foods to lure them in. When Grace and Leo realized this, my house became the go-to spot for movie nights.

"What in the world is going on in here?" Grace exclaims as we walk into my kitchen. Dad is lying on the ground, the cabinet doors under the sink wide open and half of his body tucked underneath. Cleaning supplies, water bottles, vases, and a ton of other miscellaneous items have been pulled out and are scattered on the floor around him. He backs out of the cabinet, sitting up and banging his head on the door as he does.

"Ouch!" he yells, rubbing his head.

"Did you lose something?" Leo asks.

Dad sighs. "Yeah. I dropped my wedding ring down the drain. I took it off while I was chopping the vegetables and set it on the edge of the sink. One bump and down it went." He looks at me. "Please don't tell your mom."

"Tell me what?" Mom calls from the entranceway.

Dad groans. "Perfect timing."

"Big yikes. Well, good luck with that one Mr. Jones," Grace says, laughing as she plops on the couch in the living room. Leo follows suit.

Mom walks into the kitchen, a strange look on her face. "What's that smell?" she asks.

Dad jumps up from his spot on the ground, immediately reaching for the oven. "Crap!" he says. As he opens it, a plume of smoke flows out. "I forgot to set a timer." He turns it off, then grabs a towel while Mom starts opening windows.

"And you dropped your wedding ring down the drain again, too?" Mom asks, taking in the mess in the kitchen.

Grace and Leo laugh from the couch. I try to hold back a grin.

Dad looks defeated. "We can order pizza?" Then Mom laughs, too.

"It's fine, we're good with pizza. Right guys?" I reply, chuckling.

"Pepperoni, please!" Grace calls out.

"Hawaiian!" Leo adds.

"You sinner," Grace rolls her eyes at him.

"I'm not even going to have this argument again," Leo replies. I can't help but laugh at them.

Dad goes back to his spot under the sink to keep looking for his wedding ring and Mom pulls out her phone to order the pizza. I move into the living room, where Grace and Leo have already started fighting over what movie to watch.

"Let's watch an action movie," Leo says.

"You *always* want to watch an action movie. What's wrong with the one about the dog?" Grace replies.

"Why would you want to torture yourself like that?"

"You're just afraid you'll cry in front of us."

"Okay, you two," I jump in. "Stop bickering like an old married couple. If I do recall correctly, it's *my* turn to pick the movie."

When no one protests, I choose a new movie, an action-filled comedy, and it appeases them both.

About thirty minutes in, the doorbell rings.

"I'll get it. Don't worry about pausing it, I've seen this movie a million times," I tell my friends. I walk into the kitchen and find Dad still sitting on the floor. He holds up his left hand, a ring on his finger.

"I found it!"

"Thank goodness," I reply.

"Here," he holds out a wad of cash. "Can you get it? I've still got to put all this stuff back."

"No problem," I tell him, grabbing the cash from his hand and heading to the door. A minute later, I come back into the kitchen bearing three warm boxes of pizza. I open my mouth to announce the food to Grace and Leo but stop when something in Dad's hand catches my eye. It's a vase.

"Hold on, let me see that," I say quickly, setting the pizza down on the counter.

Dad holds out the vase to me, and the second it's in my hand, I have a flashback to the echo I heard earlier in the week.

"*...we did want to bring you this*," Annie, Maverick's mom had said.

"*Wow, thank you so much! This vase is gorgeous.*" Mom had replied.

"*Don't be fooled, it's only some fancy paint, not real stained glass,*" Annie had explained.

I look at the vase in my hands. It looks like it's made of stained glass, little pieces intricately placed in yellows, blues, and greens, creating a beautiful floral design. But like Annie had mentioned, upon closer examination, I can see spots on the edges where the paint has chipped off, revealing clear glass underneath.

I recall a faint memory of the vase sitting on the counter after we moved in, a few long, yellow flowers standing in it, but I still can't remember Annie or Maverick.

"Do you know when we got this?" I ask Dad.

He shrugs. "I've never seen it before. Your mom might know?"

I walk to the other side of the house to find her. She's sitting in her office, typing something into her computer.

"Mom, do you remember where we got this vase?" I ask her.

Mom turns to me, reaching for the vase to examine it. "Wow. It's beautiful. I forgot we had this."

"Where did you get it?"

"I didn't get it, actually. I think it was just here when we moved in. I only put flowers in it once."

"But didn't we have this house built? No one lived here before, so how could it have gotten here?" I ask her.

"I'm… not sure. Maybe it was a gift from someone, then?" She raises an eyebrow.

"A gift from who, though?" I press.

She shrugs. "Honestly, I don't know, Laura. It might have just been one of those things we forgot we had and it showed up again when we moved. I don't really remember. Why do you ask?"

"I just…" I struggle for an explanation. "I really like it."

Mom smiles and shakes her head. "I do, too. But it's a mystery to me. If I see something like it, I'll let you know, though." She turns back to her computer, letting me know the conversation is over.

"Thanks," I say, then go back into the kitchen. I try to tell myself that it's all just a coincidence and that this isn't the same vase I'd heard Mom talking about in the echo. But the problem is that if it *isn't* the same vase, then Maverick might not actually exist, which means there's something wrong with the echoes. If it *is* the vase, then he might exist, which means there might be something wrong with *me*.

Unfortunately, neither of those explanations leaves room for my sanity.

CHAPTER 6

OVER THE WEEKEND, I continue to listen for any more echoes that might include Maverick or more information about him, but I get nothing. I keep an eye on the roads, too, searching for the black Suburban everywhere I go and come up short there, too. By Monday, the paranoia has subsided, and I've almost brushed off the entire past week as nothing more than a random incident that I'd forgotten about.

At school, Grace has news.

"Andy gave me flowers," she tells me and Leo at the lunch table.

"Seriously?" I reply. She shows me a photo on her phone as proof.

Leo rolls his eyes. "He's only trying so hard because he feels like he can't have you now. Once you give in, it's going to be the same thing all over again."

"I agree with Leo. This is ridiculous."

Grace's face falls. "Maybe you guys are right."

"Just don't worry about it. It's over. Live up your single life," I tell her.

"Easy for you to say. You don't even try to date people."

I open my mouth to reply, but stop, letting out my breath.

She's not wrong. Dating is the last thing on my mind most of the time. Even though I've heard the echoes my entire life, it still takes a lot of my focus to tune them out, to focus on the present. It's hard enough for me to have friends who want to go out to places that are really, really loud. Grace and Leo may have gotten used to me not wanting to go out very often, but I can still see that it disappoints them every time I don't tag along. I can't even imagine trying to hold a relationship with someone, having to explain why I don't ever want to eat at a restaurant or go to a movie. Sure, it sounds nice to have a person to do those things with, but when I don't even want to do them in the first place, I don't really *need* a person like that in my life.

"I don't need to date to be happy," I finally say.

"It's not about needing someone else to feel happy. It's about being close to someone. Having another person on your side, someone you can count on," Grace replies solemnly.

I imagine having someone like that. Maybe if there was someone I could be completely honest with, someone that knew about my ability to hear the echoes, it would be nice. To not have to hide my sometimes strange behavior. To be able to talk to them about it. I mean, I have my parents, and they know. But the topic of the echoes has become such a taboo thing with them. They don't know how to respond, or how to deal with it. What *can* you say to someone who's hearing things you never thought possible? I don't even think I'd know what to say to myself, either. So it *would* be nice if someone understood that part of my life.

But that could never happen. No sane person would believe that I hear echoes of the past. Even my parents, the people who love me most and know me better than anyone else in the world thought I was mentally ill for years. What would happen if I tried to tell Grace, or Leo, or some boy I liked? I shudder at the thought.

"I'm not sure I'd say Andy is someone you can *count on*," Leo tells her when I don't respond.

"He was, at first. He was the perfect guy, honestly," Grace replies with a sad smile.

"Everyone is at first," Leo fires back. "The more time you spend with someone, the more you learn who they really are."

"Okay, guru Leo. Fill me with more of your wisdom," Grace replies sarcastically.

Leo rolls his eyes at her and shakes his head.

"I'm not sure if I can even take advice from someone who's so biased, anyway." Grace's tone tells me it's meant to be a joke, but I can immediately see the tension forming in Leo.

"Biased or not, Leo has a point," I jump in to avoid the direction I see this conversation heading. "The last time you two broke up was because Andy violated your trust, too. That's not someone you should be thinking *long term* about."

"The last time we broke up was because of a simple misunderstanding. And *he* broke up with *me* because I was stupid enough to snoop through his phone."

"But there's a reason you felt the need to go through his phone, right?" I reply.

"And some of the things you found didn't exactly prove his innocence—let's not forget about that, either," Leo adds.

Grace just sighs. I can tell she's not enjoying this conversation, so I change the subject by asking her about her costume progress for the Halloween dance. She welcomes the change, but as she goes into a detailed explanation about what she has and what she still needs, Leo's words swirl through my mind.

The more time you spend with someone, the more you learn who they really are.

More time. Maybe that's what I need to figure out this whole Maverick situation. More echoes, more information. Maybe with enough waiting, I'll learn who he is and if he's even real. But how long will it take to figure it out? A year has passed since the first echo I'd heard of him. Would it take an entire year of listening to finally understand?

AFTER SCHOOL, MOM IS in the kitchen cooking dinner and I'm sitting at the dining room table working on my Chemistry paper when I hear an echo of the front door opening from last year. I stop working, listening to the footsteps walking into the dining room. Then I hear the office door open.

"Laura, is that you?" Mom's echo calls.

"It is!" my echo replies.

I'm already starting to gather my papers, ready to move into the office so that I can write my paper in the quiet, but I stop when I hear the next line.

"How was Louise's?" Mom's echo asks. I think back, trying to remember if I'd ever been there before last week. But I would have remembered the place, I'm sure of it.

"It was surprisingly good!" I hear myself reply. Okay, so that's definitely not true.

"That's great to hear."

"And..." my voice trails off. I can feel my heart speeding up in anticipation. Will I learn more about this Maverick guy?

There's a brief pause, then Mom says, "Honey, could you run out to the car and check for another grocery bag? I'm missing a couple of cans."

It takes me a few beats to realize that the Mom that just spoke is from the present. I look over at her, frozen, straining to hear the rest of the conversation from last year.

"Did you see the boy? Maverick, right?" Mom's echo says on the other side of the room. I look in that direction as if there's going to be another Mom standing there to have a conversation with.

"I did," my past voice replies at the same time Mom's present self says, "Laura? Can you?"

"Uhh, yeah," I reply quickly, but I don't move. I'm still listening.

"He seems pretty nice," Mom's echo says.

"He paid for my food," I hear myself tell her.

I'm hearing double now, because Mom's echo says, "*Really now? That's* really *nice,*" a beat before her present version asks, "Are you okay, sweetie?"

"Yeah," I reply, even though my heart is thudding in my ears, and I can't make sense of anything I'm hearing. I want to freeze time and remember everything so that I don't feel crazy anymore, but I can't. I can only sit here and listen.

"Hey, don't worry about it, I'll go grab it," Mom says, putting a hand on my shoulder for a moment before she leaves the room.

"*Do you think he* likes *you?*" Mom's echo asks in that nosy-motherly sort of way. It makes me want to roll my eyes even today.

"*I don't know. I can't think about things like that, though,*" comes my reply.

"*Hey, that's not true, sure you can. That's what we moved here for. A fresh start. A chance to feel normal.*"

"*I'll never feel normal,*" my echo replies. I feel the same way now. Hearing this conversation that I don't remember is the least normal thing I've experienced since moving to Shorewick.

Mom of the present comes back into the house just as her echo says, "*Don't rule it out just yet, okay? Promise.*"

"*Okay, Mom. Promise,*" I answer with a sigh, but in the present, I can make no such promise.

I listen for a minute more, but the conversation seems to be over, so I sit back down.

"Doing okay?" Mom asks me across the kitchen counter. I want so badly to open up to her, to explain all of the unexplainable things I've been hearing lately, to let her tell me I'm not crazy. But what if I am?

Instead, I settle for, "Yeah, I just got a little dizzy. Probably just hungry."

"Well, you're in luck because dinner is ready," she replies.

And as I eat, I cling to the idea that the stained-glass vase is the same one from the first echo. It's the only real, physical evidence I have from the echoes I've been hearing lately. It makes me feel like there's some possible way these things actually did happen and it's not just all in my head. I use that hope to get me through the rest of the evening.

CHAPTER 7

THE NEXT MORNING, I walk out to my car a little bit earlier than I need to leave. I've decided that I'm going to figure out what's going on in the past, and that the best way to do it is to try and listen to as many of my own echoes as I can. I'd heard myself run into Maverick one morning, so I imagine it's bound to happen again, and I want to make sure I'm there for it. So I wait outside in the brisk morning air, listening for the sounds of myself leaving. I sigh in disappointment when I hear the car engine starting, then driving away. Maybe next time.

As I'm backing out of the driveway, I glance over at the abandoned house across the street and a thought pops into my head. If Maverick exists, and he used to live at that house, there's got to be lots of echoes inside, sounds that could give me more information about the stuff I've been hearing. If I could just get inside…

I shake my head. I'm not ready to cross the breaking and entering line quite yet. But I tuck the idea away somewhere safe, in case I need it later.

When I get to school, there's a squishy white convertible parked in my regular spot. I pull my car up next to it and Grace rolls the window down, flashing a grin at me.

"No. Way." My jaw drops.

"It finally happened! The Beast is gone forever!" she exclaims.

"Why didn't you tell me?" I squeal, jumping out of my car and half-running to the passenger side. I open the door and slide into the dark leather seat next to her.

"I wanted to surprise you!"

"This. Is. Insane."

"Right? We're taking it for a ride after school."

"I've never wanted to skip school as bad as I do right now."

"Seriously, though. Too bad we have that Chemistry test."

My eyes widen. "Wait, what?"

"The test. In Chemistry." Grace raises an eyebrow at me. "You seriously didn't forget, did you?"

I slap my forehead, realization hitting me. "I must have written the date down wrong. I thought it wasn't until Friday."

Grace grimaces. "That really sucks. But hey, maybe I'll finally do better than you."

I roll my eyes, then open the door. "Time to panic study, wanna come?" I ask.

"Panic studying is my favorite kind," she grins.

When we get into the classroom, I pull out the study guide I'd prepared over the weekend and start reading through it as quickly as I can. Unfortunately, the bell rings before I get to the second page, and then Mrs. Andrews is telling us to put away our notes. Her echo from last year begins a lecture, and I silently wish that last year's class during this period had been Chemistry instead of Biology. Perhaps then I might be able to listen in and get some help for my test. But instead, the echoes are simply a nuisance like usual, not a cool superpower that can actually help me out for once. I'll just have to try my best to tune them out.

"Good luck," Grace whispers to me just before Mrs. Andrews comes by to hand us our tests. I give her a thumbs up and a nervous smile.

I get to work, and after struggling with the first few questions, I start to feel more confident, remembering things from class as I work out the problems.

Until a sudden, blaring noise fills the air.

I jolt in my seat, startled, and end up knocking my pencil off the desk. It rolls across the floor, out of reach. The noise continues, and I look around, disoriented. It takes several seconds for me to figure out what's going on.

A fire alarm.

But no one in the classroom is moving.

Because it isn't from today.

I rub my temples, squeezing my eyes shut. No, no, no. Not today. Not *right now*. How long does a fire drill last? Fifteen minutes? Twenty? I glance at the clock, realizing that I only have thirty minutes left to finish the test. And I'm not even halfway through.

Someone taps me on the shoulder, and I spin around to face Macy Blackburn, a girl I don't know very well. She holds my pencil out to me with raised eyebrows. I pluck it from her fingers and mutter a soft "thank you," turning around before she can notice the blush forming on my cheeks. She must have seen me jump at the noise of the fire alarm. The noise that she can't hear.

Crazy. I must look *crazy.*

I lean forward, resting my head on my palm, and try to stare at the paper in front of me.

Beep. Beep. Beep.

A chemical equation. All I have to do is balance it. Easy.

Beep. Beep. Beep.

The next question is about covalent bonds. I remember reading about those.

Beep. Beep. Beep.

Or am I thinking of ionic bonds?

Beep. Beep. Beep.

By the time the fire alarms stop, Mrs. Andrews is already collecting the tests. I scribble out an answer to the second-to-last question, knowing fully well that it's going to be wrong, but hoping I'll get points for at least attempting it.

When we get into the hallway after class, I can only think of five words to describe how the test went. "I did not do well," I say.

"Guess you should have studied last night," Grace replies. That, and I shouldn't have heard a fire alarm blaring for half of the exam. "I actually feel pretty good about it." I hang my head in defeat. I'll never live this one down.

"Heard you got a sweet new ride," Leo appears at Grace's side, grinning.

"I did, and—"

"Shotgun. Called it." Leo cuts her off, pointing at me.

It takes me a beat to catch up. "What? No way. You can't do that!" I look between him and Grace. "He can't do that!"

"Actually, he can," Grace shrugs.

"Not fair. You told *me* we were going for a ride first!"

"But I didn't even have to tell Leo," she fires back. She has a point, but I still shoot a scowl at Leo.

WHEN I GET HOME LATER that evening, Dad has the TV on and is sitting in his chair, snoring. Mom is tucked into her office, and there's a casserole dish on the counter, a sheet of foil on top. To my surprise, the food is still warm. I make a plate, then go and sit down on the couch.

I try to look for the remote, but I can't find it anywhere close to me, so I settle for watching what's on. The news is playing, and after ten minutes of half-listening to the stories, a photograph comes on the screen that piques my interest. It's just the front of a house and isn't notable in any way except for one thing: an old, red truck in the driveway. Something about it seems familiar.

"We got a report about a break-in two nights ago on Highland Street," the reporter says. "The resident has security cameras set up throughout the house, and when he was checking the footage recently he discovered a masked person entering his home at around two in the morning." The screen plays a clip from the footage, of someone wearing all black opening the front door and walking into the house. "The footage shows the perpetrator walking through the house, entering multiple different rooms, and then leaving. Strangely enough, no items were taken from the house." The photo of the house appears again, and I know why the red truck looks familiar. It was from the night I'd been followed by that black Suburban. I'd pulled into *that* driveway and waited there until the car left.

"The video failed to capture any information about a possible vehicle, but this incident should serve as a warning to us all to keep our doors locked and to report any suspicious activity to authorities immediately."

I stare blankly at the TV, realization hitting me. Someone broke into the house that I was followed back to. No items were taken, meaning they weren't looking for money or anything to steal. They were looking for someone. And that *someone* could quite possibly be *me*.

ALL NIGHT, I TOSS AND turn, unable to fall asleep because I can't stop thinking about the black Suburban and the person in the mask. What would have happened if I had gone straight home that night? Would they have figured out where I actually lived and tried to kidnap me? But why me? I can't stop thinking about it, and the one time I'm finally able to drift off to sleep, I wake up from a nightmare of the dark figure chasing after me.

An hour before my alarm is supposed to go off, I roll out of bed and go stand in the shower, double-checking that the door is locked before I hop in. None of it makes sense, and there's nothing I can do about it except hope they weren't really after me, and that this will all blow over soon as some type of misunderstanding.

When I step out into the hallway wrapped in a robe, a hand touches my shoulder and I shriek, jumping away from it.

"I'm sorry, I didn't mean to scare you!" Mom says, hands up in defense.

I put a hand to my chest, breathing hard. "It's okay, sorry. I'm just a little jumpy."

"I heard you up extra early. Did you sleep okay?" she asks, eyebrows drawn.

"Not really," I admit, but I have no further explanation to give her.

She pulls me into a hug. "Sorry, sweetie. I hate those nights. Let me make you some breakfast."

I hug her back, just a little too long. "Thanks, Mom."

When I come downstairs several minutes later, there's a plate of pancakes sitting on the kitchen table and a glass of orange juice next to it. I start to eat, hoping the food will give me some extra energy to make up for the lack of sleep.

When I walk out to my car half an hour later, I'm so tired that I almost don't hear the echo of myself calling out from next to my car. Almost.

"*Hey, Maverick!*" my voice rings out in the quiet morning air.

"*Hey, Laura!*" Maverick's voice calls back from the abandoned house. Then gets closer. "*I see you didn't die from food poisoning, so that's good.*"

"I've actually been deathly sick, I had to go to the hospital," I retort, followed by a fake cough, and then we both laugh.

"I'm just going to blame it on Tony, then," Maverick replies, chuckling. I remember Penny calling the guy in the back Tony when I'd gone to Louise's the other day. Would *he* remember Maverick? Would that finally let me have some solid evidence that this isn't all in my head?

"The food was pretty impressive. Although I'm not sure if that's only because I didn't have to pay for it..."

"Don't think too hard about it." More laughter. Then a pause. *"So..."* Maverick continues, *"Are you... doing anything tomorrow night?"*

"I don't believe I am, why?" my echo replies.

"Well, I was wondering if you wanted to, like, go out? To dinner, or something. Or whatever you want to do." His voice raises a little in pitch. Nervousness?

There's a pause, and it stretches on just a little bit too long.

"It's fine if you don't want to, I just—" Maverick quickly starts to add.

"No!" my echo cuts him off. Another awkward pause. *"I mean, yeah. Yes. I— I would like that."*

"Are you sure?" Maverick's echo chuckles.

"Yes. I'm sure," my voice replies firmly.

"Okay, then," I can hear the smile in his voice. *"What do you want to do?"*

"Dinner sounds nice. I like ice cream, too."

More laughter. *"Okay, so ice cream, and maybe dinner on the side."*

"Sounds perfect to me," my echo replies.

"Cool. Well, I gotta go. But I'll see you tomorrow. I'll come by around 6?"

"6 works."

"Sweet. I'll see you then."

"Cool," I hear myself reply, then Maverick's footsteps retreat. My car door opens, then closes, and the sound of the engine running drifts away. Again, I'm left standing there, all alone, confused by the echo. But this time, I'm not left clueless, wondering when I will hear an echo of Maverick again—or if it will even happen. This time I have a day and hour that I can expect it to happen, and somehow that helps me feel a little bit better.

CHAPTER 8

THE FOLLOWING DAY drags on, and I find myself checking the clock every few minutes. The anticipation is almost as bad as if I was actually about to go on a first date with a guy. Maybe it is as bad. I wouldn't know because I've never actually been on a date with a guy—at least one that I remember.

Lunchtime brings a much-needed distraction because Grace is in full-on planning mode.

"So we're all gonna ride together to the dance on Saturday, right?" she asks Leo and me.

"I'm down," Leo replies.

"I think I'm gonna drive myself," I tell her.

She frowns. "You're not gonna ditch last second, are you?"

I put my hands up. "I already bought the cat ears. I'm fully committed now."

"I'm not even going to complain about your costume choice, because you actually sound like you might show, and that's a first." Grace grins. I shrug in response. "You *have* to let me do your hair and makeup."

"I think I can handle a nose and a few whiskers myself," I say, imagining Grace going all out just for a cat costume. I mean, no doubt she'd make me look *good,* but I'm not sure there's a point when I'm not into the whole dating scene.

"Please?" she begs. "Or at least let me get ready at your house."

I sigh. "Alright, you can come to my house. But no promises on whether I'll let you touch my hair or face."

"I'll come prepared anyways," she winks.

"I'm not really into the whole getting-ready-together thing, so maybe I can just come over when y'all are done and ride with one of you?" Leo asks.

"Sounds like a plan."

After school, I try to kill some time by hanging out in the parking lot with Grace. I'm standing by her car waiting when I see her walking towards me with Andy by her side. They seem to be having a great conversation, laughing about something as they get closer. When Grace looks up and sees me standing there, she says something quick to Andy and then turns in my direction, leaving him behind.

"What's that about?" I raise an eyebrow at her.

"Nothing. It's whatever," she shrugs it off, but I see through her lie. I decide not to press the issue, though, since I'm not sure if I really want to know about whatever is going on.

"I need something to do for the afternoon. Are you busy?"

Grace hesitates, glancing across the parking lot toward where Andy is walking. "A little."

"You know, I still think you deserve better," I tell her.

She makes a face; whether it's anger or regret, I can't tell.

"But it's fine. I'll find something else," I add before she can reply. Then I wave goodbye and hop into my car.

For the rest of the afternoon, I can't seem to do anything productive. Every time I sit down and try to do homework, I end up getting lost in thought and stop after a few minutes. I try cleaning my room, but I just end up pulling a bunch of junk out from the closet, laying it on the floor, and then leaving it because I can't focus enough to sort through it. I'm pacing back and forth in my room by the time six o'clock rolls around. At 6:03, I'm waiting downstairs about to give up hope entirely when the doorbell rings, an echo from last year. I sigh, then wait.

A beat later, footsteps thump down the stairs and the door opens.

"*Hi,*" Maverick's voice is smooth, warm.

"*Hey,*" I hear my echo reply.

"*You ready?*"

"*I am. Where are we going?*" I listen carefully now, knowing that this is my chance to figure out where the echo is going to end up. If I can figure out the destination, I'll be able to go to it and then hopefully be able to listen for the echo of us there.

"*It's a surprise,*" Maverick answers, that smile in his voice again. The sound of it makes me feel warm.

"*Well alright then,*" my echo replies, and I want to reach through time and shake her, demanding answers. This isn't good. If I don't know where we were going that night, I'll have to try and guess the location, which leaves a lot of room for error. But I'm more determined than ever to figure out what's going on, so I follow the echoes out the door and hop into my car. I roll my window down, hoping to be able to listen to the echo of the car's engine and tires so that I can follow it. It works pretty well while we're in the quiet neighborhood, but as soon as we hit the main road, the car's noise gets drowned out by the rest of the traffic, past and present alike.

I think, examining my options. Shorewick isn't that big of a town, so there can't be too many places to look. Or listen, really. I decide that downtown is probably the best date spot in town, so I drive there to start my search. I park in the large parking garage in the center of the city, and from there I walk along Main Street toward the busier strip of businesses. There are all kinds of places to eat around here, and I'm not even sure where—or how—to begin listening for the echo. It's not very busy today, but it was definitely busier last year based on the abundance of echoes surrounding me. I don't know how I'm going to pick out my own voice in the bustle of downtown noise, but I listen intently anyway.

I pass by a flower store, a bar, a burger restaurant, and a photography studio. As I walk, I try to imagine what my first ever date must have been like—if it even actually happened. What did we talk about? What was Maverick like? What did he *look* like? The questions never seem to end, and before I know it, I'm lost in thought, aimlessly walking down the street.

Eventually, I reach a stoplight and realize I'm at the edge of the cityscape. Up ahead are some large warehouse buildings, but to my right, there are some smaller business buildings. I turn in that direction, feeling desperate. About a hundred feet down the road, I pass an alley, and when I glance down it, I find myself staring directly into the grill of a big, black Suburban.

I stumble, recognizing the vehicle immediately, but then try to play it cool, keeping my eyes forwards and continuing my walk at a brisk pace. Maybe it's not the same Suburban. Maybe they aren't looking for me.

Out of the corner of my eye, I see the door of the Suburban pop open as I'm passing, and I know that I'm wrong. It is the same Suburban, and they must have recognized me. I pause for a second, wondering. What if the Suburban and echoes of Maverick are somehow connected? What if the Suburban guy *is* Maverick? I hesitate, my desire for answers growing stronger.

"Hey, you!" a voice calls from the direction of the Suburban. It's light, casual. And definitely not Maverick's voice.

I make the mistake of looking back, and a hooded man is standing a few feet away from the Suburban holding something that looks like a wallet out to me. "I think you dropped this," he tells me.

I look at the guy, knowing fully well that I didn't drop anything. I can't see his face because it's shaded by the hood, and I'm not about to try and get a better look, either. Neither of us moves for a few seconds. I blink once, then twice.

And then I bolt.

A moment later, footsteps follow.

As I race down the street, a few thoughts go through my mind. First: why did I wander off to the edge of downtown where there aren't any people, alone, at this time of night? Second: who is chasing after me? And third: why?

I run faster, adrenaline coursing through my body. At school, I'm not the fastest runner in gym class—but I'm not the slowest, either. I just hope that my speed can get me out of this. Or at least back to the main road, where there might be people around who can help.

Up ahead, the block ends and on the next one are the buildings I'd originally intended to go to. I strain to look at them, searching for some indication that they could be used as a refuge, but I can't even see a neon "Open" sign, so I decide not to risk it. My chances of losing my pursuer might be better if I zigzag through the streets anyway. I make a hard right, sprinting along the backside of the shops I'd walked past minutes earlier. At my first opportunity, I dart right again, sprinting through a thin alley toward Main Street. When I hit the sidewalk, I veer left and use the few seconds I have out of the hooded guy's sight to rush to the nearest door. To my relief, it opens when I tug on it, and I slip inside, attempting to get as far away from the windows as possible.

"Bathroom's in there," a bored voice says from the counter, and I pause to look at her. A woman, probably mid-twenties. Dark hair, thumb pointed at the back corner of the room. "But you gotta buy something."

I nod, realizing that I better move quickly or else the guy might catch up, look through the window, and find me. I half jog to the bathroom, where I lock myself in and stand against the door, panting. A mirror across from me reveals a disheveled, anxious girl that I barely recognize. I walk over to the sink and splash water onto my face, trying desperately to catch my breath.

After spending a longer amount of time than is socially acceptable in the bathroom, I push open the door and step into the shop. For the first time, I notice the strong smell of coffee. The walls are painted bright pink, bearing a logo that says, "Coffee and Cream." It's a small shop, but there's enough room for a few tables and chairs. I recognize it suddenly, remembering that this is where Grace and I went for ice cream the day she and Andy broke up. I remember that their cookie dough ice cream was exceptionally good, too.

The place is empty except for the two of us and seems to have the same amount of business during previous years based on the low level of noise I hear. I walk up to the front counter, angling my body so that I can keep an eye on the front of the shop in case the guy decides to make another appearance. The woman looks up as I walk over, then smiles warmly.

"Rough day?" she asks.

I sigh, feeling my body slowly returning to a non-panicked state. "You wouldn't believe it if I told you."

"Trust me. I understand," she says. But I don't think anyone can understand what's been happening to me lately. I peer up at the menu. The "Coffee" side has a bunch of different drinks listed, and the "Cream" side has ice cream flavors. "Let me guess, you'll have a single scoop of cookie dough in a waffle cone?"

I blink, surprised that she remembers my order from last time. "Yeah, actually," I tell the woman.

"It seems to be your usual." She winks, then turns to the back counter where the ice cream tubs are.

"Usual?" I repeat, confused because I've only been here once, but she doesn't hear me. Wasn't it someone else at the counter when Grace and I stopped in here that day, too? An older man?

"How's your… friend doing?" she asks, back turned, oblivious to my confusion.

I think of the day Grace and I stopped here. Grace had just broken up with Andy, but she hadn't seemed off at the time, so it seems like an odd question to ask.

"Um…" I start to reply, and the woman turns around, holding a delicious-looking ice cream cone in her hands.

She takes two steps, then looks up and pauses for a second, searching my face. "Oh no, you didn't… did you?" Her eyes widen in horror.

"I—" I start, eyebrows cinching up in confusion, but she cuts me off.

"Oh my gosh. I'm so sorry. Forget I even said anything," she says in a rush. She shoves the ice cream into my hands. "I should have known since y'all haven't been here in months. I didn't mean to bring it up. I'm so sorry. This one's on the house. Please, stay as long as you want. I'll leave you alone." The words tumble out of her mouth, panicked. Before I have time to process anything that she said, she turns around and rushes into a back room, the door banging shut behind her.

My heart rate escalates. *Y'all haven't been here in months. Y'all*, as in *me* and *Maverick*?

Just then, I hear an echo of the door opening last year. I turn my head as if I will see someone standing there and listen, hoping to get some type of answer for the questions swirling in my head. But my hope dies a second later when I hear the voice of a young girl say, *"Mom, can I please get the big one this time? Pleeeease?"*

I stand there for a minute, tuning out the rest of the echo, both wanting to barge into the back room to fire a million questions at the ice cream girl and get out of this shop as quickly as possible. Instead, I walk to the back corner of the shop and sit down at a table facing the window. I stare out of it, the cookie dough ice cream slowly melting in my hand as I wonder who the hooded figure chasing me was, and what he wanted from me. Wonder if the ice cream girl simply mistook me for someone else, or if she somehow recognized me because I've been here before... with Maverick. The guy I have no memory of and I'm still not sure exists. It's all enough to make my head spin.

Eventually, after I feel confident that the hooded guy has lost me and is probably long gone, I peel myself out of the chair and make my way to the front of the shop. The ice cream girl is still nowhere to be seen, and I'm too freaked out to want to question her more, so I open the door and step out of the store, a blast of cold air hitting me.

Earlier, before I was chased, the sun was still hanging slightly above the horizon. Now, however, the only evidence of the sun's existence is the pale pink hue of the sky. I pull out my phone, checking the time. Seven-thirty. I wonder where my past self was right now. Was I still on a date with Maverick? I'm not sure if I even know where to look anymore, so I decide I should just go home.

I walk towards where I parked, my head whipping around every few seconds to make sure there's no sign of the hooded guy. The area is pretty empty right now, and the past is quiet, too. So I should know if someone is following me.

When I get to the parking garage, I take my time, peeking around corners and cars before I walk farther. As I'm checking the perimeter, I spot the black Suburban parked discreetly behind a pillar, a few hundred yards away from my car. I stop in my tracks, realizing they might be waiting for me to leave so they can follow me home—to my actual home this time. I wonder if seeing a car nearby a few times is enough grounds for the cops to do anything. I wonder if they would believe me if I told them someone from the Suburban tried to chase me. I don't remember seeing any other people around, so there wouldn't be any witnesses.

I don't have any more time to think, because just then, I hear the Suburban crank up, and the headlights come on. I back away, realizing I'm standing near the parking garage's exit, and if they leave, I'll be in plain sight. I dart around the building, spotting a couple of bushes that I quickly crouch behind. Ten seconds later, the black Suburban comes rolling out of the parking garage. It stops at the edge of the road, and I strain to get a glimpse of anything that might set it apart from other vehicles. But it's just a black Suburban with tinted windows. There are no bumper stickers or anything that makes it unique. It turns down the road, and I'm unable to make out any of the characters on the license plate.

After waiting for a few minutes to make sure it's gone, I rush to my car, then peel out of the parking garage as fast as I can. The entire drive home, I check and double-check the rearview mirror and scan the roads around me for any sign of the Suburban. At home, I pull my car into the garage next to my mom's car. Usually, I just leave it in the driveway, but I don't want to risk anything since my follower seems to know what my car looks like.

And that night, as I'm lying in bed going over everything that's happened in my head, I hear an echo of my bedroom door opening and then closing. It's ten o'clock now, four hours after I heard Maverick and I leave on our date. It makes me wonder where we went, what we did. What kinds of things we talked about, what Maverick was like. But more than anything, I wonder how it would be possible for me to go on a date with someone, and then a year later have no memory of it at all.

CHAPTER 9

OVER THE NEXT COUPLE of days, I don't hear any more echoes that involve Maverick, but there is an increase in the number of times I hear echoes of my phone buzzing in my room while I'm trying to sleep. It makes me wonder if the texts are between me and Maverick, leading me to the question of why those texts aren't in my phone still if they ever existed at all.

Luckily, the Halloween-themed dance is getting close, meaning I have Grace to distract me both at school and after it since she still hasn't completed her costume and insists on me going shopping with her.

"You have to see this, *now*." Grace calls to me as I'm sifting through the used shirts, once again at the thrift store we've now been to a total of three times to look for costume pieces. I step around the rack, my eyes shifting to the garment she's holding up.

"Uhh, I didn't know you were getting married," I tell her. It's a wedding dress straight from the '80s, complete with extremely poofy shoulders and copious layers of fabric.

She ignores me. "Two words: Zombie. Bride."

"I thought you were going to be a scarecrow?"

"A girl can change her mind. Come on, I need your help trying it on."

She needs my help carrying it, too, because when she tries to walk towards the dressing room, half of the dress drags on the floor. I laugh to myself but help her anyway.

"It's perfect," she tells me once she has it on.

"Maybe for our *moms*," I reply. "But I'd never be caught dead in that dress—even if I was a zombie."

"Oh don't worry. I'm going to be making a few alterations," she assures me. "Tomorrow, when I come over to get ready, you won't even recognize the dress."

Except, the next morning, Grace doesn't show up when she's supposed to. And an hour later, when I try to call her, she doesn't answer her phone. I wonder if she's just caught up trying to figure out how to de-ugly the dress, so I let it go. But as the day drags on, and the hours tick by bringing the time closer and closer to the dance, I start to lose hope. I've called four times and sent seven texts, but there's still no sign of Grace.

I'm in the bathroom, drawing a nose and whiskers on my face with eyeliner when the doorbell rings.

"Finally, I thought—" I begin to say as I open the door, but stop when I realize it's just Leo. He's wearing a green turtleneck and pants, a red belt, yellow leg warmers, and what look like ace bandages up and down his arms. I give him a puzzled look.

"Rock Lee? Naruto?" he says with an undertone of "duh."

I nod, though I have no clue what he's talking about. "Sorry, the red hair threw me off."

"Don't even bring it up. My wig was supposed to arrive yesterday, but that obviously didn't happen," he says, frustrated. He steps into the entranceway, closing the door behind him. "Where's Grace?"

Now it's my turn to be frustrated. "I don't know," I tell him. "I've been calling her all day."

He drops his eyes. "She better not be ditching us."

A twinge of anger hits as I remember seeing her with Andy in the parking lot a few days ago. I push it down. "Should we wait for her?"

"Maybe for a little bit. She does like to show up fashionably late."

So we do, and five minutes before the dance is supposed to start, I finally get a text. I hold my phone out so Leo can read it with me.

I'm so sorry. Got caught up trying to fix this dress. Meet you at the dance?

I let out a sigh.

"Typical," Leo says, then gets up from the couch. "I'll drive myself, in case you want to ditch early."

"You're a saint," I tell him, pulling out my keys.

When we get to the dance, Grace's car is nowhere to be found. The parking lot is filling up quickly, groups of people in various colorful costumes making their way into the school's gym. Reluctantly, I force myself to follow Leo towards it all.

When I step inside, the noise hits me like a train. The deep thumping of the music and voices of people trying to talk to each other over the music fills my ears in a way the echoes of the past never have. It's loud. Today, right here, right now loud. So loud that it drowns out the possibility of me ever being able to distinguish what sounds are from today and which ones are from the past.

"The best part about these school dances," Leo practically has to yell over to me, "is that everyone is so caught up trying to keep track of their crush, or their ex or whoever, that no one actually eats the food. So we can pretty much eat whatever we want."

I smile at his comment, still trying to decide if I'm okay with this new level of noise or if I despise it. I follow him to the food table, watching as he piles the appetizers on a tiny plate. As we stand off to the side, munching on our food, more and more people pile into the room, costumes and bodies pressed tighter and tighter together. I search the room for Grace, but I don't see a trace of her. I don't see Andy, either, and I'm starting to wonder if she has a reason other than the poofy dress to be late when Leo takes the plate out of my hands, drops it in the trash, and grabs my arm.

"This is my jam, come on, you've got to dance to this one." A new song has just started, and I can see people on the dance floor cheering at the DJ.

I resist, backing further away from the crowd. "No, I can't. I don't even know how to!"

"It doesn't matter!" Leo replies, voice loud above the music.

"But I—" I try to protest, but another hand grabs my other arm.

"Just one song?" Grace asks from beside me. I sigh, both relieved that she's finally here and sad because I know there's no point in trying to argue when it's two against one.

"I thought you'd never show," I comment as she drags me into the crowd behind Leo. In the dim lights, I can barely recognize the wedding dress she bought from the thrift store. She has cut the shoulders out, torn it in places, and shortened it so that strips of cloth only hang down to her knees. She's added a short veil and done her hair in such a way that it looks both frazzled and perfectly placed all at once. It suits her perfectly.

We make our way into the center of the crowd, pushing past warm bodies and big costumes. Some of the faces are recognizable, and others are so heavily covered in makeup that you'd never know who is underneath. Grace and Leo immediately start bouncing to the beat of the music, moving with the deep, vibrating bass, blending in with the crowd. I stand there, watching, unsure of what to do.

"Come on!" Grace calls over the music.

"I don't know how!" I call back.

"Just move!" she replies.

So I do, starting with a little bit of head nodding and foot tapping. And then, slowly, I start to loosen up, more and more of my body moving with the music. The volume of the music and the crowded room makes me feel trapped, and I can't hear myself think over the sound. But as the songs beat by, I start to embrace the feel of it. The stifling noise becomes a welcome distraction from all of the crazy occurrences lately, and I lose myself in the music.

I'm not sure how much time has passed before I realize that neither Grace nor Leo is nearby anymore. I snap out of the strange trance the music has put me in, straining my neck to see through the crowd. From the corner of my eye, I see Leo standing by the food table and start to make my way toward him.

"Woah. Where did you guys even go?" I ask him.

"Take a look for yourself," Leo replies, a twinge of bitterness in his voice as he points across the room.

It takes me a second to find Grace, still amid the crowd, thumping to the music. Two hands are on her waist, and a tall figure is behind her. Just then, she turns to face him and I watch as Andy leans in, kissing her on the mouth.

I turn back to Leo. "You've got to be kidding me."

"They've been doing that for a while now," Leo says.

I sigh. "Guess it was bound to happen eventually."

"I guess," Leo replies, disappointed. "I wouldn't be surprised if he's the reason she didn't show up earlier."

Anger flashes through me, then, as I think about Grace hanging out with Andy all day, completely forgetting about Leo and me. Not even bothering to let us know where she was until right before the dance.

"Hey, Laura, can I talk to you for a second?" Grace comes up beside me a few minutes later, flashing a grin.

"Yeah, I think that would be good," I reply, not even bothering to try and hide my irritation.

Grace doesn't seem to notice, just grabs my arm and pulls me over to the back door of the gym, stepping outside into the bus parking lot behind the school. Leo trails behind us. The brisk air hits my warm, sweating body and sends chills down my spine. I fear that a small breeze might give me hypothermia. As soon as the door closes behind us, it's like I've put earplugs in. All that's left is the distant thrum of the bass vibrating through the dark.

"Look, I need you to do me a solid," she says. When she finally looks at me, her expression shifts from excited to concerned. "Everything okay?"

I hold in an outburst, barely. "What's going on in there?" She looks confused until I add, "You and Andy?"

She gives me a sheepish grin. "I think we're getting back together."

"Oh really? I never would have guessed, with the mouth-on-mouth action and all."

"What's your problem?" Grace bristles.

"Oh, I don't know. Maybe the fact that you completely ditched me today, instead of coming over like we planned?"

"I didn't mean to—"

"And for what? So you could go screw around with your ex-boyfriend?" I burst.

Grace looks taken aback for a moment, but then she shakes her head. "It had nothing to do with Andy. I promise. Please, I'm really sorry. It took me forever to create this look."

"Which you said you were going to do at my house."

"Look, I'm really sorry. I screwed up. Please forgive me?"

I take in a deep breath. Then let it out. "Fine. But I want details. What's up with you and Andy?"

Grace grins. "He's been so sweet to me lately. And earlier he pulled me aside and said he couldn't stand to live without me anymore. He was practically begging, Laura. And I've just been so miserable without him."

Leo scoffs from beside us. Grace pointedly ignores him.

"But hey, listen. I need a favor," she continues. "Andy wants me to go with him to this after-party with some of his friends. I really want to go, but my mom wants me to come home after the dance. But if I tell her I'm staying the night at your place, she won't worry if I'm out a little extra late…"

I blink, realizing what she's asking.

"I'll come to your house right after the party's over. I promise."

I think about it for a minute, but only one thought keeps popping into my mind. I'd heard some kids talking about it at school. "You're not planning on going to Jet's Warehouse, are you?"

Jet's Warehouse is an old, abandoned warehouse at the edge of town. It's part of an old industrial park that hasn't been used in years. It's a popular spot for parties because it's tucked deep into a pocket of woods, and, according to Andy, there are lots of places to hide if the cops show up. But it's dangerous. And illegal. I've heard rumors about kids going up to the second floor and almost falling through the rotting floorboards. One guy got a concussion from a wall caving in on him. I've even heard about close encounters with bears since it's so close to the base of the mountains just outside of town.

"No," Grace tries to deny it, but I know a lie when I see one.

"You've heard of the things that have happened there, haven't you?"

"I'm aware of the rumors." I can almost see the frustration building in her. "But I'm not stupid. You know that. And it's not like anyone has died or anything. I'm going to be perfectly safe, I promise."

"I still don't think it's a good—"

"I don't need you to judge my decisions right now, Laura. I just need you to cover for me, as my best friend."

I can tell she is getting desperate. But I shake my head. "I can't just do that. What if something happens to you? It's dangerous out there."

"Dangerous?" Grace looks outraged. "What do *you* know about dangerous? Miss stay-at-home-and- never-have-any-fun wants to tell *me* about dangerous?"

"What's that supposed to mean?" My voice raises unintentionally.

"It means you're a party pooper, Laura. It means I'm sick and tired of you dragging me down. I want to go out and party. Have fun. And your idea of fun is sitting in your parents' living room watching a lame movie once a week. I can't do this anymore."

Her words hit me like a slap in the face. I open my mouth, hoping to come up with a retort that might sting just as bad for Grace, but all that comes out is a pathetic, "I thought you liked our movie nights."

Grace sighs, rolling her eyes. "Seriously, Laura?"

"I—" I begin, but Grace puts a hand up, stopping me.

"You never want to do anything with me. Not school dances, not the mall, not even a *movie*, Laura. Literally all you have to do is sit there and eat popcorn! And you can't even *pretend* like you want to do that!"

The words are like a thousand little pinpricks, stabbing me into silence.

"What is it? Do you hate being seen with me, or something?"

I want to grab her by the shoulders, shake her, and scream, "No!" I want to open my mouth and tell her everything—how I hear the echoes, how it makes everything so loud and overwhelming, how it isn't her at all, it's me and this stupid, uncontrollable problem I'm trying my best to deal with.

But I don't. I just stand there, my mouth hanging open like the terrible friend that I am.

Grace drops her gaze, disappointed. "Forget it, Laura. I'm just… I'm done. I'm going out with Andy, and I don't care if you tell me it's stupid. I love him, and there's nothing you can do to change that. Don't worry about covering for me. I'll figure it out on my own." When the words are out, she turns on her heel and marches into the building, the door slamming shut behind her. I watch her through the window, linking arms with Andy as I'm left there, my heavy breathing leaving clouds of mist and the cold air stinging my cheeks.

Leo is the first to move. "I'm going to follow them. I'll make sure nothing happens," he says, the determination in his voice surprising me.

"You…are?" I blink. Leo isn't exactly well-liked by Andy and his friends, so going to the party would mean facing a plethora of ridicule. They might not even let him in.

Leo looks as if he's surprised by his statement, too. "Yeah, I am. I just… don't want anything to happen to her."

"O—okay," I reply. Leo turns toward the door but glances back at me before he opens it.

"She probably didn't mean any of that. It'll blow over soon," he tells me. Then he's gone.

93

CHAPTER 10

I STAND THERE IN THE parking lot for a minute, turning the words Grace said to me over in my head. *You're a party pooper, Laura.*

It hits me hard because I know that it's true. I don't like parties. I don't like malls. I don't like anywhere that's loud, or heavily populated—which are the places that most teenagers love to hang out. Grace always wants me to go out and do stuff with her, but most of the time I'd rather sit at home in the blissful silence of the office.

But I can't do anything about it. I can't just make the echoes of the past go away. They exist wherever I go, and though I've gotten good at tuning them out when I need to, it doesn't mean I like to. And I wish that I could just explain this to Grace. I wish that she could understand, but I know that's not an option. I can't just expect her to believe me.

Which means I can't expect her to be my friend, I realize. *I'm sick and tired of you dragging me down,* she'd said. And that's what I was doing. I wasn't a friend to her; I was a burden.

I don't realize I'm crying until someone opens the door of the gym. A couple of kids spill out into the parking lot, and I turn away so they can't see my face. When I wipe the tears away, my hands are streaked with eyeliner.

I can't stay here anymore, and it's clear that Grace doesn't want me to anyway. I don't want to walk back through the party where everyone can see me, so I start walking along the side of the building. There's a gravel road that runs behind the school just around the corner of the gym, and I can follow it to the parking lot my car's in. This way, no one sees me.

The road is fairly well lit, with light posts dotted along across from me. There's a big chain-link fence just behind them, separating the school's property from the one adjacent to it. As I'm walking, I hear the sound of tires on gravel behind me and light appears, getting brighter as the car gets closer. I peer at it as I move closer to the building to give the car room to pass by me, but when it's about ten feet away it stops. The passenger door opens, but that's all I can see as I squint at the bright headlights. I pause for a second, trying to make out the shape of the car. It's big, and a chill runs down my spine.

Is this the Suburban that's been chasing me?

Just as I think it, a figure steps around the open door, slams it shut, and starts moving towards me. Quickly.

I don't wait any longer. I turn back around, breaking into a sprint. I hear the engine rev up, tires crunching on the gravel close behind me. There's still a long stretch of road ahead of me, and though I might be able to outrun the person on foot, I can't imagine being able to outrun the car.

As I run, I pass a few back doors along the back of the building, and there's another one coming up in front of me. I could try getting inside where the Suburban won't be able to follow, but I'm not sure I want to risk pausing for a locked door. Behind me, I hear the tires crunching closer, and I realize that I might have to because there's no way I'm going to make it much further. So I skid to a stop, put my hand on the door, and tug on it, but as I'd expected, it's locked. Now the car's even closer, and I don't know what to do.

Then, up ahead, I see two small dots of light. Headlights, I think. There's someone else coming down the road. Maybe they can help me.

The two small dots grow into large, bright lights faster than I expect them to. The sound of the engine and the tires screaming across the gravel follow a split second later. It's coming straight at me, so I flatten myself against the building to keep out of its way.

A gust of wind hits me as a small, expensive-looking sports car whips past me. I watch, my eyes widening as it veers to the left, drifting sideways towards the Suburban in a cloud of dust. The sound of a collision comes a second later.

I stand there, stunned for a moment, trying to process what I've just seen. But then, my instinct to escape comes rushing back to me when I see the figure on foot slide past the sports car, still moving—quickly—in my direction. I turn around and continue my flight, realizing that the sports car has just halted the Suburban. If I can outrun the person on foot, I may be able to escape after all.

So I run, and up ahead I finally see the edge of the gravel road and the parking lot just to the left of it. I throw a glance over my shoulder to see how close my pursuer is, and just as I do, the sports car speeds up behind them. It veers around the person, then pulls in front of them, coming to an abrupt halt as it blocks their path to me.

The person in the sports car is helping me. They crashed a very expensive car to stop whoever is doing this. Could they somehow be involved in all this?

I set the thought to the side, continuing my rush towards the parking lot. The sports car seems to have stopped everyone from chasing me for the moment, but I don't slow down.

After what seems like ages, I reach my car, and I go through my pockets for my keys, my stomach dropping when I don't find them at first. Finally, though, my hand touches the metal of my key ring and I whip it out, throwing my car's door open and jumping inside as quickly as humanly possible. I hit the lock button on the door as soon as I'm in, and fumble to put the key in the ignition because my hands are shaking so bad.

Once it's on, I back out of the parking spot and speed toward the exit. In my rearview mirror, I see the sports car moving off of the gravel road and through the parking lot in my direction. I hesitate, wondering what to do. Whoever is in that car seems to be protecting me by blocking my pursuer's path. But what if *it* tries to follow me?

When I glance back again, I see the bright headlights of the Suburban shining over the top of the sports car, headed in the same direction, and I realize that I need to leave, *now*. But before I look away, the sports car makes a wide turn to the left, taking up the entirety of the drivable space in the parking lot. And then it sits there, blocking the path of the Suburban.

I slam on the gas and whip out of the parking lot, losing sight of them both. I speed home, taking a route I don't usually take, making as many twists and turns as I can. I circle the neighborhood once, then twice, on edge. When I'm sure no one has followed me, I finally pull into my driveway. I open the garage door to find that Mom and Dad have both parked their cars inside and sigh, knowing I can't leave my car in the driveway because I don't want them—whoever *they* are—to find me.

As I rush inside to find the keys to Dad's car, I once again think about coming clean to my parents. About telling them everything that's been happening lately. What would they think? Would they believe me? Throughout my life, they've always tried to be supportive of me, but for the longest time, they thought that I'd been lying about the echoes. Making them up, or hallucinating. It wasn't until this past year they've finally believed me, and we've gotten to the point where they don't ask questions anymore, they don't treat me like I'm broken. At least, not as much. So what if I do break? What if this ruins everything we've worked so hard to build?

I shake the thoughts away as I step inside. The house is dark, and it appears that Mom and Dad aren't even awake. I sigh in relief, grab Dad's keys off the key rack, and move his car into the driveway.

Inside the house, I double-check that all of the doors and windows are locked before going upstairs to my room. And when I finally curl up in bed, I can't stop the tears from flowing down my face. I'm confused and angry, and I can't figure out how to fix anything that's going on. I want to know who's chasing me and what they want, I want to know who Maverick is and where he went, and I want to explain everything to Grace and continue to be friends with her. But I can't. I'm just stuck here, curled up in a ball in my bed, not knowing what to do about any of it.

CHAPTER 1

MONDAY MORNING, I roll into the school parking lot, sleep-deprived, and still a bit jittery. One glance around tells me that Grace's car is parked on the opposite side, as far away from mine as possible. I take a deep breath before going inside, unsure of what to do about Grace. I could try talking to her, but what's the point? She made it abundantly clear that I'm holding her back, and who would I be if I kept doing it?

In Chemistry, she's sitting at our usual table, but one of Andy's friends is in my spot. I bite my lip and scan the room, finding an empty table to sit at a few rows away. For the entire class, I avoid looking in their direction because I'm afraid I might burst into tears if I do.

"Alright everyone, I graded your tests over the weekend, and I have to say I'm impressed by the overall performance of the class," Mrs. Andrews tells us. She begins handing out the papers, and I remember the morning Grace showed up with her new car, how I'd forgotten all about the test. How the fire alarm echo had interrupted my already struggling attempts to answer the questions.

Mrs. Andrews passes me by, placing my test on the desk facedown without making eye contact. I flip it over, and at the top, the number 47 is circled in bright red. I take a deep, shaky breath. I usually do excellent in school, and I've never had a grade this low. But with everything going on lately, I've been way too distracted to study well.

"Oh my gosh!" I hear Grace exclaim from behind me a minute later. I try to tune her out, but I still hear her tell someone that she got a 92 on the test, the best she's ever done in Chemistry.

I try to hold in my emotions through the rest of the class, and when the bell rings, I wait until everyone has cleared out before making my way toward the door.

At lunch, I sit at our usual table, but I know that Grace won't be joining me. Instead, she goes over and plops next to Andy without even glancing in my direction. Leo slides into the seat across from me.

"Yikes, you don't look so good," he says.

"Gee, thanks."

"Look, I know what she did sucked, but you know how she is. It'll pass eventually."

"Do you think I'm boring, too?" I ask him, serious.

Leo makes a face, the corners of his mouth pulling to one side. "I think you're just… you. I enjoy our movie nights. I also enjoy going out and stuff, but that doesn't make you boring. It just means you're not the person I'm going to invite to those kinds of things. And if you're okay with that, then I don't see the problem."

I throw my head and arms down onto the table, my voice muffled through my sleeves. "Ugh. Why can't Grace be in love with someone else? I feel like Andy is the one making her think she can't be friends with me because I'm not 'fun' enough, or whatever."

When I look up, Leo is looking across the cafeteria at the table Grace is sitting at, a strange expression on his face. Then he looks down at his food. "He's honestly the worst."

"How did the thing go on Saturday?" I ask him.

"Not well." Leo sighs. "I followed them, but I wasn't about to go inside, since I probably wouldn't be welcome anyway. So I waited outside until Grace left. Everyone was fine, but my parents weren't too happy about me coming home so late. So I'm grounded, for who knows how long."

"Yikes," I reply. I wonder why Leo was so persistent about following Grace to the party. I understand that it's a dangerous place and that he was worried she could get hurt, but to sit outside of the building for hours just to make sure she was okay... that takes dedication. I admire Leo's loyalty, even when Grace isn't returning it.

AFTER SCHOOL, I DECIDE to do some digging to figure out more about this Maverick guy. I remember the echo between me and Maverick about my supposed trip to Louise's. Maverick had talked about Tony, the chef as if he knew him. If they worked together, Tony should know who Maverick is, so I need to ask him about it.

I drive to Louise's alone, and when I pull into the parking lot there are two other cars parked out front. I enter the building and immediately Penny greets me with a smile.

"Welcome back!" I go to the bar, listening to the echoes of busy chattering, just like last time. It's pretty empty today, except for an older couple sitting in a booth to my right. "Friends couldn't make it this time?" Penny asks as I sit down.

I cringe a little bit at the word *friends* but smile back at her. "Just me today," is all I can reply.

"Well, what can I get you to drink on this fine afternoon?" She asks.

"Cherry Coke," I reply, smiling. I'm not sure how to go about asking if I can talk to Tony, so I just sit and look at the menu for a few minutes while Penny pours my drink. When she comes back, I order a burger, remembering to ask for chips as my side since the fries weren't any good last time. She heads back into the kitchen to put in my order, and I catch a glimpse of the older man Penny had called Tony as the door closes.

Once she's gone, I look around the diner, spotting a bathroom sign just past the kitchen door. I get up from my seat and walk over, then down a small hallway that leads to the back of the building. To my left are two doors marked as restrooms, and to my right is a third door with a small window on it, the kitchen on the other side. If Maverick really worked here, there will probably be plenty of echoes of him in there. Maybe if I just slip in for a second and listen, I'll be able to hear something.

Slowly, I push on the door, checking left and right to see if anyone is nearby. As I enter the room, the echoes change from a loud stream of chattering to the sounds of pots and pans clanging, water running, and a knife hitting a cutting board repeatedly. The sounds from today are also quieter in comparison.

Then, to my right, I hear someone's voice. "*Hey, did you finish order number sixty-six?*" it calls out, filling up the space of the room. It's Maverick's voice, from last year.

"*I finished the salad, but that's it,*" another male voice replies to his echo.

"Looking for something?" the same male voice asks, except it's not an echo. I whip around, and the older man I'd seen through the other door is standing a few feet away. He's big, mostly bald, and scowling at me.

"I—uhh, sorry!" I spit out. "I thought this was the bathroom!" I back up, ready to turn to head out the door. The man—Tony, I presume—points out the window of the door I'd just come through.

"Bathroom's right there," he says. I nod, then exit through the door, practically running across the hall to the bathroom.

When I finally get back to my seat, Penny is wiping down the table that the old couple had been sitting at earlier. I take a deep breath and sip on my Coke, my heart rate slowly returning to normal. A few minutes later, the door of the kitchen opens up, and Tony comes out holding a plate with a burger and a bag of chips on it. He sets it down in front of me while I try to avoid his gaze, then puts his hands on the edge of the bar, looking at me pointedly.

"Alright, sweetie. Now you and I both know that the bathroom was clearly marked and that you could see the kitchen through the window. So I need to know what you were really doing back there."

I struggle for a reasonable explanation that doesn't make me sound crazy. "I—uhh—thought maybe I could…" I trail off.

"Steal something?"

"No! Of course not!" I burst, though I can't deny that I do look pretty guilty.

"Then why?" he presses.

"I just—" I stutter, then take a deep breath. Maybe I just need to tell him what I was really looking for. "I needed to ask you something."

Tony raises an eyebrow.

"Do you know someone named Maverick?" I blurt out.

A flash of emotion—surprise?—crosses Tony's face. "Why do you ask?"

"I just… someone told me that he worked here." I can't think of a better explanation.

Then, without saying anything, Tony goes to the cash register. He opens a drawer, digs around for a second, then opens another. He shuffles through some papers and miscellaneous items, then pulls something out of the drawer and walks back over to me, holding out the item. I take it, turning it over in my fingers. It's a nametag, one identical to the one Penny wears. Glancing at Tony, I notice he has one, too. But this one says "Maverick."

I suck in a breath.

"Now listen. I don't know anyone named Maverick. I've never known a Maverick, and I can promise you that one has never worked here. But last week I was cleaning out underneath the oven, and I found this nametag. I'm not sure where it came from," Tony tells me, searching my face. I don't know how to respond, so I just stare at the nametag in my hand. "Do you know anything about it?"

I shake my head. I'd heard Maverick's echo back in the kitchen, *talking* to Tony, and yet, Tony has no idea who he is. "I don't know," I tell him because it's the truth. "I'm just trying to figure it out."

"Well," he says, his face brightening up, "it's a mystery to me. But obviously, it means something to you. I won't pry anymore, but you can keep it."

"Thank you," I tell him, curling my fingers into a fist around the nametag. It *has* to mean something. "I'm sorry for snooping," I add, giving him an apologetic look.

"It's in the past," he replies. He turns to the door, takes a few steps, then stops, facing me. "Sometimes," he adds, "the past is in the past for a reason. Sometimes it's best to leave it there." He gives me a sad smile, then saunters back into the kitchen.

If only it were that easy for me.

CHAPTER 12

THE NEXT FEW DAYS pass in a blur as I try to make sense of the name tag. Just like the vase, it seems to be actual evidence that Maverick exists, but the fact that Tony has no idea who Maverick is seems to negate that. It could have been possible that Tony *did* know Maverick, and Maverick had used a different name, but then why would there be a name tag with *Maverick* printed on it? It doesn't make any sense, and there's nothing I can do except wait and listen, hoping that the echoes will reveal more information eventually.

I don't hear any more encounters with Maverick, but I do continue to notice echoes of my phone buzzing and ringing more often. I don't remember texting anybody that much back then, because even Grace and I weren't quite close friends yet. So the only explanation is that somehow Maverick was involved. Did I like him? Was I seeing him, and simply missing the echoes? I don't know what to think.

Grace avoids me at school, so I spend my lunches with Leo. Since he's grounded, I have no one to hang out with after school, so I end up just heading home. I don't venture too far from the house anymore, especially since the days are getting shorter and I don't want to have any more close calls with the Suburban. I remain on edge, checking my mirrors and scanning the traffic around me for any sign of it.

And then one morning, I finally witness another appearance of the mysterious Maverick.

I'm walking to my car, following the sounds of my own echo leaving for school as usual, when I hear his echo.

"*Laura Jones,*" his voice appears right next to my car, calm with a hint of mischief. I stop in my tracks.

"*Oh!*" My echo replies, surprised. "*Hi.*"

"*How are you?*" he asks, and I can hear echoes of my past self opening the passenger door, dropping something inside, then closing it.

"*I'm well, how about you?*" I hear myself reply.

"*I'm good. But I've got the strangest feeling that you've been avoiding me.*"

My echo lets out a short laugh, then replies, "*What do you mean?*"

"*Come on, really?*" he starts, his tone light. Playful. "*We go on this wonderful, magical date together. I had fun, I thought you had fun. Then for the next week, every time I ask you if you want to hang out or go do something together, you're not home, or you have 'stuff' to do. And now I don't know if you're just playing hard to get, or if you actually don't like me."*

There's a pause, and finally, my echo replies, *"Well, I haven't been avoiding you, actually."*

Maverick makes a noise of shock, then laughs. *"Did you just roll your eyes at me?"*

"Why would I ever do that?" comes my innocent reply.

Maverick sighs in disdain. *"Gosh, now you just think I'm clingy."*

"Maybe just a little," my echo replies, laughing.

"Fine, I can play this game too. Pretend like I don't care. That's okay with me if you really want to do it that way," Maverick challenges. I hear myself laugh, then what sounds like a slap on an arm.

"Stop it. You don't have to do that."

"And why shouldn't I?" I can almost imagine his expression, eyebrows raised, half-smiling, but I can only put the image on a blank face since I have no idea what he looks like.

"Because..." my echo trails off. There's a long pause.

"It's okay if you're not—" Maverick starts, but my voice cuts him off.

"Because I like you?" It sounds like I tried really hard to make it a statement, but it came out as mostly a question.

"You like me?" Maverick replies, mimicking my unsure tone.

"I like you! Okay? I said it," my echo finally replies, laughing. It's less of a question and more of a statement of desperation this time. Maverick just chuckles. *"Oh, so that's it? You have no reply?"*

"*Hmm. I'll think about it,*" he replies. Then footsteps move further away from the location of the conversation, towards the abandoned house.

"*You're the worst!*" my past voice calls out to him.

"*But you like me! You said it yourself!*" he calls back.

I hear myself laughing, then sighing. My own footsteps move around the front of my car. The door opens.

"*But Laura?*" Maverick calls from across the street. I look in the direction of it, my gaze landing on the empty driveway and bushes with little yellow flowers growing on them. "*I guess I like you too.*"

My echo laughs softly, then I call back, "*Go to work!*" The car door closes, and then the engine starts.

As the echoes leave me behind, I stand next to my car, staring at the abandoned house across the street. I feel like I've just witnessed a conversation between strangers, not one that I partook in a year ago. I feel like I don't even recognize the girl that was talking to Maverick. She's flirty and funny and seems normal enough to have someone like Maverick as a boyfriend.

And I'm just a confused, boring version of her that can't even keep her own best friend around.

SCHOOL FEELS MUCH longer than normal, and after what seems like three full days, the bell rings for lunch. Grace is still avoiding me at all costs, and I'm starting to wonder if she'll ever come around.

"It's like I don't even exist to her anymore," I say bitterly as Leo sits down at the table.

"She'll get over it, eventually," he replies.

"I'm starting to think *eventually* means *years* from now."

Leo glances over at Grace's new lunch table. She's sitting next to Andy, her head thrown back in laughter. "It could be a while. But she's not usually one to hold grudges forever."

"She isn't even justified in holding a grudge. I did nothing wrong," I reply.

"I know," Leo sighs. We've probably had this same conversation at least three times now. But I can't stop thinking about it. Grace was the first person who'd ever called me her best friend, and it hurt to have that ripped from me. She took me under her wing when I first moved here and became someone I truly cared about. She helped me feel like I was starting a new life. A normal life. And now, because she's gone, I feel like my ability to be normal is gone with her.

"Maybe I should just try talking to her," I finally say.

Leo shrugs. "If you think that would help."

I put my elbows on the table, pressing my palms to my temples. "I just don't know."

"I'll probably be un-grounded by next week. We could try stopping by her house to chat after school one day? It's probably best if we get her when Andy's not around, anyways," Leo suggests.

I nod, glad to have something even slightly normal to look forward to. "I think that's a good idea."

The weekend passes by uneventfully, and on Monday after school, Leo hangs out at my house for a couple of hours before we go to Grace's. We spend most of the time deep in the trenches of homework, but finally, a little before dinnertime, I take a deep breath and close my book.

"Alright. Let's get this over with."

As we make the familiar drive over to Grace's house, I try to think about what I will say to her. "I'm sorry and I just want to be friends with you again," makes it sound like the whole ordeal is my fault but I imagine saying, "You were a jerk and you need to get over it," isn't going to fix any problems, either. I'm still at a loss as we walk up to her front door, but I ring the bell anyway.

Grace's mom, Clara, opens it, and immediately I can tell we've made a mistake.

"Is Grace here?" Leo asks before I can stop him.

Clara's eyebrows crinkle in confusion. "I thought that Grace was at your house, Laura?" Her eyes dart between us.

I think, quick. "Crap! I totally forgot we were supposed to meet her there!" I grab Leo's arm a little too forcefully, starting to back up as I do.

"Hold it right there," Clara puts a hand up. "I texted Grace an hour ago and she told me she was already there."

I'm a deer caught in the headlights. "I… she must have just gone inside. I forgot about our… meeting. We better go—" I try to escape again, but Clara shakes her head.

"I guess you're not the one that gave her a ride to school, then? Right?"

"I…" I start, but I know it's futile. I glance at Leo.

Clara sighs. "Alright. I think I see what's going on. Why don't you two head home, now, okay?"

"Mrs. Williams—" Leo starts, but Clara puts a hand up.

"It's obvious that Grace has been lying to me, and I can't let her get away with this. I won't mention your names, okay?"

I take a deep breath, knowing that Grace will eventually figure it out, then tug on Leo's arm. "Let's go," I say.

And so we do, and as we're driving away, I realize I may have just gotten Grace into the biggest trouble she's ever been in.

"I think I just killed my chances of ever being

friends with her again," I tell Leo.

"Maybe she won't know it was because of us?" he replies, hopeful.

But the next morning as I pull up to the school, Grace is standing next to my usual parking spot, arms folded.

"What is wrong with you, Laura?" she bursts as soon as I'm out of the car.

"Grace, I'm so sorry—"

"Sorry? For getting me grounded for the rest of my *life*? For showing my mom that she needs to 'put tighter restrictions on my behavior'?" She makes the air quotations with her fingers. "You got my phone revoked, my car taken away, my entire life ruined!" she practically yells at me.

"How was I supposed to know you were using me as a cover? I just went by there because I wanted to talk to you! Grace, please—"

"You wanted to talk to me? Why, Laura? What do you not understand about the words 'I'm done,' huh?"

Leo appears beside me, hands in front of him as if he's approaching a dangerous animal. "Look, Laura just wanted to make things right, you can't blame her for this."

"Oh, so you were in on this too, then?"

"I just wanted us all to be friends again," Leo tells her.

"Well I already told Laura that we were done, and maybe I should've told you the same thing," she spits.

"And what would you know about being done with someone? How many times have you been 'done' with Andy, and still you end up back in the palm of his hand?" Leo fires back, the hurt from her words evident on his face.

"Don't even go there. You're just biased because you don't like him!" Grace attempts to defend herself.

"No, Grace. I'm biased because I'm in love with you!" Leo blurts out, his words knocking the wind out of me. There's a moment where we all stand there, processing what he said. I watch as Grace's face freezes in confusion, and Leo's eyes widen in fear. I look between the two, realization dawning on me. It suddenly makes so much sense. *That's* why he insisted on following her to that party at Jet's Warehouse. Because he cares about her, and he cares enough to take a grounding for her.

We stand there, a triangle of awkwardness, none of us knowing how the conversation took this unexpected turn, none of us knowing how to end it. Then, finally, Grace moves, the anger returning to her expression just before she turns on her heel and walks towards the school building without another word. I turn to Leo.

"I didn—" I start to say, but Leo puts his hand up.

"Just forget about it," he says, then turns to the school building, too.

I want to catch up to him and say something that will help. I want to figure out how to smooth things over with Grace, too, but I don't know how to. So instead, I walk slowly to class, sitting down at my new desk away from Grace, and listen to the echoes of Mrs. Andrews's Biology class for the entire period.

115

CHAPTER 13

LATER THAT NIGHT, I've just curled up in bed and turned the light off when there's a knock at my window. Three distinct taps. I freeze, my stomach dropping as I jolt up in bed to look towards it, but I relax when I hear an echo of footsteps walking to the window. The sound is from last year, not someone trying to break into my house right now.

I turn my light back on, my curiosity piquing when I hear the window sliding open.

"What do you want?" I hear myself call softly. I get out of bed and creep over to the same spot, opening the window today, too, so that I can hear the echo better.

"You. To come with me," Maverick's smiling voice replies from the ground outside.

"Seriously? Right now?"

"Right. Now."

"But it's so cold!" And it's cold tonight, too, a soft breeze sifting through my curtains into the warm, cozy house.

"Problem solved. Catch!" he calls, and I hear the sound of fabric shuffling, then being pulled through the window. I imagine my past self holding one of Maverick's hoodies—if he even wore hoodies at all. Was it big or small? What did it smell like? What did *he* smell like?

"You want me to wear this?" my echo deadpans.

"That is kind of the purpose of a jacket."

"It's fifty degrees, not negative fifteen. This thing is huge.*"*

"I didn't want you to be cold," Maverick replies simply, and my echo laughs from the window.

"Okay, fine. Give me a minute. I'm not jumping out the window."

"What, you don't think I can catch you?"

"I don't. However, I'm pretty sure this jacket would break my fall," my echo replies.

Maverick chuckles. *"Meet me around back then?"*

"Sure." I hear footsteps retreating, then my window closing. Sneaking out at night to see a boy. What a strangely normal thing for my past self to be doing.

I follow the sounds of my echo moving through the room, then down the stairs. The back door opens, and I race after the noise, grabbing a coat off the rack as I pass it by.

Outside, Maverick's voice greets me. *"Warm enough?"*

"I think I'd be sweating even at the north pole."

"Good. Walk with me?"

"Sure. But only if you tell me what brought this strange guy to my window at nearly eleven in the evening?" The sound of my echo starts to drift away from where I stand, so I follow it, moving in the direction of the woods at the edge of my backyard.

"Hold up, strange guy? I thought you would at least consider me an acquaintance by now," comes Maverick's reply.

My echo laughs. *"Fun fact. Your status actually does depend on the circumstances."*

"So like, what kind of circumstances, exactly?" I can almost hear the eyebrow raise in his sentence.

"Hmm. Well, for starters, the time of day. I'm technically supposed to be in bed, so I had to bump you down a bit for rule-breaking."

"Noted. What else?"

"I guess the location can change things, too. Because right now it looks like you're leading me into the woods so you can murder me."

"Wow, I didn't think this through, did I?" Our echoes join in laughter at the comment. A few beats of silence pass and I continue walking in the direction the echoes had been headed, listening. A breeze drifts past, rustling the tree branches above and I shiver, pulling the coat tighter around myself.

I'm beginning to think I've lost track of the echo when a few feet away, Maverick's voice appears again. *"So if we stop here, does that move me up on the list?"*

I walk toward the sound, listening as my echo says, *"Not really. You're still at strange guy, but you've dropped the risk of falling to ax murderer."*

Another gust of wind blows through the trees, but Maverick's voice is easy to pick out, its low pitch standing out against the rustling of the leaves. *"Okay, okay. So how can I move up on the list?"*

My reply comes a beat later. *"Well, you did bring me a jacket to stay warm, so you get points for that. But my hands are freezing."*

Another few seconds pass. *"Does this help?"*

"See, now I'm just confused. Because you were just at strange guy, but holding hands is definitely creeping into boyfriend territory." I feel my heart flutter a bit at the thought of holding hands and boyfriends, but it just leaves me longing to remember this moment. To remember Maverick.

"Oh snap. Laura just used the b-word. Who are you?" Maverick gasps.

"Whatever. Just tell me why you brought me out here!"

"What, I can't just surprise my girlfriend with a scandalous stargazing session whenever I want?" I hear my echo laugh, then Maverick adds, *"Also, there happens to be a meteor shower tonight."*

"Seriously?" my echo replies, and I look up at the sky. It's cloudy tonight, but there's a gap in the trees right above where I stand that would be perfect for stargazing on a clear night.

"Seriously. Of course, we'll be lucky if we see two or three. The peak isn't supposed to happen until two or three, but assuming you want to go to school tomorrow, you'll probably want to go back to bed a lot sooner."

"Oh, okay," my echo replies but doesn't sound too terribly disappointed.

"Really it just made for a good excuse to get you out here with me."

"I think that actually bumps you back down to strange guy," my echo teases.

Maverick laughs, a low, gentle sound. *"Alright, we need to watch, because we could only have so many chances to see one."* At that, there's a rustling sound in the grass. Us lying down?

A long silence stretches into the night and I stare up at the sky, waiting to hear the continuation of the echo. It seems like such a sweet, romantic gesture, an interesting addition to the playful flirting from a few days ago. I wonder what, if anything, had happened between now and then.

"Look!" my echo exclaims, though there's nothing but clouds for me to look at in the present. *"Did you see that?"*

"I did! Hurry, make a wish."

There's a brief silence, and I close my eyes. *I wish I remembered this moment. I wish I knew what happened to you.*

"What'd you wish for?" he asks.

"Wouldn't you like to know?" my echo counters.

"I would, actually."

"I can't tell you, or it won't come true."

"That's totally a myth," Maverick fires back.

"Maybe. But I'd rather not take any chances," my echo insists.

"So what if I guess what you wished for, and you just tell me if I guess it right? Because technically then you're not telling me," Maverick suggests.

"Hmm. It's risky, but I guess you can try if you want," comes my reply.

"*Challenge accepted. Okay, so what would Laura Jones wish for? Let me think,*" Maverick pauses. "*I know. A scoop of cookie dough ice cream, on a waffle cone.*"

I shiver, partially because of the cold and partially because I remember the worker at Coffee and Cream knowing the exact same order Maverick just recited. It *is* my favorite. "*Really good guess, but no.*"

"*An endless supply of French fries?*"

"*Why do you think I would want that?*"

"*Have you seen yourself around a plate of French fries?*" He chuckles. "*You're pretty ravenous, actually. And you get territorial about them, too. Anyone who takes one—or even thinks about taking one—gets this horrifying glare.*"

"*Oh my gosh, stop it!*" Both of us laugh, and I imagine the moment, lying on the grass next to a guy, joking around. It just seems so… normal. I envy my echo, wishing I could feel that normality right now.

"*It's super cute, honestly,*" he says.

"*Whatever,*" the word comes out muffled as if my face is buried in my hands.

A minute later, Maverick speaks again. "*Alright, I have one final guess, and then I give up.*"

"*Better think carefully, then.*"

There's a long silence, and the wind sifts through the trees again, gentler this time. I look up, watching the dark shadows of the leaves moving.

"*That's my final answer,*" Maverick finally says. I frown, feeling like I'm missing part of the conversation.

"You might be right," my echo replies, barely above a whisper.

"Knew it!" he exclaims.

"And my wish came true because I didn't tell you what it was. Point proven," my echo says matter-of-factly.

"Actually, I would have kissed you whether you told me or not, so point not *proven,"* Maverick replies, and my stomach drops. *Kissed?*

"Whatever," my echo huffs. There's another pause and I feel like I'm eavesdropping on an intimate conversation that was only meant for the people involved. Like I'm hearing another person's life unfold in front of me. Not mine.

"You don't have to wait for another shooting star to get another kiss, you know," Maverick finally says.

"I'm okay with that being a permanent rule."

"Deal, but only if I'm permanently upgraded to a rank higher than strange man."

"I guess I can do that," my echo teases.

He laughs, and silence falls across the backyard. I've heard myself meeting, flirting with, and going on a date with this guy, and I still have no recollection of any of it. And now, I'd apparently kissed him, though I definitely don't remember kissing anyone, *ever*.

This happened a year ago. An entire year, and I have no idea what happened after this. Did we keep dating? Did we break up? And where is he now?

These echoes are giving me a glimpse into the relationship that Maverick and I must have had, but there isn't any useful information about who Maverick is or what happened to him. I've got two pieces of solid evidence that he actually exists—the vase and the nametag—but how can they mean anything when no one seems to remember anything about him?

CHAPTER 14

TWO DAYS LATER, it's Halloween. It's a day I've dreaded for a few years now, ever since I grew out of my trick-or-treating days. Now, all the day brings is a constant stream of doorbell ringing, both from the past and the present. It's a day where sitting in the office can't even bring me peace and quiet, and going out is even worse because *everyone* throws parties on Halloween.

"You're not going to dress up?" Mom calls to me from the stairs just as I'm about to open the front door to leave for school.

"Not a chance!" I call back, waving. There's a decent amount of my peers who do dress up for the holiday, but I'm not one of them. I imagine that if Grace and I weren't on such bad terms, she'd have convinced me to dress up with her—but under the circumstances, that wasn't going to happen this year. Even

Leo has been avoiding me since the confrontation on Tuesday where he confessed his love for Grace. I've seen glimpses of him in the hallways, but he hasn't shown up at the lunch table or in the parking lot since.

Though it sucks eating alone, I've been using the time to focus on my studies. I can't afford to get another bad test grade, at least not without risking parental involvement, which I don't ever want to have to go through. I've put my parents through enough stress throughout my life, and the last thing I want them to worry about is my grades.

So after school, I head straight home, hoping to use the few hours I have before the doorbell starts ringing nonstop as effective study time. And I do, for the first forty-five minutes or so, until I hear an echo of my front door opening. Footsteps walk into the kitchen, the sound of plastic bags along with them. I hear things being set down on the counter, then Dad's voice. "*Kara, honey, are you home?*" he calls out.

"*I'm coming,*" Mom's voice echoes from her office. Her footsteps enter the kitchen.

"*I got the stuff you asked me to get from the store. What's all this about? I thought we were just going to order pizza tonight?*"

"*We were, but we've had a slight change of plans,*" Mom's echo replies.

"*What do you mean?*"

"*Laura texted me. She invited Maverick to come over tonight!*" Mom sounds *way* too excited.

"*Did she?*" Dad replies.

"*Yes, and I don't want to scare him off. I'm going to make my famous meatballs.*"

"You shouldn't be worried about scaring him off, Kara. This is our chance to find out more about him. Intimidate him a little bit and see if he's even a good fit for Laura," Dad says. I almost laugh at the idea of my dad trying to intimidate a guy I brought over. If I'd ever actually brought a boy over, which I don't remember doing.

"No, Jeff, we can't scare him away," Mom replies.

"Why not? If I don't think he's good for Laura, I have no problem telling him exactly that."

"This is her chance, Jeff. The first boy she's ever dated— even though she won't call it that. If this goes well, she might gain some confidence and realize that she can live a normal life, just like the rest of us," Mom tells him, concerned. I repeat the words back in my mind, closing my eyes. I know my parents always wished they'd had a normal kid, and I've felt so bad about it. They didn't ask for this life, none of us did, but there's nothing we could do about it.

"I get that, but if he's not treating her right, then things could get even worse," Dad points out.

"I don't think we have anything to worry about. You remember him, right? He helped you move all that furniture. He seems like a total sweetheart. And I've never seen Laura so happy before," Mom replies, and I can hear the smile in her voice. I try to imagine feeling so happy, with no chaos or confusion surrounding me. But I can't. Not while listening to an echo of something I don't remember anything about.

"I know. But I still want to make sure his intentions are in the right place," Dad adds. Then I hear the plastic bags shuffling,

the fridge opening and closing, and the sounds of food preparation beginning.

Mom and Dad must have both known about Maverick, too. But they don't seem to remember anything about him, either. Do they? How could someone exist in the echoes of the past, yet no one from the present has any clue about them? Not me, not my parents, not even Penny or Tony, who he supposedly worked with. No one seems to know who he was…

Except for that girl at Coffee and Cream. She seemed to recognize me and might have remembered Maverick. But I'm not sure if that was solid evidence or just her mistaking me for someone else.

For the rest of the afternoon, I listen to the echoes of dinner being made while I work. Mom comes home while I'm deep in focus, more on the echoes than my homework. She sets two giant bags of candy down on the counter, then walks into her office without saying another word.

Then, around four-thirty, the echo I've been waiting for appears. The front door opens, then closes, and a moment later I hear my own voice in the kitchen.

"*It smells delicious in here!*"

"*Hey, guys!*" Mom's echo replies.

"*Well, well, well. It's about time you showed up here again,*" Dad's echo adds.

"*Hello, Mr. Jones. How are you doing?*" Maverick's voice appears, just across the room from where I sit now.

"*Oh, just fine. And you?*" Dad replies. I imagine a handshake ensuing.

"Good, thanks. Do you need help with anything?" Maverick asks.

"No, no! We'll take care of it, you two just have a seat!" Mom replies.

"I am a cook over at Louise's, Mrs. Jones, so it's no problem, really," he adds from by the sink.

"You could chop these tomatoes for me if you want to?" Dad offers.

"No, no. Don't even listen to him! Jeff could use the practice, anyway," Mom throws in, laughing. After a few beats, she asks, *"How is your Mom doing? I still think it was so sweet of her to bring over those flowers. Is she busy tonight? She's welcome to join us for dinner, of course!"*

"She's volunteering for her school's trunk-or-treat tonight. She teaches Kindergarten over at Lakefield Elementary."

"Oh, how sweet! We'll just have to catch her next time, then."

"Definitely," Maverick replies, then adds, *"Are you sure you don't want some help with that?"*

"Oh, Jeff! I said slice, *not* mash. *Maybe I should let Maverick do this,"* Mom laughs.

"I agree," Dad replies.

"On it," Maverick says. I hear a drawer opening, then the faucet running again.

"So you're a cook at the diner, huh?" Dad starts, his voice on the other side of the counter now. *"Do you plan to work there for a while?"*

"For now, yeah," Maverick answers, and I hear the sound of a knife cutting through what sounds like lettuce. *"I'm taking a*

couple of classes at the community college right now while I finish my high school credits through a homeschool program. I hope to get into State next year." It's the same college I'd been looking into. Grace wanted me to go there with her and be roommates, but I'm not entirely sure I *want* to go to college, a place where thousands of students have been through for years. Maybe online school is the best route for me.

"That's nice! What do you want to study?" Dad's echo asks.

"For undergrad? Biology, probably. I eventually want to specialize in neuroscience, though."

"Neuroscience! Wow, how'd you decide on that one?" Dad sounds shocked.

"I'm just... fascinated with how our brains work, I guess."

"Interesting," Dad replies. *"So what's your dad up to, then?"*

There's an awkward pause until Mom finally speaks up. *"You don't have to answer that. Jeff—"*

"No, it's okay," Maverick jumps in. *"My dad isn't around. I never really knew him."*

"I am so sorry, Maverick. Jeff is just really... interested in getting to know you. He didn't mean to bring up anything painful," Mom says hurriedly.

Maverick laughs, though. *"It's okay. I think you have a right to know more about your own daughter's boyfriend."*

There's a pause, and then my own voice echoes from the other side of the kitchen. It surprises me because I'd almost forgotten that this entire conversation is an echo and that I'm not actually seeing it unfold in the present. *"Why is everyone looking at me like that?"* I hear myself ask.

"*Maybe because we're all wondering if you're going to correct my use of the word* boyfriend, *or if you're going to finally let it go,*" Maverick answers. The room fills with laughter.

"*You know, I think I'm starting to like this kid,*" Dad says, chuckling.

The conversation continues, and I listen, hoping to catch some chunk of information that might help me in my search for answers. Dad starts telling stories about some of the crazy things he did with his friends when he was in high school, and then Mom makes small talk, careful to avoid anything that may be too personal, I notice.

Around six o'clock, I hear the front door opening today, and Dad enters the kitchen carrying a shopping bag. He looks at the two bags of Halloween candy on the counter, then down at the bag in his hands.

"Kara," he calls to my Mom. She enters the kitchen, eyeing the bag in his hand as she does. I hear the echoes of the past around the table laughing at the same time.

"You bought some too, didn't you?" Mom asks, just after I hear her echo say, "*Well we'd better start cleaning up before the trick-or-treaters make their appearance.*"

Dad of the present sighs. "I guess I'm just going to have to eat it all," he says, and I strain to hear the echoes over him. There's the sound of kitchen chairs scooting across the floor, then plates being collected.

I hear an echo of the doorbell ringing, and then my own voice saying, "*I'll get it.*" A beat later, the doorbell rings today.

"I'll get it," I tell my parents, feeling a strange sense of deja vu. I grab one of the bags of candy from the counter and head to the door, hearing it open in the past just before I open it today. After I hand out the candy and close the door, Maverick's echo appears next to me.

"So what do you say about that haunted house tonight?" he asks. I stop in my tracks, listening.

"I don't know. I'm sad to admit, but I'm a bit of a scaredy-cat," my echo admits. It's a lie, of course, but an expected one. I had to find some excuse not to go to a loud place, I guess.

"That's what I'm here for. I'll save you from the monsters," Maverick teases. My echo laughs.

"Yeah, but still…" I trail off.

"It's not that scary, honest. And we can leave if you decide you don't want to go in," Maverick assures.

"I'm not sure…"

"Hey," Maverick's voice goes serious. *"Do you trust me?"*

I count one, two, then three seconds before I hear my reply. *"Of course I do."*

"Then what do you have to worry about?"

"Okay fine. I'll go with you. But no promises I'll go inside," my echo finally gives in.

"That's fine with me," Maverick replies, and our footsteps start back towards the kitchen.

Later that night, I hear the echo of me and Maverick leaving the house between doorbell rings. I feel strange, like I should be leaving, following the sound, taking part in the echo. But after what happened the last time I tried to follow myself on a date, I know that it's not the best course of action. So instead, I stay inside, taking turns with my parents passing out candy to kids, wondering what the night was like for my past self one year ago.

I don't remember going out that night, but I do remember having Mom's meatballs. When I try to remember how I spent the latter part of the evening, my memory comes up blank.

Toward the end of the night, I finally work up the courage to ask my Mom a question. "Do you know anyone named Maverick?"

Mom's sitting on the couch across from me. She yawns, flipping through the channels on TV. "Not that I can think of, why?"

"I just… heard the name somewhere, is all," I tell her, feeling disappointed. Mom not remembering Maverick isn't helping my case.

Mom looks over at me, like she wants to ask more about it, but decides against it.

"What about that house across the street? To the right of Kate's. Do you know who lived there before?" I press.

"To the best of my knowledge, it was foreclosed a while ago, years before we moved here," Mom replies. "Why? Have you been… you know…?" Mom trails off. I can fill in the blanks for her: *hearing things?*

"It's not important," I reply, shaking my head. I get up from the couch.

"You know you can talk to me, if you need to," Mom tells me as I'm walking away.

I turn to look at her for a second, a sad smile pulling at my lips. "Thanks, Mom," I say, wishing that I *could* just talk to her, and come clean about everything I've heard lately. But I don't, because I'm afraid of what might happen if I do. Will I finally be able to put the puzzle pieces together, or will I only end up with more questions?

CHAPTER 15

THE NEXT DAY AT school, Leo appears at the lunch table, setting down his tray in front of me. I blink in surprise.

"Before you say anything, I already know I'm an idiot," he says.

"Leo—" I start.

"Don't even try to deny it. I was stupid to think…" he closes his eyes. Sighs.

"I had no idea," I tell him.

"It doesn't even matter anymore." He shakes his head.

"You don't know that," I say. I think of all the times I'd heard Leo and Grace bickering about random things. How they frustrated each other but were always best friends at the end of the day. They'd be a good match.

"I *do* know that Grace is probably never going to speak to me again."

"You and me both," I reply. "I'm pretty sure I actually ruined her life."

"For now. When things go south with Andy again, she'll come around."

"Is it bad for me to hope it will happen soon?" I ask.

"If it is bad, then I'm the worst." He pauses, pushing a piece of salad around on the plate with his fork. "I just hope I didn't screw everything up with her."

"I doubt it. She'll come around, like you said," I tell him, hoping he's right. She can't just throw away an entire year of friendship like that. *Right*?

"Maybe to you. But I made things weird. I can't ever take it back," he replies. It dawns on me that he's probably also wondering if she'll ever want to be more than friends with him.

It's an interesting thought, Grace and Leo dating. I'm not sure how that might change our friend group. Would it be more fun, or would I always feel like a third wheel?

The thought of dating leads me to Maverick. The boy that only seems to exist in the echoes of the past. And a name tag. And maybe a vase. But what other evidence do I have that he exists?

The lady at Coffee and Cream, perhaps. She had recognized me that day when I ran in there to escape the person chasing me. Either that, or she thought I was someone else. But the fact that she knew I'd ordered cookie dough ice cream makes me think that it wasn't just a weird mistake. And I'd been so frazzled from the whole ordeal, I hadn't thought about going back to talk to her.

If she remembers me, even from what could be months ago, maybe she remembers Maverick, too. Maybe she can lead me to him.

I look directly at Leo, a new idea crossing my mind. "Do you want to grab some ice cream with me after school?"

Leo narrows his eyes. "If this is your way of asking me on a date, I don't think you understand what happ—"

"Ha, ha," I cut him off, rolling my eyes. "No. I just need to go do something. Distract myself from all this drama."

Leo shrugs. "I mean I guess if you want to. You know I'm always down for food."

I sigh in relief. I don't want to end up alone downtown again, being chased by a stranger.

So half an hour after school, Leo and I push through the doors of Coffee and Cream and the deep, rich smell of coffee fills my nose. No one is in the shop besides us, but I can hear a conversation at the back of the shop mixed with the sound of a child laughing. The noise must be a few years old, however, because it's low and so muffled that I can't make out any of the words.

Good. Nothing to distract me from getting answers.

No one is at the counter when we get there, but after a few seconds, the door to the back room opens up. My heart speeds up when I recognize the girl walking in our direction.

"Hello," she says, a flash of recognition crossing her face when she sees me. She looks over to Leo, then back at me. "How can I help you?" she asks, avoiding my eyes. I glance at the nametag pinned to her shirt. Elle.

"I'll have the usual," I say. Elle blinks at me, nods, then turns to Leo. She knows what I'm talking about. She recognizes me again, meaning it probably wasn't a mistake the last time.

"And you?"

Leo stares at the menu for a minute. "Chocolate chip mint. Double. In a cup."

"Sounds good," Elle replies, then walks over to the back counter to get our order ready. When she pulls out a waffle cone and scoops cookie dough ice cream onto it, I realize how close I might be to finally getting answers. She passes my cone across the counter, then goes to scoop Leo's.

"Come here often, then?" Leo asks me.

"I guess I do," I reply, worried that it might be true. What happens if this girl—Elle—confirms Maverick's existence? How do I explain my lack of memory and the fact that no one else seems to remember him either?

When Elle comes back to hand Leo his ice cream, I almost fire all of my questions that second, but I hold back, remembering that none of it will make any sense to Leo if I do it in front of him.

After we pay, I lead us to the opposite end of the shop and sit down at the table. I wait a couple of minutes before making my move. "I need to get some napkins," I tell Leo, then stroll over to the front of the shop. Elle has already gone to the back room again, and although I can clearly see the napkin dispenser along the counter, I ring the bell. I just hope that Leo doesn't question it.

When she comes out, I take a deep breath.

"Can I talk to you for a second?" I ask. She eyes me suspiciously but nods. I move closer to the counter, my voice low. "Last time I was in here, you recognized me. You said that I hadn't been here in months, right?"

Another nod.

"Here's the deal," I say. I'd rehearsed this story a hundred times since I came up with it at lunch, but I still hesitate before I continue. "I was in a car accident recently, and I got a bad case of amnesia." The story almost doesn't feel like fiction, because amnesia would explain a lot of what's happening. "I don't really remember much from the past... well, year of my life. And I was just hoping you could help me clear up some things since it seemed like you knew something I didn't."

I watch, my heart pounding in my chest, as Elle's expression changes from confusion to shock to realization. "Oh my gosh," she says, putting a hand to her mouth.

I wait, trying to listen over the blood rushing in my ears.

Finally, she speaks. "So you don't remember anything? Ever coming here? With that boy?"

My heart stampedes in my chest at the word *boy*. "No," I barely manage to say.

She covers her face with her hands. "This is so tragic."

I don't know how to respond, so I wait.

"Listen, I don't know much, honestly. I'm probably not the best person to ask." She shakes her head.

"I need someone to tell me. Please," I beg. I don't have to fake my desperation.

She sighs, nods, then starts talking. "It started last year around this time, I think. You and this guy started coming in here every week, it seemed. You'd always get a scoop of cookie dough on a waffle cone, and he'd always get a hot chocolate with extra whipped cream. Even when it got hot outside."

I blink, trying to process what she's telling me. "Got hot outside?" is all I can say.

"Yeah. You two were, like, *so* in love. You'd come in here and sit down for hours, just talking. But then, maybe around June, you just stopped coming. I didn't see you again until the last time you were here."

A string of chills runs through my body, from my neck down to my toes. "June?" I choke out. June, as in four months ago? As in, *eight months* after meeting Maverick for the first time?

"Yeah. It didn't even cross my mind that y'all might not be together anymore. You seemed so… happy. I thought maybe you'd gone away for the summer or something."

I have to focus to control my breathing. "What happened to him?" I say, barely above a whisper.

Elle gives me a pained look. "He wasn't in the accident with you, was he?"

I breathe in slowly. There was no accident. There is no explanation. He's gone, vanished from my life, leaving nothing behind, not even a memory of him. Except for this girl, in this random coffee shop that I'd never have stumbled into if I hadn't been chased that night. Why would *she* remember, when neither I, my parents, or even Tony can remember him? None of it makes any sense.

"I'm so, so sorry. I had no idea you—" Elle begins to say, but I cut her off, feeling my eyes starting to water.

"Thank you for telling me," I choke out, then turn around. It takes everything I have to pull it together as I walk back to Leo.

"I thought you were going to grab some napkins?" Leo asks as I sit down across from him. He glances up, then frowns. "Are you okay?"

I stare down at my melting cookie-dough ice cream cone. "I'm fine," I say.

"Look," Leo shakes his head, "everything's gonna be okay with Grace, just give it some time."

I nod, wishing he knew that there was so much more going on in my life. "I think I should get home," I tell him.

Leo nods and doesn't say another word to me as we exit the shop. He gives me a small wave as he walks past my car towards his own, and then I drive home in silence.

THAT NIGHT, I CAN'T sleep, something that's becoming a recurring pattern in my life. I pace back and forth in my room for hours, thinking I might eventually tire myself out, but every time I lie back in bed, I end up just staring at the ceiling, wide awake. Over and over I try to make everything make sense, but I can't. The ice cream girl had seen me and Maverick coming into her shop for *months*. And then, in June, we'd just… stopped. What had happened in June? Would I have to wait until then, listening to these echoes for months, to find out? The idea sounds like torture.

Sometime around two in the morning, I'm pacing around my room again when I pause by the window, peering out at the street.

I do a double-take when I realize that there, sitting in the driveway of the house that's been abandoned—Maverick's house—is a car. I can't exactly see it very well through the dark, but the shape of it is unmistakable.

My heart skips a beat. Someone is there, right now. Could it be him?

I don't even think about it, I just move, grabbing my coat, rushing downstairs, and slipping on my shoes. Then I'm quietly opening the front door, slipping outside into the cold night air, moving towards the house.

When I get closer, the car in the driveway becomes more visible in the moonlight, and my stomach drops. It's a black sports car. I don't recognize the brand or model, but it looks exactly like the one that showed up the night of the Halloween dance.

When I get even closer, I see that the entire right side is crushed. I pause, the pieces falling into place. This could be Maverick's car. *He* could have been the one protecting me from the Suburban chasing me. If we were so *in love* like Elle had explained, then it would make sense that he'd want me to be safe. Right?

But, then, who was chasing me? And more importantly: *why*?

Slowly, I creep closer to the house. I crouch down as I get to the front, not wanting whoever's inside to see me. I step past the bushes covered in slowly dying yellow flowers, peering at the front. The door has a padlock on it, the same kind I'd seen on houses that have been foreclosed. The blinds in the windows are drawn, and I can't see anything inside, not even a hint of light.

I slowly shuffle across the front of the yard, making my way to the side, then the back of the house. Whoever parked the car must have gotten inside somehow, and I intend to use the same point of entrance.

At the back, I crouch as I move past each window, trying to see inside. Eventually, I spot what I'm looking for: just past the padlocked back door, a window is wide open with the screen on the ground beside it. The glass is broken through in one corner, a hole just big enough for someone to reach their hand inside and unlock the window.

I sit crouched a few feet away from it, contemplating. If I go, I could run into whoever is inside. If it's Maverick, I might be able to get some answers. But if it's someone else, or if Maverick isn't the sweet, fun guy he sounds like in the echoes…

I shake the thought away. I'm willing to take that risk more than anything right now.

So I wait just outside the window for a few minutes, listening. There's no noise coming from inside, not even from the past. When I peer into the house, I don't see any movement, so I throw a leg over the windowsill and slip inside.

It takes a minute for my eyes to adjust to the dark, but when they do, I'm surprised by what I see. I'm standing in the living room, and instead of being empty like I'd expected the abandoned house to be, it's full of furniture. Couches, a TV, end tables, and lamps are scattered across the room. Further down, the kitchen and dining room look pretty well furnished, too. Almost as if someone is still living here, or, I suppose, like they had to leave in a hurry without taking anything with them.

After I take it all in, I move deeper into the house. The echoes are just as quiet as the house is right now, and I'm sure I could hear a pin drop from across the room. My eyes are peeled, looking for any sign of movement, and I'm crouched low to the ground. But as I move from kitchen to bathroom, I don't see any signs of life.

Eventually, when I'm sure that the downstairs is empty, I creep over to a staircase I'd passed earlier, listening for any sounds from up above. When I'm sure nothing is coming, I quickly and quietly climb the staircase, pausing at the top to look around before I go any further. The upstairs opens into a hallway with three doors, two on the right and one on the left. The door on the left is slightly ajar, so I slide towards it, peering inside.

It's a bedroom. A glance around tells me that no one is here, either, so I slip inside and take in my surroundings. A queen-sized bed stands in the center of the room with a dark plaid comforter spread on top. In the silence, I can hear an echo of someone breathing softly on the bed, probably sleeping. Who was it? Maverick?

There's a bookshelf next to a dresser on one side of the room, and on the other, a desk and an office chair. I walk over to the desk, noticing a stack of papers on it as I get closer. In the dark, I can barely make out the letters that form the words, "Argumentative Essay," at the top of the first page. It looks like a school assignment, so my eyes are immediately drawn to the top left corner.

I try to control my breathing as I read the name at the top. *Maverick Schall.*

A sudden noise cuts through the darkness, startling me. Downstairs, it sounds like a window being closed. I wait for a second before I go to the bedroom window and make a small gap in the blinds to see out of. I can see the driveway, the little black car still parked there. After a few seconds, a figure appears from the side of the house, walking toward the car. I spring into action, exiting the bedroom and rushing down the stairs. I can't let him leave. I need answers.

When I get to the window I'd climbed through earlier, it's closed. The screen is replaced and the only sign that it was ever tampered with is the small hole in the corner of the glass.

I throw it open, kicking out the screen with as much force as I can muster. When I finally get outside, I break into a sprint, whipping around the side of the house.

When I reach the driveway, disappointment hits me. The car is gone. My chance of finding answers is lost.

I turn back to the house, shivering as a cold breeze blows across the yard. I want to go back inside and turn every square inch of the house upside down to find more information, but instead, I just stand there, trying to catch my breath.

For the rest of the night, I toss and turn, questions running through my head. Was the person in that house Maverick? And if he was, what was he doing there? Why was the house foreclosed, and where do they live now? Around 4, I come to the decision that attempting to sleep is futile, so I flip my bedroom light on and pull out my laptop to do some research.

I start by typing the name "Maverick Schall" into the search bar. In seconds, a list of various people with the same name pops up and I begin to scroll. Unfortunately, as I click on each link and scan through, I don't find anything that stands out. Most of the people listed are from different states or aren't close to my age.

I type in "Annie Schall" next, and the first link that comes up takes me to an obituary for Annie Elizabeth Schall, who passed away on April 19th of this year.

My eyes drift down the page.

Annie Elizabeth Schall, 49, passed away Sunday morning at her home in Shorewick.

In honoring her wishes, no services will be held.

Annie was born in Shorewick, the daughter of Eliott William Schall and Angela Rose Schall. Annie worked at Lakefield Elementary as a Kindergarten teacher for 23 years until retiring in January of this year.

Surviving is her son, Maverick Schall.

I swallow hard.

Maverick's mom passed away. The same woman I'd heard an echo of that first night we'd moved into our new house. I want to feel sad at the knowledge of her passing, but because I can't remember her, I can't seem to feel anything other than confusion.

And that's it. Nothing else. No other family, no cause of death, no information about where Maverick is now. It isn't helpful at all, but it does strike me as odd that Annie was so young when she passed. And no cause of death is listed.

Now I have more solid proof that Maverick really exists, and yet, I'm no closer to finding him. It's relieving to know that I'm most likely *not* hearing things that didn't happen, but at the same time, it's unnerving.

Because why can't I remember him?

CHAPTER 15

THE ENTIRE NEXT WEEK I can barely focus on anything but the echoes around me. Everywhere I go, I listen, hoping for more information about Maverick. Nothing comes up, as usual, but I stay on edge, just in case.

At school, Grace still won't have anything to do with me. I watch her sitting at the lunch table with Andy or walking through the hallways holding his hand. She looks so happy, like she's thriving without me, and I'm beginning to believe that I really was holding her back.

Then, on Friday night, an unexpected echo appears in my house while I'm reading a book downstairs. The front door opens, followed by the sounds of multiple feet walking into the kitchen.

"Welcome to my house. I'd offer to give you a tour, but it's nothing compared to yours," I hear my echo saying.

"At least it's homey. My place feels like an empty castle," Grace's echo replies from the same direction. I turn my head, interested. I remember this day, the first time Grace had come over to my house. I'd been to her house once already to hang out, and I'd invited her to mine a few days later.

"Laura, is that you?" my mom's echo calls out from her office.

"It is!" my own replies.

"How was your day? How did the—" Mom's voice moves into the kitchen, then stops in the doorway. *"Oh hello there! What's your name?"* I remember, now, being a tad annoyed by Mom's enthusiasm at meeting Grace. She acted like Grace was the first friend I'd ever brought over to hang out. And I mean, she was, but I didn't want it to *seem* like that.

"I'm Grace."

"It's so nice to meet you!" Mom exclaims. They'd shaken hands, I remember.

"Sorry I didn't call. I was hoping you wouldn't mind if we hang out here tonight?" my echo says.

"Of course not! You're welcome any time. Seriously," Mom's echo replies. I roll my eyes, picturing Mom's giddy smile as she said the words. I remember the moment of this echo, and yet, I have no memory of any of the echoes of Maverick. If I can remember this small encounter with Grace and my Mom from a year ago, why can't I remember him? Maybe the story I'd told the ice cream girl wasn't far from the truth: maybe I do have amnesia. Me, my parents, and the workers at Louise's. All at the same time.

"I appreciate it," Grace's echo says. She'd tested Mom's offer many, many times since that day. For the past year, we'd hung out at my house every couple of days. I've been so focused on solving the Maverick dilemma that I haven't noticed how strange the past few weeks have felt without her. A part of me wishes I could be friends with her again, that none of this crazy drama had ever happened.

The echo moves into the living room, and a wave of nostalgia comes over me as I listen, remembering the conversation like a weird, extended deja vu. We talked about our classes, about how much we hated our super-strict gym teacher Ms. Miller, and about the various books and TV shows we shared interest in. But then, something comes up that I don't remember ever talking about.

"Who is it?" I hear Grace's echo ask.

"Who's what?" my echo replies.

"The person who keeps texting you! Who is it?" Grace asks again.

"I—it's no one. Just a friend," my echo replies.

"You mean to tell me that someone who's 'just a friend' is texting you every ten seconds?"

"He's not texting me every ten seconds," my echo tells her.

"Oh, so it's a he?"

"He *is not important."*

"So that's why you grin like a little kid with candy every time you see his name light up on your screen? Maverick? Did I read it correctly?" Grace asks mischievously.

"I do not."

"You do. I want details, friend," she replies, serious. I can picture her knowing smirk, the glint in her eye as she said the words. I know exactly how she would look at me while saying this, but only because I know her so well, not from my own memory.

"There are no details. We just... kinda went on a few dates, is all."

"A few dates? Why didn't you tell me you had a boyfriend, Laura?"

"He's not—"

"I need to see pictures of this mysterious man I knew nothing about," Grace's voice cuts off mine. *I need to see pictures too.* I hear my echo sigh, then a brief pause.

"Here."

Grace's echo gasps. *"Oh, hello! Oh my gosh, he's* hot, *Laura. Where did you even find him?"*

"He lives across the street. He came by the night we moved here, and then we kept running into each other."

"You're kidding."

"Nope," my echo replies. *"What about you? Do you have a boyfriend?"*

Grace's echo sighs, then launches into full-on story mode, telling every last detail about Andy and their complicated history. I remember this part of the conversation, where I first learned that Grace and Andy had been together, but had broken up a few weeks prior. But I don't remember the part about Maverick, as usual. It's as if the entire night still happened the same way in both my memory and the echo, but everything involving Maverick is just gone.

I sigh, knowing that there's nothing I can do about it. I decide that the next time I talk to Grace, if I ever do, I'll have to ask her if she knows anything about Maverick, though I have a hunch that she won't.

Later that night, as I'm finally getting ready to go to bed, my phone rings unexpectedly, startling me. I reach for it and to my surprise, Grace's name is displayed across the screen. I stare at it for a minute, confused. It's close to midnight, which seems like a strange time for Grace to be calling.

I take a deep breath and pick up the phone. "Hello?" I say tentatively, part of me hoping it's just an accidental call and the other part hoping she actually wants to talk.

"Laura?" Grace's voice is strained, and by the sound of it, I can immediately tell that something's wrong.

"What's going on?" It seems weird to be talking directly to her after all these weeks of being avoided.

"Laura, I'm so dumb," she says, her voice shaking through the phone. She lets out a muffled sob.

"Is everything okay?"

There's a long pause before she replies. "I'm such an idiot. I should have listened to you. I'm so, so sorry," she chokes out.

"Grace, it's okay. Tell me what's happening."

Grace hesitates, then her words tumble out between sobs. "I went to this party with Andy tonight. Everything was fine at first. And then—then Dana showed up. She started calling me names and making fun of me. Others started doing it, too. Andy—he—" she pauses, sucking in a shaky breath. "He just sat there. Let them say all these things to me. So I ran to the bathroom to calm down, and when I came back they were sitting there, *kissing*." Her voice cracks on the last word.

I close my eyes, regretting ever wishing for this moment. I hate hearing Grace like this.

"I know you probably hate me. I was a jerk, I know that. I just… I need help," she cries.

I think about it, about how I'm still mad at her for treating me the way she did, and how I'm worried that this will happen again. But then I think of the echo I heard earlier and remember all the fun times we'd shared. I can't just throw it all away, not when she's one of my only good friends. "Where are you?"

"Jet's Warehouse," Grace replies sheepishly. I pinch the bridge of my nose with my free hand. "I snuck out, my parents don't know I'm here. I need to get back home, but Andy was my ride."

I sigh, looking at the clock just as it strikes midnight. "I'll be there in a little bit," I tell her, then hang up the phone. My parents are fast asleep and I consider waking them to tell them where I'm going, but decide against it. I should be back within the hour, and it's probably not the best time for me to be explaining the whole situation with Grace to them, either.

As I drive through the cold, black night, I try to think of how I should deal with Grace. Can I really just put everything she did behind me and be friends with her again? If she gets back with Andy eventually, I don't want to go into this circle again.

And what about Leo? How will his confession of love change the dynamic of our friend group? Will we ever really be a group again?

I'm so lost in thought that I miss the turn into the abandoned industrial park. I snap into focus, watching my GPS as it recalculates the route. When it finishes, I see on the map that the road ahead of me comes to a dead-end where I can U-turn. I follow its direction, making a three-point turn at the end, then drive back toward the turn I missed. I'm not far from the turn when in front of me, my headlights reflect off something metal, the object growing larger as I get closer to it. My stomach drops. There, parked sideways across the middle of the road, blocking my path, is a car.

My stomach falls even lower as I recognize it.

The Suburban.

CHAPTER 17

PANIC TAKES OVER as I slam on the brakes, my car jolting to a stop about twenty feet away from the Suburban. My heart pounds in my chest, and I hesitate there for a moment, sizing up the gap between the back end of the Suburban and the ditch on the side of the road. I'm not sure if I can get past it without getting my car stuck, but with the dead-end behind me and a steep hill along the other side of the road, my options are pretty slim. I'm not about to sit and wait for a friendly reunion with the guy who had chased me.

I hit the gas and swerve to the left, holding tightly onto the string of hope that I can make it out of this. A loud grinding noise hits the air as I pass the Suburban, its back bumper scraping against the side of my car. My side mirror collides, too, and gets ripped off. But I'm free. I made it past the car.

I press the gas pedal to the floor, watching my rearview mirror as the Suburban turns, racing after me. I make a hard right turn onto the road that leads into the industrial park and it follows, tires screeching.

I speed into the industrial park, taking in my surroundings. It's a maze of disintegrating buildings and parking lots overgrown with weeds taking up about a square mile. My GPS tells me to turn left to get to Jet's Warehouse, but in my state of panic, I miss the turn and end up moving in the opposite direction. I zigzag through the streets like I'd done on foot when I was chased downtown, hoping that I'll lose the Suburban. It follows closely, but after a few twists and turns, it starts to lose some ground.

When I make a sharp turn onto a side street, I spot an alley between two buildings that looks just big enough to fit my small sedan, but not the Suburban chasing me. I turn down it, and while I check my rearview mirror to see if the Suburban can follow, I almost miss the giant chain link fence blocking my path. Luckily, I spot it just in time and slam on the brakes, my tires squealing as my car slides toward it, then collides, stopping abruptly. Behind me, I see headlights shining into the alley, and I curse. *I've trapped myself.*

I pull the handle on my car's door, but it only opens a few inches before it hits the wall of the building next to me. There's no way I can fit through the space, so I roll the window down, squeezing my body upwards through the gap. I climb over the hood of my car, rushing to the fence. I put my hands on it, shaking to determine its structural capacity, but I realize that there's no way my car could generate enough force to knock it down, not without backing up to the start of the alley and then speeding up again. I shake it again, panicking. It's got a gate, but it's padlocked shut.

Behind me, I hear a set of footsteps moving toward me.

I grab onto the chain link fence, pulling myself upwards. I've got no other choice, so I climb, throwing a leg over the top, then lowering myself back to the ground.

The second my feet touch the cement, someone makes contact with the fence. I don't look back, don't even hesitate, I just break into a sprint. After a hundred yards or so, I can see the end of the alley up ahead where it runs into the adjacent road. When I'm a hundred feet away, headlights appear in front of me and the Suburban comes screeching to a halt across the gap, blocking my route of escape. I skid to a stop, trying to think quickly, trying to find a way out of this. But I'm not fast enough. The footsteps behind me close in and the door of the Suburban opens, another figure making its way out into the dark alley.

Before I can prepare to defend myself, a body collides with mine and an arm slides around my neck. A hand grabs one of my arms and forces it behind my back. I reach with my other hand, trying to rip the hands away from my body, but I'm weak in comparison. I let out a scream.

"Scream all you want, no one's going to hear you," a gruff male voice breathes into my ear. "You're not getting away this time."

"Hold her there," another voice calls from the direction of the Suburban. My captor tightens his hold on me, pushing me towards one of the buildings until I'm up against it, my cheek pressed against the cold, rough brick. I struggle, trying to kick or pull or bite, but every time I move, my captor's grip around my neck tightens.

"Give it up," he says, holding me firmly in place, the skin on my cheek burning. I'm breathing hard, and I stop moving for a moment before I lift my leg and kick backward, hard. My foot makes contact with his knee and he loosens his grip for a second as he tries to find his balance. I seize the moment, throwing all of my strength into movement, breaking free from his grasp. I try to slip away, but before I can take three steps, a hand lands on my head, grabbing a fistful of hair. I scream as he tugs, pulling me down to the ground. I land on my knees and he grabs my arm again, forcing my body lower. My cheek collides with the ground this time, and no matter how much I kick my legs and struggle, I can't seem to escape the force holding me down.

As I'm lying there held captive, I hear footsteps coming up behind us.

"Grab her—" my captor begins to say, but cuts off. Just then, the weight holding me down lifts. I roll over, scrambling to my feet. There's another figure a few feet away, struggling against the man who had been holding me down. I watch them for a second, tangled in a battle of strength.

"Run!" one of the figures calls and I snap into action, turning my head around. Over by the Suburban, a person is lying on the ground, still. Someone's helping me. I can escape. I turn toward the chain-link fence where my car still sits, headlights glowing faintly through the alley, and I've only taken about three strides towards it before I realize something.

That voice.

I recognize it.

I stop in my tracks, whipping around to look back at the fight. Both men are covered in dark clothing and the alley is dimly lit, so I can't tell which one is my rescuer. I watch as the taller of the two takes a swing at the other, fist colliding with jaw. He falls to his knees and the other guy shoves him to the ground and lands a kick right to his head. The man on the ground goes still.

I watch silently as the man still standing pauses for a moment, his chest heaving in exhaustion. Then his head lifts in my direction, and my heart skips a beat.

"You should leave. Now," he says, and my heart completely stops. I know that voice. It's the voice from the echoes. *Maverick.*

I stare at him through the dark. I can make out his figure, tall and lean, but I can't see any of his facial features. He stares back at me, unmoving. After a few seconds, he takes one step toward me and instinctively I mirror him, taking a step back.

Is this Maverick? The boy I've been hearing echoes of, the boy I'd supposedly fallen in love with but have no memory of? The boy who'd been erased from my life somehow? I'm both desperate to know and terrified of the answers. I'm not sure what to do, so I just stand there, feeling a cool breeze blow through the alley.

"Go! Get out of here before they wake up," he calls to me. His tone is urgent but isn't mean. It's cautious, desperate. But he doesn't move, and neither do I.

Finally, I work up enough courage to part my lips. All that comes out is one barely audible word: "Maverick." The name rolls off my tongue as if I've said it a thousand times already.

I don't think he hears me, because he starts to turn, stepping away from me and toward where the Suburban is parked. I watch him moving, knowing that I can't let him leave. I need to know who he is. I clear my throat.

"Maverick?" I say again, loud enough that I know he can hear me even though my voice is shaking.

The outline of him freezes, rigid in the dark.

"That's your name, isn't it?" I add, watching his movements carefully.

He turns to face me, pauses, then steps in my direction. This time, I don't back away. He stops about ten feet in front of me and I strain to see his face, but it's still too dark.

I open my mouth, unsure of what I'm going to say, and just as I do Maverick's figure flinches, then turns in the direction of the Suburban. I follow his movements, noticing that the figure that had been lying motionless on the ground earlier is sitting up, holding something in his hands.

"No," Maverick—or whoever he is—says, turning back to me. "Go—" he chokes out, then falls, hitting the ground with a thud before going completely still. My gaze snaps up to the figure by the car, and time seems to slow down around me as he raises something into the air. Something that looks like a gun.

I turn on my heel, but just as I do I feel a tiny pinch in my thigh. I look down and notice a little dart sticking through my jeans. Reaching down, I pull it out and hold it in front of me to look at.

And then the world starts to spin. I put my hands out in front of me, feeling my palms colliding with the cement just before the world turns black.

CHAPTER 18

WHEN I WAKE UP, THE first thing I notice is the silence. No noise—not from today, not from the past. Nothing.

The second thing I notice is my pounding headache. It gets worse when I open my eyes and a bright light is shining above me.

Squinting, I take in my surroundings. I'm in a white room with tile floors, lying on a plain green cot on the floor. Long fluorescent lights hang from the ceiling above me, and a dark-stained wood desk sits against the wall across from me. There's a window to my left with bright sunlight shining through and a door to my right, but other than that the room is empty.

After looking around, the panic sets in. I touch my thigh, remembering the dart that had hit me. I've been drugged, and I don't know who has done it or where I am. Maverick—if that's who he is—has too, I remember, an image of him falling to the ground coming to my mind.

Then the panic turns into urgency. I need to escape.

I try to stand, but a spell of dizziness hits me, so I have to use the wall for balance as I scramble toward the door. It's locked, of course, and my next destination is the window.

Outside it's bright, so I have to squint when I look through. Trees. Lots and lots of trees. The building is in the middle of a forest. The window itself is barred, letting me know I have no chance of escape that way, either.

My next thought is that I need a weapon, but right as I think it, I hear a click from the door—the lock sliding out of place.

I drop to the floor as soon as I realize what it is, but I'm not quick enough.

"Good morning, sweetie. Sounds like you've finally woken up." It's a woman's voice, filled with empty warmth.

Shoes click on the floor toward where I lie facing the wall, frozen. Then a fist grabs a handful of my hair and yanks me up. I try to resist, but pain shoots across my scalp, so I give in. She turns me around and I meet her gaze.

The woman's eyes are a bright, innocent blue, and despite her face looking fairly young, her hair is silver, cut short right beneath her ears. She sighs.

"I'm sorry you had to get caught up in this mess, honey, but there's not much else I can do." She sounds everything but apologetic. "Dave, bring Laura up to meet with us for me, will you?" She lets go of my hair, turning on her heel and clicking out the door. *How does she know my name?*

A middle-aged man appears in the doorway, his dark eyes fixed on me and his mouth set in a thin line. He isn't much bigger than me, so I contemplate whether I can take him in a fight, but decide against it. The drugs are still wearing off, so it's hard to move with any kind of speed.

Dave grabs my arm and pulls me to my feet without saying a word. He puts handcuffs around my wrists, then takes me through the door. He's much more gentle than the woman, but he's still got a firm grip on my arm, something I'm not sure I can get out of easily.

I'm led down the hallway, then up a flight of stairs. The building reminds me of the office building my mom works at, with sleek marble floors and pristine wooden doors on each side of the hallway. All of them are closed, and the entire place has a strange smell, almost like a hospital.

Eventually, Dave reaches out and pulls on one of the door handles, swinging it open. He jerks my arm, shoving me through the doorway first, then follows, closing the door behind us. Inside, I see a conference table with three swivel chairs evenly spaced around it. In one of them is the silver-haired lady, and in the other is a guy, his hands cuffed behind his back like mine and his head down, a gag tied around his mouth. This room, like the rest of the building, is strangely quiet, and completely devoid of echoes.

The woman smiles as I walk in, a pinched, almost creepy expression, then gestures to the empty chair.

"Please, have a seat," she says. I don't move, looking between her, the guy, and Dave, who's closed the door behind us and is moving toward the woman. He stops a few feet to her left, folding his arms and tilting his chin up like he's some kind of bodyguard. Except, even if he were to switch out his jeans and polo for a suit and tie, he wouldn't look very threatening. He's too thin, his features too washed out to be scary.

After a few seconds pass, the woman purses her lips. "I guess I should explain something to you. You can do this willingly, or you can do it unwillingly. But I promise that you're going to do it." Her voice is silvery, but her words slice like knives. This is probably not someone I want to mess with, so reluctantly, I take two steps and sit down on the edge of the seat. The woman nods, pleased I've made the right decision.

"Thank you. Now. We've got some things to discuss here, don't we? Dave, go ahead and let him talk to us," she says, a smile playing on her lips like this is all some kind of game to her. Dave walks up behind the guy in the other chair and loosens the gag around his mouth. He lets out a breath, his head still hanging down.

"Let her go," he says, voice low and taut. All at once, I remember all of the echoes I'd been hearing, and I realize that the guy sitting on the other side of the table isn't just some random guy. It's Maverick. Or at least, he has the same voice as the Maverick I'd heard in the echoes. I still don't know what to think.

The woman pulls something out of her pocket and tosses it onto the table. It skids toward Maverick and stops a few feet from him. He looks up, and for the first time, I get a good look at his face. Thick, almost black eyebrows, the same color as his shaggy hair. Amber eyes. They flick over to me, meeting mine for a split second before focusing back on the woman. Does he know me?

Does he remember the things I don't? "The key's right there," she says—as if it's that easy.

"Why are you doing this?" he asks, glaring at her.

"I'm glad you asked," she says, but *glad* isn't exactly the word I'd use to describe her expression. Maybe *amused* is a better fit. She lifts her hand, pointing a remote at the wall across from me. A section of the wall opens up, revealing a massive black screen behind it. It flashes on, displaying a still shot of a news reporter standing in front of a small townhouse. "There's something I want you to see." She clicks a button on the remote, and the image comes to life.

"Police have found a possible lead on the case of Eddie Davis from Shorewick, who went missing a couple of weeks ago," the reporter says, and a picture of a young boy, maybe in his early teens, flashes across the screen. "An anonymous witness has come forward, saying that they saw someone entering Davis's house from the front window around three in the morning the night he was reported missing. They saw the person exit holding a large object, then leave in a black 2018 Chevrolet Suburban. The witness wasn't able to get a license plate number, but this report brings us one step closer to finding answers for Davis's family, who are devastated by his disappearance. Anyone who may have any information about this possible kidnapping should contact the Shorewick Police Department immediately."

The screen goes black and I watch as the silver-haired woman glares across the table at Maverick, who won't meet her eyes. The black Suburban from the news story must have been the same one that chased me, meaning that this woman must be responsible for the boy's kidnapping. And now mine.

"Now, you might see how this could be a problem," the woman finally says. She pauses, waiting for some kind of reply, but none comes. Then she sighs. Purses her lips. "I didn't want it to come down to this, but you've given me no other choice."

"You blame me for that, is that what this is about?" Maverick finally speaks, his voice calm but his eyes angry.

The woman slaps both of her hands on the table, hard, making me jump in surprise. "You should have been more careful," she snarls.

"You shouldn't be doing this," Maverick fires back, and a chill runs down my spine. He might have the same voice as the boy in the echoes, but this angry, cold tone is not the same as the kind, flirty one I'd gotten used to hearing. It's darker. Scarier.

The woman takes a deep breath before she speaks. "You, of all people, should know the good in my work."

Maverick drops his head, his jaw twitching.

"It seems like lately, you've forgotten that. So I've brought someone along as a sort of… insurance. That your priorities are in the right place." The woman glances over at me, smiling as if she's proud of herself. I look over at Maverick, desperately trying to understand what's going on, but he just stares at the table, unmoving.

"I don't know what you're hoping for me to accomplish," he finally says.

"I want you to *make it go away*," she says the last four words through her teeth, and I watch her hand on the table clench into a fist.

"It's all over the news already. There's not much I can do now, you know that," he replies.

"Then I want you to make sure it doesn't happen again."

"And what makes you think I'm going to do what you say? Because you're holding some stranger hostage? You think I'm some hero who'll do anything you ask just to save an innocent life?"

"Nice try, but you're not fooling anyone. Except, maybe—"

"I'll do what you want," he cuts her off, his voice growing somehow louder and darker at the same time. I'm not sure who I should be more scared of, the woman or Maverick. "But you'd better start thinking about the consequences of your actions. I can only cover your crimes up for so long, and as soon as I can't anymore, it's going to be over for you."

The woman seems to be getting more and more uncomfortable with each word he says, but finally, she crosses her arms and leans back in her chair, crossing one leg over the other. "She stays here until you've finished the job."

Maverick glances at me for a brief second and I think I almost see a hint of emotion there, but as soon as he looks away it's gone. He glares at the woman from across the table but doesn't reply.

"Dave, why don't you take Laura to the third floor. I think there's some space for her up there," the woman says without breaking her stare at Maverick.

Dave moves towards me. "Wait!" I cry, unsure of what else I can say. I feel like I've just been dropped into the middle of some crazy story, and I have no idea what's going on. I want answers.

Dave doesn't stop, and no one acknowledges my cry of desperation. He comes over and grabs my arm, jerking me out of the chair.

"Who are you?" I shout as Dave tugs me along. I try to resist, but I'm too weak, my head too fuzzy. "What is going on?!" I try again, but neither Maverick nor the silver-haired lady makes eye contact with me. Dave opens the door, pushing me through it. "What do you want from me?" I demand, but it's hopeless. Dave shoves me into the hallway, and the door swings shut behind him. And once again I'm left standing there, even more confused than I was before.

CHAPTER 19

I'M SWIMMING IN thoughts as Dave leads me down the hallway. The building is L-shaped with a hallway that runs along the center, adjoining rooms on both sides. The woman had mentioned something about a third floor, but Dave is taking me down, not up. We reach the first floor where I'd woken up, then stop in front of a door at the bottom of the stairwell. Dave pulls out a card, holds it up to a little gray square on the wall, and a green light flashes, followed by a beep. A lock clicks and he tugs open the door, pushing me through.

Inside is another staircase that leads us down into a basement. This part, like the rest of the building, is strangely quiet. It's colder down here, and the hospital-like scent is stronger, too. I shiver as we walk down a long, pristine hallway.

Everything is white—the walls, the metal doors, the shiny linoleum floors.

Eventually, we come to a stop in front of a door marked with a blocky "3" and Dave has to use his card to open it as well. Inside is a small room that looks like a strange cross between a prison cell and a doctor's office. There's a security camera hanging in the upper corner, a medical examination chair, a cot with a stack of folded blankets sitting on the edge, and a toilet in the back corner. I *really* hope I'm not trapped in here long enough to have to use it.

I pause in the doorway, trying to think quickly and figure out some way to get out of this. Dave is quicker, though, and he puts a hand on my back and gives me a hard shove into the room. I try to keep my balance as I stumble inside.

"Please don't do this," I cry out, turning to face him. He gives me a long, pitiful look, then slams the door shut. I rush toward it, but my hands are still cuffed behind my back, and there is no door handle on the inside anyway.

I'm stuck here.

I pace back and forth for a few minutes, bang on the door with my foot for a little bit, and scream for help, but nothing happens. I think, trying to process everything.

I saw him. The real-life, in the present Maverick. I'd finally heard his voice, not just the echo of his voice. So that means he exists. He's not just some crazy hallucination of my brain. He's a real person. So does that mean the echoes really happened and I'd somehow forgotten?

I replay the conversation again in my head.

"And so I've brought someone along as a sort of... insurance," the woman said.

Insurance? Am I the insurance? Is she using me to get Maverick to do what she wants? *Me*, because we had once known each other? Because we were *in love*? So why don't I remember any of it? I struggle, trying to remember the rest of the conversation. I hear Maverick's voice replying to the woman in my mind.

"And what makes you think I'm going to do what you say? Because you're holding some stranger hostage?"

Stranger?

Does Maverick not remember me, either? Am I just as much of a stranger to him as he is to me? But why would he have been there in the alley, attempting to rescue me hours ago? And if he was the person in the sports car the night of the dance, why would he have been saving me then if he didn't remember me?

I don't know what to think.

I sigh. I need everything to make sense, maybe, but right now I have a bigger problem: I need to escape. I glance around the room, trying to think of a plan. I can't open the door, but someone will have to come back eventually to give me food and water. At least I hope they will.

There aren't any windows, and the only thing that could potentially be used as a weapon is the stack of blankets. But I'm still handcuffed, so even a knife won't do any good.

Before I can come up with a solid plan, the door swings open. I quickly back as far into the corner of the room as I can get. The silver-haired woman steps in and Dave follows suit rolling a stainless steel cart. On it are various medical supplies—syringes, gauze, needles. My stomach drops.

"Well, Laura, I'm so glad we've finally made your acquaintance," the woman says as she steps forward. She pulls a pair of latex gloves off the cart, then starts slapping them on.

"Who are you?" I demand.

"I know you're probably very, very confused right now," she says. Dave stops the cart at the side of the room, then closes the door.

"What do you want from me?" I try to sound brave even though I'm shaking. Dave steps in my direction, his mouth set in a thin, almost bored line.

The woman keeps talking as Dave reaches for me. "Though it's not *my* fault that you're so lost right now," she says. I duck, throwing all of my weight toward Dave's knees. "The situation definitely could have been handled better. It was some poor, hasty decision making that caused this whole mess if you ask me." I collide with Dave's legs, but he doesn't even move a muscle. Instead, he catches my arm, yanking me up with ease. I struggle, but with my hands still cuffed, there isn't much I can do.

"Anyway, I know you don't understand, but I'm excited to have you here. You might actually play a huge role in solving this issue," the woman continues as Dave drags me over to the exam chair, forcing me onto it. I struggle futilely while he straps my feet to the legs of the chair, uncuffs my hands, and does the same with my arms. "Now it's just going to be a little pinch, at first," the woman says, and I watch as she grabs a syringe off the cart, connects a needle to it, then taps the air bubbles out.

"What is that?" I panic. "Please don't do this." The woman gives me a small look of pity, then comes closer, ignoring my plea. She grabs a sanitizing wipe and attempts to rub a patch of my arm, but I struggle, moving as much of my body as I possibly can away from her. I knock her arm backward, causing her to drop the wipe on the floor. A beat later, her hand closes around my throat.

She leans close, her cold fingers sending chills across my skin. "I can make this hurt a lot worse if you don't stop," she sneers, tightening her grip just enough to cut off the air flowing into my lungs.

I try to meet her gaze in defiance, but the sudden lack of oxygen causes tears to spring into my eyes. The woman smiles, satisfied, and releases her grip. I cough.

"I'm glad you understand," she says, then grabs a new wipe from off the cart and rubs a small circle on my left arm. "I'm Alice, by the way," she tells me, her eyes connecting with mine just as she plunges the needle into my arm.

"What was that?" I ask after she slides the needle out, my heart racing. Alice goes over to the cart, sets down the used needle, then grabs a fresh one. When she comes back over to me, she ties a band around my upper arm tightly. "What is going on?" I ask her, but it's as if I'm talking to echoes. She ignores me, sticking a second needle into my arm and drawing a small vial of blood. She holds it up in front of her eye, tapping it.

"That should be plenty. Dave, you can let her go now," I hear Alice say, but it sounds far away. And her mouth doesn't move. A second later, she looks over to Dave. "That should be plenty.

Dave, you can let her go now," she says. I stare blankly at her, a strange sensation coming over me like I'm about to be nauseous.

Then there's the sound of footsteps moving, a few seconds before Dave actually starts moving to release me.

"What did you do?" I hear my voice mumble. It sounds like an echo, just like Alice's voice a few seconds ago. But I've said nothing.

"What did you do?" I ask as Dave unties me from the chair. Suddenly, the room is filled with echoes. Doubles, then triples of sounds echoing back to me, moments before they happen in the present. I hear Alice rolling the cart out of the room with Dave's footsteps just behind her. Faintly, then a little louder a second later, then I watch it happen, making the sound in the present.

"Wait!" I hear an echo of myself call, once, then twice. Then I call, "Wait!"

Alice pauses, peering at me through the doorway as I hear an echo of myself say, "What is happening to me?"

"What is happening to me?" I ask, a deep ache forming behind my eyes.

Alice's eyebrows lift in curiosity. Her echo says, "I guess we're going to find out," then she smiles and says the exact same thing. I hear the door slamming shut a second before Dave grabs it and slams it shut.

I sit there in the chair, frozen. Normally when I hear echoes, they're always from exactly one year ago, no matter where I am. They're from the past. That's how the echoes work. You can't have an echo without a sound that happened before it. And yet, right there, I was hearing echoes of things a few seconds *before* they occurred in the present. Whatever Alice put into me made something strange happen:

I'm hearing echoes of the *future*.

CHAPTER 20

I SIT THERE, LISTENING. For the first few hours, every time I decide to move, I hear the movement a second before I do it. It's like a strange deja vu where I can hear what's going to happen a moment before it does.

As the hours tick by, however, the future echoes start to grow fainter until I no longer hear them. It's as if they were just a temporary malfunction in my brain that finally wore off.

What was in that needle?

And who is this Alice lady, anyway? How does she tie into the echoes I'd been hearing of Maverick?

The hours tick by, one, then three, then six. Maybe more, maybe less. It's hard to judge the passing of time in this room with no clock and no windows. No one comes into the room to bring me food or water, and my stomach begins to grumble, aching for sustenance. I begin to wonder if the real reason I've been brought here is for Alice to watch me starve to death.

Eventually, my eyelids grow heavy. I glance up at the security camera hanging in the corner, wondering if I'm being watched at this very moment. What if they're waiting for me to fall asleep? What if I miss my chance of escape by nodding off?

The fears swirl inside of me, but as time continues to march forward, I finally give in. I climb onto the cot, pull one of the rough, itchy blankets over my torso, and lie down.

The second I close my eyes, an alarm screeches through the building, making me jolt back upright.

Above the door, a red light comes to life, spinning in circles as the alarm blares in bursts of three.

I leap to my feet and try pushing on the door, hoping that the alarm has triggered some kind of release mechanism, but it remains solid. If this is just a drill or a test of the alarm system, then it's possible that nothing will happen and the alarms will stop after a few minutes. But if it isn't, someone might end up coming to help me get out of the building.

I won't hold my breath, but if someone does come, I have to be ready to make my escape attempt. So I grab one of the blankets and stand by the door, ready to spring into action at any moment. I listen, trying to hear the sounds of footsteps outside the door, but I'm not sure I can make out anything above the sound of the alarm. And anyway, I'm pretty sure this room is soundproof, considering I never heard Alice and Dave coming when they visited me last time.

The minutes tick by, the alarm continuing its siege through the building. Then, finally, the door swings open.

The second it does, I pounce on the person entering and throw the blanket over their head. I recognize the figure as Dave, and a glance through the door tells me he's alone. I know there's no way I'll be able to hold him down, so this is my only chance. I use the extra few seconds I've bought myself to slide past him through the door and bolt down the hallway.

As I sprint, I go over the mental map I'd drawn of the place earlier. I'll round a corner up ahead, then the staircase will be on the right at the end of the hallway. I'm not sure where all of the other doors lead—maybe to more rooms with more people being held captive—but I do know that the stairs are my best chance.

I round the corner, glancing behind me, and I see Dave in hot pursuit, already catching up. So I pump my limbs faster, building as much speed as my hungry, fatigued body can muster. I make it to the door, swing it open, and run straight into another person.

We hit each other, hard, and I fall, my head colliding with the bottom step of the staircase. I roll over in a rush, peering at the figure standing above me. His back is to me, a dark gray hoodie pulled over his head.

Dave comes barreling through the door and the other person side steps. Dave runs past him, then sees me on the ground and skids to a halt, turning to face the hooded figure.

I seize the moment, scrambling to my feet. I've made it up exactly seven stairs when a voice calls out, stopping me in my tracks.

"Wait! Don't go that way!" it calls, and immediately I know who the hooded figure is. I whip around, facing him. Dave is lying on the ground facedown. Two amber eyes peer at me from under the hood.

"What?" I can barely say the word, my heart thudding in my chest.

"Come with me. I'm here to help you escape," Maverick says.

I stand there, trembling. I can't get myself to move. All I can manage to do is say three little words: "*Who are you?*"

"There's no time to explain, I just need you to trust me," he tells me. I remember that same voice from the echo on Halloween.

"*Do you trust me?*" he'd asked.

"*Of course I do,*" I'd replied.

But that was a playful, fun exchange, not a dire situation where my life was in danger. And I don't even remember it. Obviously Maverick exists, meaning the echoes quite possibly could have happened, but I wonder how well I knew him back then. And how little I know about him now. I'm not sure I can trust him.

But right now, I'm not sure I have a choice.

I take a step forward. "Okay," I whisper.

"Follow me," he says, and I do.

We take off, sprinting back down the hallway in the direction I'd just come from. Maverick is faster than me, but he slows down when he notices I'm struggling to keep up. He leads us around the corner and just before we get to the room I'd been held in, there's another staircase entrance. When we get to the first floor, Maverick peers through the window on the door into the main hallway.

"Wait here. I'll take care of the guards. Don't let them see you," he whispers, staring directly into my eyes to make sure I understand. His eyes don't miss a thing, not the fear in mine, not the tremble of my hands, not the heat that forms in my cheeks under his gaze. I can tell by the depth of them, the endless pools of amber that don't drift a millimeter away from mine.

I steady my breath and nod, and then he slips through the door. I watch through the small rectangular window as he rushes to the first guard and places his hands on the guard's arms, shoving him toward the ground. It doesn't look like that hard of a shove, but the guard falls, rolling onto his back, and goes still.

A second guard rushes toward Maverick, pushing him against the wall. They move just outside of the range of vision provided by the small window, and I strain to see what's happening. I hear a loud thump, the sound of a body hitting the ground, and I wait, my breath coming out in short gasps. A beat later, Maverick appears in front of the window, then pulls the door open.

"Come on," he says, voice low, gesturing for me to follow him. I slip through the door and he leads us down the main hallway. I can see two double glass doors directly in front of us, a hundred yards away. Outside, the sun is shining, but there's a faded, reddish tint to the light that tells me it must be sometime in the evening.

When we get about halfway to the door, a person steps in front of it, blocking our path.

"Not so fast," Alice calls out, her voice echoing down the hall. Maverick grabs my arm and pushes me behind him protectively. "Don't. Move." Alice says, and then I notice the gun. Pointed directly at us. We both freeze.

Behind me, I hear footsteps. I whip my head around, noticing two guards who are also holding guns.

"Did you think you could get away so easily?" Alice asks, then tilts her head back and lets out a short laugh.

Maverick doesn't miss a beat. Just then, in one swift movement, he places his hand on a door next to us, pushes me inside, and slams it shut. He grabs the closest piece of furniture, a chair, and wedges it under the doorknob just as I hear Alice yell, "Get them!"

The door vibrates as the guards bang on it, the sound kicking my adrenaline to a new level. Maverick goes over to the window on the back wall and gives it a hard kick with his shoe. The glass shatters, and a gust of cold air bursts into the room. This window, unlike the one in the room I'd woken up in, isn't barred. Either we got lucky, or Maverick knows his way around this place.

"You go first," he tells me, and I throw my leg over the windowsill. It's a relatively short drop and I land on a bed of pine needles, shrubs on either side of me. Maverick drops a second later, and from inside the room, I hear the scraping of furniture along the floor. "Run," he says, and he doesn't have to wait for my response.

We take off, tearing across a small lawn, then crashing into woods. Thorns and branches reach out at us, scraping as we move through the vegetation. I ignore them, my need to escape outweighing the pain of a few cuts. I glance behind us and see two figures making their way across the turf behind us. They're a good distance away, so we might have a decent chance of losing them.

I face forward and press on, sticking as close to Maverick's side as I can. I'm not sure where we're going, but it seems like Maverick has a destination in mind because he makes purposeful turns through the woods. Eventually, we reach a small clearing and at the opposite end, a small car is parked. When we get closer, I recognize it: the little black sports car. The one I'd seen at the school and in the driveway of the abandoned house across the street.

"Get in on this side," Maverick gestures toward the driver's side as he opens the door, and I remember seeing the entire right side crushed in. Because he'd pulled in front of the Suburban, stopping it from chasing me.

I climb in, scooting across the center console into the passenger seat. It's tiny, with barely enough room to fit my legs. And sure enough, the right side door is crushed in; even from the inside it looks pretty badly damaged.

Maverick slides in next to me, cranking the engine up. He drives forward slowly, winding the car between trees until we reach a road. Maverick makes a right turn, pressing his foot down on the accelerator.

The car's powerful engine hums beneath us as we drive. Maverick doesn't take his eyes off the road, and I don't take mine off the speedometer slowly creeping upward. I'm not sure where we are—or where we are going, for that matter—but I know that even I have a limit to how far I'll go over the speed limit. Maverick, apparently, doesn't.

We drive for a long time on a two-lane road, nothing but trees on either side for miles. My ears pop as the road drops in elevation, letting me know we must be somewhere up in the mountains. I wonder if Maverick knows where we are or if he's just heading in an arbitrary direction. I don't ask him. I don't want to break the silence.

Fatigue hits me as my heart rate finally slows, the adrenaline wearing off. I'm not sure how long it's been when we pull off onto a dirt road, but I feel heavy like I've been asleep. The sky is a bright orange, the sun probably setting somewhere behind all the trees.

At the end of the dirt road is a mobile home, and next to it, a garage. I wonder if this is where Maverick lives. He obviously doesn't live in the house across the street from mine anymore.

"One second," he tells me, then hops out of the car and walks into the house. A moment later he comes back out and the door of the garage slides up. Inside is another car, a blue Toyota Corolla that looks about a decade old. He hops into it and backs up next to the sports car, then comes over and opens the door.

"We don't want them to be able to follow us in this, so we need to move to the other car. Is that okay with you?" he asks. As if I have a say in the situation. As if I have any idea what is going on.

"Where are we going?" I ask, my voice gravelly.

"Somewhere safer than here," he tells me. It's purposefully not much information, but I'm too exhausted to dig for more. Maverick helped me escape from Alice, at least, so for now, I don't care where we go. As long as it's far away from her.

Climbing into the Corolla feels strange after riding in the sports car. The sports car was cramped and had a brand-new car smell. The Corolla is more spacious and smells stale like it's been sitting for a while. Maverick pulls the sports car into the garage, closes it up, and gets back in the car with me.

As we pull out of the driveway and back onto the road, I try to think of something to say, but I can't even begin to imagine where to start, so I let the silence be our companion. I don't know what's happening, but I know that at least for right now, I feel somewhat safe. And I let that feeling carry me down to sleep.

CHAPTER 21

"LAURA." THE VOICE IS soft, like it's from the past, but echoing back and forth through my mind, growing louder and louder as time shoots towards me.

"Laura," the voice calls again. I open my eyes.

Two golden eyes are staring back at me. The door of the Toyota is open and bright, artificial light shines onto my seat. I sit up, squinting.

"Where are we?" I ask, looking around. We're parked on a hedge-rimmed, stone-circle driveway, a massive water fountain jutting from the center. It's dark outside now, but there's a surprising amount of light coming from something behind me.

"This is—" Maverick begins, then pauses. "My, uhh… house."

I slip out of the car, turning around to take in the house. Or, I guess I should say, *mansion*. The sight of it makes my jaw fall open.

Spotlights light up the front, explaining the glow that reaches out into the driveway. Four stone columns line the front, and there are more than a dozen windows along each side. It has a pristine white exterior and a front door that's at least twice my height.

"This is your *house?*" I exclaim in disbelief.

He scratches the back of his neck. "Kind of, I guess. Come inside."

I follow him hesitantly, wondering if this is all just some wild dream.

When we step into a massive, brightly lit entranceway, I gasp. I can see a swimming pool through giant, floor-to-ceiling windows at the opposite end of the room, and then the house continues behind the pool. There's a grand staircase to my left, and directly above me is a glass dome that I can see the stars through. The hallways to my left and right appear to go on forever.

As I stand there, gaping, I notice how quiet it is. There are a couple of echoes of footsteps tapping across the marble floor and voices talking in a distant room, but they're all so old they're barely there. Other than that, the house is silent.

"Jacob, will you find Laura a room? And some clean clothes, too" Maverick calls. I look down at my muddy jeans and torn shirt, feeling suddenly improper in this massive, gorgeous house. An older man in a suit walks out of a side room and nods to me. Is he the *butler*?

"You may follow me," he says, turning on his heel. I glance over at Maverick, suddenly wanting desperately to stop and ask him all of my questions. But he gives me a nod that says *go on,* so I follow Jacob. I'll ask the questions soon.

Jacob leads me down a hallway, up a hidden staircase, and down a second hallway. At the fourth door on the left, he stops and pushes it open. The room is as massive as the rest of the house, with a four-poster king-size bed in the center. Two windows with dark blue curtains pulled to the sides provide a nice view into the front yard, and a door attached to the room leads into a similarly grand bathroom with marble countertops and white tile floors. Even here, the house's past is eerily quiet.

"I will be back in a moment with some clothes," Jacob tells me.

When he says a moment, he literally means a moment, because I've barely had time to take in the massive mirror and dark, intricately carved headboard before he's back with a stack of clothes.

"You may shower if you'd like. Maverick will come for you when dinner is ready," he tells me, then pulls the door closed behind him. *Dinner,* I think, my stomach waking up with a soft grumble. How long had it been since I'd eaten?

I watch the door for a second, then carry the clothes to the bed. In the pile, I find a few different options: a pair of sweatpants, a pair of jeans, and some dark leggings. I also find a large, solid blue t-shirt and a gray and pink striped shirt. I stare at the striped shirt for a minute, an odd thought forming in my mind. *Don't I have one like this at home?* I try to remember it. It's the same one, but I hadn't seen it since... May? Maybe?

I realize with a start that this might be my shirt. *Have I been here before?*

I shake the thought away, snatching the pair of sweatpants off the bed. I hesitate for a second, then grab the striped shirt, too.

After I shower, I'm too anxious to sit around in my room waiting, so I decide to explore. I peek my head out into the hallway, and when I'm sure no one is there, I walk towards the staircase Jacob had led me up earlier. When I get to the first floor, I turn left, the opposite direction we'd come from. I quickly realize that the house forms a rectangular shape, surrounding the pool in the middle.

As I'm wandering down the hallway aimlessly, I'm about to round a corner when I hear footsteps just on the other side of it. I don't want anyone to think I'm snooping, so I whip around and dart into the closest room, shutting the door without a sound. I wait behind it for a second, and when the footsteps pass by without stopping, I let out a breath. Then I turn and look at the room I'm in.

It's dark, so I feel along the wall for a light switch, and when I flip it, two lamps come on in opposite corners of the room. It's an office space, with a wall of bookshelves lining one side and windows covered in thick, dark curtains on the other. There's a desk in front of one bookshelf and a fireplace on the wall opposite of it. The desk is empty except for a small lamp, a few pens, and a notepad.

The fireplace's mantel is covered in a variety of decorations, so I walk over to get a closer look. There are some decorative candles, a mini globe, some fake flowers, and a framed photo. I almost skim over the photo, but it catches my eye just in time.

My jaw tenses.

The photo is of *me* standing on a patch of grass in front of a line of trees, with Maverick next to me. He's got his arm around me, and he's kissing my cheek while I smile at the camera. I lift the picture and stare at it for a long moment, then reach my hand up to touch my cheek, the same spot his lips are touching in the picture.

I've barely had time to process what I'm looking at when the door creaks open behind me. I hurry to set the photo down where it was and turn around. Maverick stands in the doorway, looking past me at the photo. After a moment, he meets my gaze.

Neither of us knows what to say.

"I need you to tell me—"

"I think we should—" we both start at the same time.

Maverick takes in a breath. "You go first," he says.

I don't hesitate. "I need you to tell me who you are."

He pauses, then takes a step forward, watching me carefully. "You don't remember me, then?"

"No," I say. He drops his gaze.

"I'm… Maverick," he says slowly.

"I know your name," I reply.

"What else do you know?" he asks, searching my eyes.

"I don't know for sure."

"That's okay," he says, taking another step closer to me. I put a hand up.

"Stay back," I say—a little too harshly, but it stops him in his tracks. I stare at him, watching every movement. I'd heard echoes of myself talking to him, I'd listened to what the worker at Coffee and Cream had said, and now I'd seen a picture of us together. And yet, I still can't seem to believe my eyes.

He's taller than me, but not by much. He wears a black long-sleeved shirt that shows off his sturdy, toned frame and his hair is much longer than it was in the photo of us, nearly touching his wide hazel eyes.

We study each other for a long time until he finally asks, "What *do* you remember?"

I sigh, closing my eyes for a moment. When I open them, I have to blink away tears. "Remembering and knowing are two very different things for me right now," I tell him.

He keeps his gaze on me but doesn't respond. I don't know how to explain to him what's going on. That I know who he is and what we were, because I heard it happening, but I don't remember any of it. I'm not sure there's even a good way to explain it. What if I'm wrong? What if he doesn't know me, and everything in the echoes was just in my head?

I take a deep, shaky breath. "This is going to sound crazy," I tell him.

I don't want to continue, but Maverick's eyes fix on me, never wavering. They pull the words right out of me.

"I have this… ability," I start, then pause. "I hear things." I haven't told anyone about this since my parents, and that took a long time to get them to understand. It might not make any sense to him, but I'm not sure what else to do. There are so many clues pointing to the fact that we were once a big part of each other's lives, a *really* big part, and it doesn't make sense that he simply disappeared. That I just forgot about him.

Maverick doesn't look away from me, not for a second. He doesn't even blink.

"Echoes. Of the past," I continue. I close my eyes. "Wherever I am, I can hear all of the sounds made in that same spot, at that exact time during previous years."

When I open my eyes, Maverick is still staring, but his expression softens.

I go on, the words flowing like water. "It sounds crazy, I know, but it's something I've always dealt with. I can hear the past. Every conversation, door opening, footstep—any noise at all. I hear it, always." I'm shaking as I speak. "I don't know why, but I can't remember you. At all. But I've heard you in the past. I heard you come to my house and drop off flowers when my family first moved in. I heard you ask me out. I heard us talking late in the night in my backyard. I heard you come to my house for dinner on Halloween." I take several gulps of air, then finish with two words: "Last year."

Maverick opens his mouth, the expression I'd seen forming earlier solidifying into what looks like realization. But then it darkens into something else, like he's angry and sad and disgusted all at the same time. I know I should stop, but I can't.

"I heard all of that, but I don't remember any of it. I didn't even recognize you when I first saw you, but when you spoke, I knew your voice. I don't know how it's possible, I don't know if I'm just going crazy, or have amnesia or what. But I need to know, I need you to tell me *who you are*. If it's all true." I'm borderline hysterical now.

Maverick puts his head down, chin touching his chest. He opens and closes his mouth once, then twice, but no words come out. Then he looks up, one single word escaping his lips. "Yes."

I wait.

"Yes," he says again, his eyes darting to the place where the picture sits on the mantle. "What you heard did happen. There's so much more than you know." He closes his eyes.

"Tell me," I plead.

He shakes his head, his gaze dropping again. "I'm so, so sorry. This is all my fault," his words hit me like two hands around my throat.

"Why? What do you mean?"

He's frozen in place, and now he won't meet my eyes. "I have an… ability, like you." The hands tighten, stopping my breath.

"To do *what*?"

He finally looks at me, and his next words squeeze the last bit of life out of me.

"I can take away memories."

CHAPTER 22

THE WORLD STARTS to spin around me, tilting, teetering until I'm falling. Maverick crosses the room in three quick strides, bracing me as I slump to the ground. My vision goes black, and my heart pumps double-time. When I open my eyes again, I'm looking at Maverick's face through a million stars. His hand presses against my forehead for a second, then he shines a light into my eyes.

"Laura, can you hear me?"

I squint, turning my pounding head away. "Yeah," I choke out.

"Listen, I think you're dehydrated. And you probably need food. Let's go eat something."

My stomach rumbles as if on cue. "Okay." The stars flooding my vision are still clearing. When Maverick pulls me to my feet, I'm shaking. Whether from dehydration or shock, I'm unsure. He pulls my arm across his neck, supporting me as I walk.

My thoughts are spinning so fast I can't keep up. Over and over, all I can focus on are the words, *I can take away memories.*

It takes us a long time to get to the dining room—since the house is about ten times the size of my own—and the entire walk I try to formulate words. As Maverick helps me sit down at a long, elegant dining table, I finally find them.

"You took my memories away?" It's more of a statement than a question, but I still pause, holding on to a sliver of hope that it's not true and that Maverick will deny it.

He doesn't.

"*Why?*" The word comes out barely above a whisper.

Maverick doesn't meet my eyes, he simply reaches across the table to grab a pitcher, pours water into a glass, puts it in my hand, and says, "Drink."

I lift the glass to my mouth, gulping the water down as I think. Why would he take my memories away? Did it have to do with Alice? Did I know about something I shouldn't have? Did Maverick decide he didn't want to be with me anymore and erase himself from my life to avoid confrontation?

I feel a stab of pain when I think of the last scenario. It catches me off guard; I don't remember him anyway, so why should I care?

It strikes me, too, that to any normal person, someone telling you they could take memories away sounds pretty far-fetched. But with my own strange ability and the pile of evidence I'd already witnessed, I hadn't even given it a second thought.

A woman in an apron enters the room as I put down my water, carrying a steaming plate in each hand. She sets one down in front of each of us, smiling. "Enjoy," she tells us before walking back through the door.

I look down at my plate: breakfast for dinner. My favorite. Two pancakes covered in only butter, a slice of bacon drenched in syrup, and scrambled eggs with a side of ketchup. I blink in surprise. "This is exactly how I like all of these foods."

Maverick doesn't look at me. "I know."

Of course he knows. He knows me. But I don't know him, and apparently, it's because he doesn't want me to. I'm not sure what to say to that, so we eat in silence. I should be starving, but the latest news has killed my appetite, so I end up just nibbling for a long time.

Maverick finishes his plate in mere minutes, then sets down his fork. He waits until I put down mine to speak.

"I did it to protect you," he croaks, defeated.

I blink a couple of times before replying. "What do you mean?" I ask. To protect me from Alice? Or to protect me from heartbreak? Or both?

"It's..." a pained expression crosses his face, and he drops his gaze. "Complicated."

I don't know what to say, so I just look at him, my fear deepening. What if I came all this way, digging up the past just to find out I should have left it buried? What if I have to let go of a love that I don't even remember having? I'm not sure if that would be worse than remembering.

I look up to find Maverick staring at my striped shirt.

"This is my shirt, isn't it? From...before."

He nods. "You…" the corner of his mouth tilts up slightly, "…spilled some chocolate milk on it. It was pretty bad, so you borrowed one of mine. I forgot to give it back to you."

It's weird, listening to him tell me about something I did and have no recollection of. Almost as weird as hearing it happen myself. "So it's all true, I really did know you."

He nods again.

I bite my lip, afraid to say the thoughts racing through my mind. But then I say them anyway. "And then what? You decided you didn't want to know me anymore, so you erased yourself from my life?"

Maverick's eyes widen in surprise, and he shakes his head. "No, Laura, you've got it all wrong. I've *always* wanted to be in your life. Since the day I met you."

I frown. "Then what did you mean when you said you did it to protect me? Protect me from what?"

"From me," he stares at the table.

"What—" I begin, but he puts a hand up.

"Let me explain, it's kind of a long story." He pauses, waiting for me to protest. When I don't, he launches into the story. "Last year, around the time I met you, my mom was diagnosed with an early onset of Alzheimer's. It's this disease, it makes you—"

"Forget things," I finish for him, realizing the irony as I say it. The boy who can make people forget things and his mom, who can't help that she's forgetting them.

"Yeah. She started to decline rapidly. She would misplace things, forget which day of the week it was, and then around December, she had to stop going to work because she would forget how to get there, or forget she had a job altogether. One day when I came home, she didn't even recognize me." He looks down after he says the last few words, a deep sadness in his eyes. An image of Annie's obituary flashes across my mind.

"We tried everything, all of the remedies in the books. But nothing was helping. By the time January rolled around, I'd almost given up hope." His eyebrows draw together and he pauses for a few seconds, squeezing his eyes shut.

"Throughout my life—because of this ability I have—I've been seeing this psychiatrist. Alice, the woman who kidnapped us." I nod, trying to put the pieces together. "She specializes in people who have… special circumstances. Like us. She was the first one to actually believe that I had this ability to manipulate memories, and she helped me learn how to control it.

"When I came in for my yearly session, I told her about how my Mom was sick and I wasn't sure what to do. Then she told me she had been researching this new drug that she thought might be able to help, but that it was an experimental drug that technically wasn't cleared for use yet. At that point, I was so desperate that I asked if we could try it anyway. I got her to agree, and she gave us a month's supply. Surprisingly, it worked. Mom was back to normal within a week, it was like a miracle.

"When the month was over, however, I went back to Alice and asked if she would be willing to get me some more. I was prepared to pay any amount she wanted, but she didn't want money. Instead, she said she needed me to do something for her before I could have it. I was willing to do just about anything at that point." He drops his head, sighing heavily.

"She told me she needed my ability to help her. She asked me to erase a few things from someone's memory. It was a simple task, one I thought would be harmless, and I didn't question it. I just wanted to cure my Mom. When I completed the task, she gave me another month's supply, and everything was fine again for a while.

"But then, the month after that, I went back, and this time she had a list of people she needed me to take memories from. And not only that but instead of simply erasing a few small memories, she wanted me to erase an entire person from existence."

Maverick hangs his head in defeat. "It was so, so stupid, but I did it. I just wanted my mom to be okay."

I try to put myself in his shoes. How far would I go to save someone I love? My mom? Dad? Grace, even? It scares me to think about what I *wouldn't* do for them.

"That time, Alice only gave us enough medicine to last two weeks, so I was forced to go back to her sooner. But when I did, I decided I was going to confront her about what was going on— why she wanted me to get rid of certain people. That's when she showed me her laboratory—the building you were locked up in. It's where she does her research."

I have a flashback of Alice sticking a needle in my arm, then the strange future-echoes I'd experienced. "What is she researching?"

Maverick meets my eyes, the disgust plain on his face. "Us. People with strange abilities. 'Anomalies,' she calls us. There are more, a lot more. She has them locked up in there like lab rats."

"What is she hoping to accomplish?" I ask.

"She tells me she wants to find a way to block our abilities, to prevent people from using them in the wrong ways."

I imagine a world where my "ability" could be blocked so that I wouldn't have to listen to the echoes. It doesn't sound too bad. Not worth kidnapping and hurting people to get it, though.

"There's more, though. I think she's up to something else," Maverick tells me.

"Like what?"

"Weaponizing us. Finding a way to replicate certain abilities, then using them to her advantage."

My eyes widen.

"Once I found out about everything, I told her I wouldn't work for her anymore, but because of it, I couldn't get the medicine for my mom." His head goes down, a hand running through his hair. "She... passed away back in April."

Instinctively, I reach a hand out towards his. He looks up at me when we touch, his eyes meeting mine, and my heart skips a beat. "I'm sorry," I say, pulling back my hand and averting my gaze. I'm not sure why I reached for him like that. I still don't know him.

He blinks a few times, then sighs. "You and I... we were together," he tells me. It's something I've sort of known for a while, but it's strange hearing him say it. "You knew my mom pretty well, too."

Of course I would know his mom. "Did I know about Alice? And the medicine? Your ability—any of it?"

He grimaces. "No. I didn't know how to tell you, I guess."

I expect a feeling of hurt, betrayal, or anger to come, but there is none. I obviously hadn't told him about *my* ability, either, or he would have known that erasing my memory never would have worked. I can understand why he wouldn't; it's not exactly the easiest of subjects to talk about.

"But after she died, I tried to go back to a normal life, I tried to put it all behind me. It was fine for a while, but then I started receiving threats from Alice. If I didn't go back and work for her, she was going to start taking everything I had from me. Everything I loved." He meets my eyes as he says the word *loved*.

I hold his gaze for a moment, understanding the pointed look he's giving me, but then look away. It's strange to think that he could have been in love with me when he feels so much like a stranger right now. Had I loved him, too?

"I didn't know what to do. I tried to get the police involved, but they couldn't track her—I'd covered up her crimes too well. And no one's going to believe me when I say I can take their memories away. So I tried to wait it out, but she started terrorizing me. My tires were slashed, my house was broken into—all kinds of things. I couldn't escape her."

Understanding hits me all at once, knocking the breath out of me. "You were afraid she would come after me."

He nods solemnly. "I couldn't stand the idea of you being hurt because of me."

"So you erased yourself from my life," I finish.

"Yeah," he says, his eyes shut. "I couldn't just leave, I needed to make sure you wouldn't know anything about me, I needed to make sure she couldn't use you against me. I erased myself from you, from everyone we'd come in contact with together."

I glance up at him. "You missed someone."

He frowns. "What do you mean?"

"I didn't understand it at the time, but a worker in this shop downtown recognized me. Coffee and Cream. She told me about you."

It dawns on him. "Oh. Right," he says. "I can't believe I forgot about that."

We sit in silence for a few minutes after that, and I go over everything he's told me in my head. The story makes sense. It makes complete sense. I've finally gotten my answers. But I still feel empty inside. Like something is missing.

"So it was as if you'd never met me, after that?" I finally ask him.

"For you, yeah," he answers, his eyes burning into mine. The color of them seems to change with his emotions—amber one moment, then greenish, then yellow. Right now they're dark.

I watch him fiddle with a piece of string coming off his shirt as I think about it. Maverick still remembered me, the whole time. Even now, he remembers everything about our relationship. I hate it, knowing that he knows about every moment we shared, and I'm a blank slate.

"Is there some way I can get my memories back? Can you... restore them, somehow?" I wave my hand in the air, a little bit of hope creeping into my voice.

Maverick simply shakes his head, and the hope dies.

"I erased your memory because I thought she didn't know about you, I thought making you forget me would protect you from being used as a pawn in a game."

"Obviously that didn't work out," I mutter. Maverick's plan made sense, it was great that he was trying to protect me, but I feel a twinge of anger bubbling up inside me. How could he just delete me from his life like that? How could he just let me go? Couldn't there have been some other way?

Maverick grimaces. "I didn't know that she had been watching me and already knew about you. I didn't think she would use you, since you weren't in my life anymore. If I had known…" he trails off.

I feel my anger building, hot and sudden. "You would have done what? *Not* done it? A few days ago, I was listening to the coffee shop worker tell me about how we were so *in love* and now I'm learning that you cut me out of your life just like that? How could you?" My heart is thrumming in my ears by the time I finish.

Maverick looks like he's just been punched in the gut. He shakes his head. "I didn't know. I thought it was the best decision."

"The best decision," I scoff. I can't control the anger inside of me. I've had a part of my life ripped from me, and there's nothing I can do about it.

I can see Maverick trying his best to stay calm, but when he speaks, his words are saturated with frustration. "Do you know how hard it was to live with the memory of you every single day, knowing there was nothing I could do to get you back? Do you know how hard it was to find out that my enemy knew about you all along, and that it was all for nothing?" His eyes burn into mine like a million suns. I'm speechless for a moment, a tear streaming down my cheek. Then I find my voice.

"Do you know how hard it was for *me*? To hear myself talking to you, getting to know you, and not remember any of it?

To wonder whether I was going crazy or not? Then to find out you're real, but you're also the reason I don't even remember my *first kiss*? The first guy I supposedly *loved*?"

"I—" Maverick chokes out. "I didn't know about your ability, I didn't think this would happen."

"But you were okay with just accepting that I was gone forever?" I spit, not bothering to hide my anger.

"No!" he replies, angry, too. "If I could take it all back, I would. Laura, I'm so, so sorry. You have to believe that." The look in his eyes tells me he truly means it, but I can't stand the thought of sitting here for another second.

"I'm sorry, too." Tears flowing freely now, I stand, knocking over a glass as I do. It topples over and shatters, spraying water and glass across the table but I ignore it, turning towards the door we came through, and run. When I finally get to my room, one glance in the mirror tells me I look like a tired, frantic mess. I spread out across the bed, taking deep breaths, trying to calm myself down.

When my heart finally slows and my breathing is normal again, fatigue hits me. Aside from the brief nap in the car, I haven't slept in a long time. My eyes feel heavy, and I don't fight them as they close. I embrace the sleep, letting it take me down into a dark, silent abyss.

CHAPTER 23

WHEN I WAKE UP, the sky is a light gray, the sun beginning its ascent somewhere far away. I turn away from the window, blinking a few times before I notice an alarm clock on the stand beside me. 6:06 A.M. In the corner, there's the date. *Sunday.*

It dawns on me that I haven't been home in over 24 hours. *Mom and Dad.* They're probably out of their minds, wondering where I could be. The police are involved by now, no doubt, and there's probably a massive search party out looking for me.

I stand up in a hurry, opening the door and poking my head out before I leave the room. Something about the grandness of this place makes me feel like I have to move in secrecy so I don't disturb the peace.

I walk down the almost-familiar hallway, down the staircase, and into the entranceway. I peek my head into the doorway I'd seen Jacob come from yesterday. No one is there, so I continue down the hallway, checking inside each door as I pass by. I'm backing out of a doorway when I bump into someone, startling me. I whip my head around, meeting Maverick's eyes. He looks down at my hand, still on the doorknob.

"I—" I start, feeling a little bit guilty. The tension of our fight last night hangs in the air between us, making it hard to breathe. "You're up early," I say, trying to break it up.

Maverick blinks his yellow eyes at me. "So are you."

I'm not sure how to respond, so I just cut to the chase. "I think I need to call my parents, they're probably worried about me."

Maverick blinks again, taking a deep breath. "Actually, they... uh... probably aren't worried yet," he says tentatively, like he knows he has to say it but he doesn't want to.

I blink back, confused.

"After Alice let me go yesterday, before I came to break you out, I... made sure they weren't worried about you. They think you're at Grace's for the weekend," he explains.

"How did you...?" I trail off, realization hitting me. "Oh. Right. You can make people forget things." The words taste bitter in my mouth, and I can see the hurt in Maverick's eyes after I say them.

"I just wanted to get you back and take you home. I didn't want there to be any further disturbance in your life," he tells me.

"Oh, so you made my parents *forget about me*?" My voice cracks.

"Not completely, I just thought—" he stops short, closing his eyes tight. "I'm sorry," he finally finishes. I stare at him as he runs a hand through his dark hair awkwardly, then something dawns on me.

"Wait, were you going to erase *my* memories too?"

Maverick grimaces.

"Oh my gosh. You were! So what, you were just going to make me forget everything that happened this weekend? Getting kidnapped, meeting you, all of it?"

"I… that was the plan until I found out about your ability." He waits for my response, but I simply glare at him. Then, finally, he adds, "I just wanted to keep you out of this."

"I'm sure you did," I spit, then shove past him. I'm not sure where I'm going, but the last place I want to be right now is standing here with Maverick. He was going to erase my memory. Make me forget meeting him, all of it. If he had, I'd have been stuck in the same endless cycle as before, hearing echoes of him and questioning my sanity because I couldn't remember any of it.

Instead, I'm here, and I understand what has happened. Maverick erased my memory, and he thought he was protecting me by doing it. But now I'm not sure if I can even trust him.

I'm not sure which situation feels better.

"Laura, please," I hear Maverick call from behind me. He's following me down the hallway, which I quickly realize comes to a dead-end, and suddenly I feel trapped.

I stop in my tracks and spin around, facing him. "How can I trust you?" I ask, trying to make my shaky voice sound brave. "How can I trust anything that you say or do, when you can just wipe the memory from my mind if it doesn't go well for you? How do I know you haven't tried this conversation before and just hit the reset button when things went wrong? How can I trust that you won't do something like that to me again?"

I watch his chest moving up and down a few times. I can tell he doesn't know how to respond, but I wait anyway. We stare at each other, and I can almost feel the sun rising a few inches in the sky as we do.

Then, finally, I can taste one last question on my lips, less bitter than the previous ones. "How do you even do it?"

Maverick's eyes burn into mine, questioning.

"Take away people's memories," I add.

He looks down, and I think I see his hands shaking the tiniest bit, but I can't be sure. He inhales and exhales slowly. When he speaks, darkness clouds his eyes. "I have to touch them," he tells me, and his hands curl into fists. "If I make contact with them, and I focus hard enough, I can reach through their skin, all the way into their mind. It's like snipping the little strings that hold their memories together." His face contorts in disgust, and he lowers his head solemnly. "It only takes a moment."

Immediately, I become aware of the distance between us—maybe ten feet. I take another step back for good measure. "So then there's just empty holes in the person's memories?" I ask. I hadn't noticed any weird gaps in my memory—the only thing that taught me about Maverick's existence was the echoes, which any normal person wouldn't have been able to hear.

"Technically, yes. But the mind is powerful. It's good at filling in the gaps when it needs to. Most people don't even notice at all. Sometimes—like with your parents yesterday—all I have to do is take away one small detail, and they come up with the rest themselves. I simply took away their worry when they couldn't find you yesterday morning, so they assumed you were at Grace's."

I listen to his words, my own swirling through my mind. This ability that Maverick has is completely different than mine. It affects other people, while mine only affects me. It's useful, while mine is nothing but a burden. It makes sense that someone like Alice would want to abuse his power and use it for her own gain. It makes him powerful. *Dangerous.*

My thoughts are interrupted when I see movement: Maverick, taking a small step towards me. I throw my hands up in front of me. "Stop!" I blurt, my eyes wide.

He does, his hands going up defensively. "I'm sorry."

"I don't know if I can trust you," I tell him, "but if I'm going to try, I need to know that you won't use your ability on me. Ever. Again."

"I promise—"

"And the only way to be sure is to make sure you don't touch me. So I don't want you getting too close."

A sadness glows in his eyes, but he nods, backing away and lowering his hands. "I won't," he says.

"Good." I sigh, calm acceptance flowing through me. I know the truth now. I know I'm not crazy. That's what matters, right? That's all I've wanted for weeks now. But now that I have it, I'm not sure I can handle it anymore. "I would like to go home now," I tell Maverick.

He nods. Then, without saying anything, he turns around and gestures for me to follow. So I do.

In the entranceway, he disappears into a side room. Then he emerges, Jacob trailing behind. Maverick stops several feet away from me, but Jacob closes the distance, holding out a couple of items to me. The first: my car keys. The second: my phone. I realize I must have left them in the alley when I tried to run. My car must be pretty beat up, too, after scraping against the Suburban. I recall a faint memory of the side mirror getting knocked off. I wonder how I'm going to explain that one to my parents.

"Your car's out front," Maverick tells me.

Not only is my car out front, but it's fixed, too. The mirror is back, and there's no evidence that it has even made contact with another car.

"I got it… fixed. I wanted to make sure everything was normal, as it was before you started getting chased. I wanted you to have your life back," Maverick tells me when he sees me eyeing the car suspiciously.

I nod, hitting the unlock button on my keychain. I remember the grinding noise I'd heard when my car scraped against the Suburban. There must have been some serious damage to the exterior, and it probably had needed an entire new paint job. Wasn't getting a car painted expensive, and didn't it take a long time? I hadn't even been gone for a full forty-eight hours yet.

"My number is in your phone now. In case you… need anything," Maverick tells me sincerely. I can hear what he really means in the space between his words: *in case you want to talk.*

"What are we going to do about Alice? What if she tries to kidnap me again?" I ask him.

"I'm going to look into it. I'll figure something out, but for now, just try and stay safe. Don't go out alone, lock your doors, stuff like that. I don't think she knows where you live. Call me if you notice anything suspicious—anything at all. Okay?"

I search his hazel eyes for a long moment. "Okay."

Maverick starts giving me directions on how to get home from here. We're right at the edge of town, so it's almost a thirty-minute drive back to my house. But as I stand there, listening, my focus changes to something else.

Maverick's house. His massive, elegant, very expensive-looking house. I take in the perfectly mowed lines in the front lawn, the spotless windows lining the front. The art and furniture I'd seen throughout the inside, the sports car he drove—all of it pointed towards one simple truth: Maverick must be rich. *Really* rich.

"—I'll keep you updated if I find anything," he finishes. My eyes pull into focus and I look at him. He's wearing an old, gray t-shirt and a pair of dark jeans today. Black sneakers. If he wasn't standing in front of a mansion, I'd never suspect him to have lots of money.

"Okay," I reply, though I'm sure I've missed some part of the conversation. I take a couple of steps towards my car, then turn, looking at him. "Thanks," I tell him.

His mouth twists up in a knot. "Drive safe," he replies.

As I get in my car, and as I pull out of the glorious stone driveway, a thought wanders into my mind. If Maverick can essentially manipulate people's memories, he can make anyone forget ever meeting him. Or seeing him do something wrong. What kinds of things could he have gotten away with throughout the years?

I see a flash of the speedometer creeping higher as we'd driven away from Alice's laboratory. If he had gotten pulled over, he could have simply made the cop forget it had ever happened.

To get to the main road, I have to pass through a tall, intricately woven metal gate that swings open when I get close to it. If Maverick has lots of money, how did he get it? He could have easily robbed a bank or stolen the money from someone and covered up the act by making them forget about it. He could have taken the mansion from someone and left them on the streets, and they'd never have even known they were rich.

I take a deep breath, my fingers tightening around the steering wheel, turning my knuckles white.

What kind of person *is* Maverick—the kind who'd be honest and true, or the kind who'd use his ability for personal gain?

CHAPTER 24

SUNDAY PASSES BY in a haze of spending my time avoiding my parents, moping around in my room, and trying to sort through the endless spiral of thoughts coursing through my mind. On Monday, I stay home from school, certain that sitting in a classroom attempting to focus while I have so many things to process will just make me crazier.

I'm not sure what I want to do about Maverick. Sure enough, when I'd checked my cell phone later on Sunday, his name was lit up across the screen in my list of contacts. I'd started typing, then erased a message to him at least four times since then, unable to figure out the right words.

I feel a strange mix of emotions, some stronger than others at times. I'm afraid: afraid of what Alice is going to do next. She could be hunting me down, trying to take me hostage again. How can I be sure that I'll ever be safe again? I'm mad, too: mad at Maverick for getting me into this mess—and also for keeping me out of it. If he had just been honest with me, maybe we could have worked something out instead of him erasing himself from my life. Maybe I would remember how I felt about him before all of this, and maybe I'd know what it's like to be a happy, normal teenager who could actually have a boyfriend.

As Monday creeps into Tuesday, my emotions all end up in the same place: anticipation. What's going to happen now? How are we going to stop Alice? How are we going to save all of the other anomalies she has locked up in her laboratory? When I'd been locked up there, Alice had injected me with something that had temporarily caused me to hear echoes of the future. What else could she be doing to the other anomalies? We have to find some way to help them.

My head is starting to hurt, even as I walk into Chemistry Tuesday morning and throw my backpack down on the table. The echoes of last year's classroom are especially annoying today, even before the bell has rung, and today's students are in a buzz about the football game that happened Friday night. Everything is so *loud*.

I'm pinching the bridge of my nose when a person appears in front of me. I look up, meeting Grace's dark eyes. She looks frustrated and worn out.

I open my mouth, trying to think of something to say, but come up short. I have a flashback of her phone call to me, just before my world exploded. She'd needed me to pick her up. But I'd never shown up.

"Before you say anything, I just want you to know that I don't blame you," Grace tells me.

I try to speak, but again, no words come out.

"But that was kind of a jerk move." She throws her backpack down on the table next to mine, scooting out the chair so she can sit.

"Grace—"

"I kind of deserved it. But seriously?"

I try to figure out how to respond. How can I explain to her everything that has happened? How can we repair this fractured friendship?

Luckily, I'm spared from having to figure it out right now because the bell rings and Mrs. Andrews calls the class to attention, preventing any further conversation. For fifty-five minutes, I sit there, listening to both Mrs. Andrews's Chemistry lesson on bonds and the echoes of Mrs. Andrews's Biology class learning about the carbon cycle. By the time the bell rings again, I still have no idea what to say to Grace.

"I get that you don't want to talk to me. Just… let me know when you've come up with a good excuse," Grace tells me, then leaves the room before I can form a reply.

At lunch, she's nowhere to be found. Leo, on the other hand, is sitting at the table, staring straight at me as I walk towards him.

"So I heard what happened," he tells me.

I think of the whole Grace situation, and then I think of getting kidnapped, rescued, and my conversation with Maverick. A lot of things *happened.* "What'd you hear?" I ask him bitterly. I plop down at the table, exhausted.

"Grace and Andy broke up. That he and Dana are back together," he replies.

"Officially? Really?" I ask him. He doesn't reply, but simply nods his head towards the table we'd seen Grace and Andy sitting at together last week. I glance over and don't need any more confirmation because Dana and Andy are sitting next to each other, mid-kiss.

"And there are rumors," Leo adds, "about how Grace handled the situation." I watch him clench his fists on the table. "The whole school is talking about how she started screaming at Andy, about how she supposedly tried to fight Dana. That she's a psycho."

"Oh, no," I blink, sliding my hands down my face. "This is so much worse than I thought."

"What do you mean?"

"On Friday, when everything happened, Grace called me. She told me that everyone was being mean to her, so she left the party for a minute to go calm down and when she walked back in Andy and Dana were kissing. Anyways, she asked me to pick her up—since her parents didn't know she was out and Andy had taken her to the party—and I told her I'd be there to get her, but... I never made it." I say the last few words slowly, hoping Leo won't need any further explanation.

"You *what?*" His eyes widen.

"She's never going to forgive me."

"How did she get home, then?"

I shrug. "I don't know. I thought she would have called you."

He frowns. "I guess I'm not even on the list of people to call when she's desperate."

"Leo—"

"No, it's fine," he puts a hand up. "Where even is Grace now?"

"She was in Chemistry. She didn't seem very happy with me, so she's probably avoiding me now."

"Or just avoiding *me*."

"Or *both* of us."

Leo and I sigh simultaneously.

"I don't know what to do. How can I convince her I'm not a terrible friend?"

"You'd better have a really good explanation for why you never showed up," Leo eyes me questioningly.

I search for some kind of response. *I was kidnapped* is a pretty good reason, but would she believe that without actual evidence or a police report? And how could I explain the reason for my kidnapping?

Fortunately, Leo doesn't press the issue when I don't respond, so we spend the rest of lunch in silence.

* ✱ *

GRACE AVOIDS ME for the rest of the week, giving me time to think about everything in my life. Every single strange, crazy thing.

I don't hear from Maverick, not that I'd really expected to. I don't expect the strange twitch of disappointment I feel every time my phone lights up and it's not his name, either. I know that I could just as easily open my phone and send him a text, but I'm not sure what I would even say. I'm still mad at him for erasing my memory, but as time passes, my curiosity grows, replacing the anger.

What is Maverick like? Right now, the only Maverick I'd experienced in person was the frustrated, angry, or desperate Maverick who was caught in a situation he didn't know how to handle very well. But what was he like outside of that? I think of the echoes I'd heard, where he seemed so sweet and gentle or flirty and playful. Which one was he: the dark, serious Maverick, or the open, lighthearted one?

Perhaps he was both. Perhaps we don't really know someone until we experience all of the different sides to them.

On Thursday night, I experience another side of Maverick.

I'm sitting at the table attempting to focus on homework when I hear an echo of the doorbell ringing. I hear my own voice, a little bit scratchy, call from the couch, *"I'll get it!"*

"No, Laura. You stay right there," Mom's echo calls back from her office. Footsteps go to the door. *"Come on in,"* Mom says, then the footsteps come back, followed by another pair. *"She's in here."*

Someone walks over to the couch while Mom heads back into her office.

"Oh, you pitiful thing," Maverick's smooth voice says, a hint of a smile in it. This time, unlike all the other times I'd heard echoes of him, I actually have a face to picture with the voice. Two bright, hazel eyes. Dark hair, short, but long enough to hang down over his forehead a little bit. I'm still frustrated with the situation he's put us in, but I can't stop the heat that forms in my cheeks when I imagine him being my boyfriend. He's definitely not hard on the eyes.

"Don't say that," the last two words are choked out, followed by a fit of coughing. *"Okay, yeah, I'm pretty pitiful."*

"Luckily, I brought you some stuff to help," Maverick's echo says, and I hear the soft creaking of the couch as he sits down. Then the sound of a plastic bag rustling. *"Peppermint candy canes for your sore throat—can you believe they're already selling them in stores?"*

"Wow, it's not even Thanksgiving yet," My echo chimes in.

"A cheesy romantic comedy that you can watch while you're holed up in here."

"And I haven't seen that one yet!"

"And last—but certainly not least—your very own tub of cookie dough ice cream."

"Oh. My. Gosh. You. Are. Amazing."

"I'm what, now?" Maverick teases.

"I was talking to the ice cream. Now hand it over." Both of our laughter fills the room, and then I hear the couch shifting again. *"Woah, not too close now. Trust me, you don't want to get this bug,"* my echo warns.

"Trust me, I think it's worth the risk," Maverick mumbles, his voice closer to where mine was. Unexpectedly, I feel my stomach flutter as if I was there, experiencing the situation myself.

"Let's put in the movie," my echo says. I hear the shuffling of Maverick getting up, walking to the TV, and turning on the movie.

The sounds of the movie we'd watched start echoing back to me, and I just sit there, listening. I remember seeing this movie, but not with Maverick. In my memory, it was someone else.

Grace? But perhaps that was just my mind filling in the gaps after Maverick removed the memory.

About twenty minutes into the movie, I hear the couch creaking again. Footsteps cross the room, and then the movie cuts off. They cross back, hovering by the couch.

"*Good night, my love,*" Maverick says, barely above a whisper. Then his footsteps leave the room.

The second I hear the door click close, I know what I need to do.

I stand, half stumbling, half running through the house, up the stairs, into my room. With trembling hands, I pull my cell phone out, scrolling through the contacts list.

On my bed, breathing hard, I touch Maverick's name, then hit the call button.

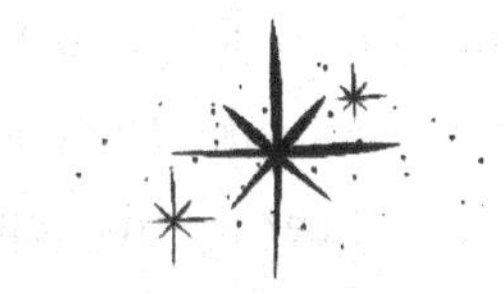

CHAPTER 25

THE PHONE ONLY RINGS once, and then Maverick's voice is on the other end.

"Laura? Is everything okay?" he asks, urgent.

"Yes," I say, clutching the phone in my hands. I take a deep breath, building the courage to say my next words. "I want to talk. Can we meet up somewhere?"

There's a brief pause. "Right now?"

I glance at the clock. 8:08. My curfew is ten on weeknights, which means we might have a little over an hour to talk. Not nearly enough time. "Yes."

"Where do you want to meet?" His answer is instantaneous. No questions, no hesitations.

"Somewhere quiet."

"A park?"

"Shorewick City Park, do you know it?"

"Yes."

"Meet me by the bathrooms, at the first entrance."

"I'll be there," Maverick assures me.

When I end the call and set down the phone, my hands are shaking the slightest bit. Hearing the echo of Maverick coming to my house and bringing me gifts when I was sick had sent me over the edge. Back then, he and I had meant something to each other, and if we'd dated for so long, then it must have been something good. I've never felt like I needed a boyfriend to be happy, but something about hearing his echo and knowing that he really does exist makes me want to know more about him. Obviously, we still have a long way to go in the trust department, but how can I pass by an opportunity to get to know someone that I'd already liked in the past?

It takes me ten minutes to get to Shorewick City Park and when I arrive, Maverick's car is already parked in the lot, his dark figure standing just outside of the bathrooms. I wonder how he got here so fast if his house is so far away, but I don't think too much about it.

I hop out of my car and walk over to him, stopping before I get within an arm's distance. I listen to the quiet evening air, the sound of the wind rustling through the last leaves still attached to their branches. Some of the noise comes in echoes, but most of it is from right now.

"Hi," I say, my breath forming clouds of mist in the air. A chill runs through my body; I'd forgotten how cold it was starting to get at night and in my rush to get here, I hadn't put on a coat.

"Laura," Maverick regards me, watching my movements. "You're freezing." Immediately, he starts to shrug out of his coat.

I put a hand up to stop him, "I'm fine," I say, but he doesn't listen. He gets the coat off, revealing another, thinner coat underneath.

"I don't need it," he tells me, holding it out to me. I hesitate, then cautiously step towards him. I reach my hand out, plucking the coat from his fingers, careful not to make contact with his skin.

I pull the thick, soft material around myself, taking in the leftover warmth from Maverick's body heat and the sweet, musky scent buried deep in the jacket. "Thanks."

We stand there for a moment, staring at each other across the cold air, the moonlight glowing around us. "Is everything okay? Do you need anything?" Maverick finally asks.

"I need the truth," I reply.

His eyebrows furrow. "I've told you the truth—"

"I know," I cut him off. "I believe what you've told me. But I want more. I want to know *everything*."

"Everything?" Maverick blinks in surprise. "Everything about what?"

"About you. About me. About all of this," I wave my hand aimlessly through the air. "Like how long we were…together. Like what your plans are to stop Alice. Like why you live in a mansion when last year you lived just across the street from me." I meet Maverick's eyes as I say the last statement and he winces. "I just need to know. I'm so confused because I don't know who you are when you obviously know me pretty well. I don't know if I can even trust you, but I feel like I should be able to. I need answers." Maverick just stands there as I spill the words out into the night, eyeing me thoughtfully.

He nods. "I understand. All you have to do is ask, Laura, and I promise I'll be honest with you about whatever you want to know."

I let out a breath I didn't realize I was holding, hoping his words are true. "Then tell me. Tell me all of it."

Maverick nods again. "Shall we walk?" he asks, gesturing into the park. I look down the dimly lit path and hesitate, wondering if it's safe to be out here alone with him. Then I think of Maverick pulling his car in front of the Suburban to allow me to escape, fighting off the men sent to kidnap me, then dragging me through Alice's laboratory, into the woods, and out of her reach. Everything he had done so far, he had done to protect me. Even though some of his methods were questionable.

"Yes," I reply, then start down the path, careful to keep a few feet of distance between us.

We walk in silence for a minute, then Maverick clears his throat. "We dated from October until June," he says.

I count the months off in my head. "Nine months?"

"Technically more like eight, since our first date was in mid-October, and then mid-June was when…" he trails off.

"When you made me forget," I finish for him.

His face twitches. "Yeah—that."

"I'm mad about that. But I'm trying to understand," I admit. It's hard, though. It's easy to just be angry and spiteful about something someone did to you, to hold onto a grudge. It's harder to accept things, to forgive, and to move on.

"You don't know how much I appreciate that," Maverick tells me, his hazel eyes cutting through the dark.

A few beats of silence pass before I ask another question. "Where did we go on our first date? I heard an echo of us leaving, but the location was a surprise, so I didn't know where we had gone, and I kind of have to be in the same place as the echoes to hear them."

Maverick looks over at me curiously. "I took you for ice cream, first."

"At Coffee and Cream?" I ask, remembering how I'd been there. But I hadn't heard any echoes. Had I just barely missed them?

"No, no. It was another ice cream place, somewhere off of Brooks Street, I think? We didn't start going to Coffee and Cream until, I wanna say, December? On our first date, we went to the other place, and you ordered a double scoop of cookie dough ice cream."

"Well, it certainly sounds like me," I tell him.

Maverick laughs under his breath, a low, clipped sound that's somehow the same, yet somehow different from his echoes. Colder. "We tried a few different ice cream shops, but one day we stumbled into Coffee and Cream and you said it was the *best* cookie dough ice cream you'd ever had. You vowed to never eat another brand again."

We both laugh, and I try to imagine the moment. I remember going to Coffee and Cream a few times now, and all three of them I'd been impressed by the cookie dough ice cream. Perhaps it *was* the best I'd ever had.

"On our first date, after we had ice cream, we had dinner at this little cafe, and then we wrapped it up with a stroll through the park. This park, actually."

I look around us, the moonlight glowing softly through the trees. It's such a strange thought, that I was with him, right here, over a year ago. That I'm with him, right now, under these unbelievable circumstances. To think that all of this happened without me knowing about any of it scares me.

A cold chill runs through me. "I want to know about your house," I say suddenly. "The one you have now."

The warm, lightness of the air between us goes cold and heavy in an instant. Maverick stiffens, his movements growing rigid as we walk through the dark. He doesn't respond for a few minutes.

"Did you..." I pause, trying to judge his body language, "take it from someone?"

Maverick's eyes flash at me. "You think I used my ability to get it?"

I shrug. "I don't know what to think."

He lets out a long, steady breath. "I didn't," he says, to my relief. "I inherited it from my father."

Distantly, I remember an echo I'd heard.

"So what's your dad up to, then?" my own dad had asked him.

"My dad isn't around. I never really knew him," Maverick replied.

"Your father who you never knew?" I mumble, repeating the words I'd remembered.

Maverick winces when he hears my words, and I can see the lines of a painful memory crossing his face. "I did know him, actually. But he didn't know me," he tells me, finally. "When I was growing up, I started to notice weird things that would happen around me. Mom would forget I had a doctor's appointment simply because I didn't want to go. Dad would forget that the game was on because I was busy playing cars with him. My teacher would forget that I didn't turn in my homework. I didn't know it was me, at first. But as I grew older, I started to figure out how it worked.

"When I was about ten, I tried to talk to my parents about it. I tried to convince them that there was something wrong with me, that somehow I could make people forget about things. But they wouldn't believe me, they thought I was just being paranoid. So they started taking me to counselors, psychologists. People who told me I simply had a disorder."

I nod, "I know how that feels."

"One day, I tried to bring it up again, and my dad got really mad. He could be short-tempered at times. He told me I needed to grow up, to stop it with the stupid little games. I begged and begged him to trust me, to listen to me, but he wouldn't. So I got mad, too." Maverick hangs his head down. "I didn't mean to do it, honestly. But I was angry, so I told my dad I wished he would just forget about me. That I hated him and didn't want him to be part of the family anymore.

"The second he laid his hand on me, I watched the memories fade from his eyes. Me, my mom, everything. I was angry, and I didn't know how to control it. So it just happened. And I couldn't take it back." I watch the muscles in Maverick's jaw twitching as he pauses. "I made my own dad forget about our family. And my mom watched it all happen."

A brief silence falls around us. It totally makes sense to me now why Maverick responded the way he did when my dad's echo asked him about his dad. This couldn't be easy for him to talk about. Even if he hadn't told us why his dad was gone, the guilt of knowing it was his fault was probably unbearable.

"I was just a *kid*," his voice falters on the word. "I ruined our family. He left that day, and we never saw him again—why would we? We were just strangers to him after that. But his name was on my birth certificate, so when he died last year, and he had no other family to pass down his possessions to, it went to me. Mom kept it from me since I was still a minor, but once I turned eighteen I got all of it."

"So your Dad was rich?" I ask him, blinking in surprise.

"Not exactly. He won the lottery a few years ago. Six hundred and seventy-five million dollars."

I suck in a cold breath.

"Of course, he bought the house, and the cars and everything. And with taxes, and estate taxes, and all that stuff, it's nowhere near that much money anymore..." Maverick scratches his neck uncomfortably.

"Wow," the word doesn't even begin to wrap around the enormity of the information I've just learned. The words hang over our heads like dark thunderclouds. "Did I know about any of this? Your Dad leaving?"

"I told you eventually that my Dad left us when I was younger and that we never saw him again. Though I kind of left out the part about it being my fault, obviously. But I told you about the house and everything right after I found out about it all. You even came over to hang out a few times."

"That makes sense," I reply, nodding.

A corner of his mouth tilts upwards, the expression catching me off guard. "Though, I was glad that we'd already been dating for several months before I got it all. Because at least I was *mostly* sure you weren't just dating me for my money."

I can't help but laugh at his comment, but it makes me wonder. How *had* I felt about him? We'd been together for a while, so I must have been happy. But he also would have been my first relationship, ever. Could I have been too afraid to end things? Afraid that I'd never find love again if I left him?

I don't *want* to think it had been like that. All of the echoes I'd heard of Maverick and I had been sweet. Sure, there had been a lot of teasing and flirting, but underneath it all, it sounded like we cared about each other. Maverick had brought me gifts when I was sick—even now the thought of that encounter makes my heart flutter in my chest. But had things changed as the months went by? I guess my only option now is to listen to all the echoes I can and wait and see.

We take several steps through the darkness before I clear my throat, changing the subject yet again. "So what's the plan? How are we going to stop Alice?"

Maverick looks at me pointedly. "We?"

I blink at him. "Yes. *We.*"

He shakes his head. "I don't think you want to get involved with this."

I stop walking, turning on him squarely. "I'm not going to sit around while you try to take down Alice alone. The woman who's chasing *me,* too, in case you don't remember." The words come out harsher than I'd intended, but they get my point across.

"I don't want you to get hurt—"

"I've already been hurt," I cut him off. "And now that I know about all of this, it's kind of personal."

Maverick looks determined to convince me I should stay out of it. "This is big, Laura. This operation she has—it's not just going to be an easy waltz-in-and-stop-her kind of deal. It's going to be messy. You don't know what you're getting yourself into."

What he doesn't know is that I'm determined to help anyway. "I don't care. I want to help."

We look at each other, eyes fixed in place like it's some kind of staring contest, and neither of us wants to lose. Part of me knows that what I'm asking for is terrible. Dangerous. But the other part of me knows that I don't really have a choice, not after learning about Maverick and our shared past, about what Alice has done to him and to others. What she might try to do to me. I'm a part of this, now. I have to be.

Finally, Maverick drops his gaze and breathes one word: "Okay."

CHAPTER 26

I PULL INTO THE parking lot, my hands gripping the steering wheel tightly. I crane my neck, but it doesn't take long for my eyes to spot Maverick, sitting on a rusty bench in front of the building.

After our conversation last night, we knew there was more we needed to discuss, but my curfew was approaching swiftly, so we decided to meet up again another time. That meeting was now, right after school on Friday, at none other than Louise's.

I park the car, then hop out and walk over to him. He stands when he sees me, and I take in the sight of him. He seems to favor dark, simple clothes, because his long-sleeved shirt looks almost exactly the same as the last one I'd seen him wearing, only a few shades lighter.

He opens the door for me, and when I step inside a wall of sound hits me. The jukebox is playing a classic rock tune that almost gets drowned out by the voices of people deep in conversation and by the clinking of dishes throughout the room. None of the noise is from the present, as usual. I follow Maverick to a booth by a window, where we are immediately greeted by Penny.

"Can't get enough of us, can you?" she says to me.

I throw her my best smile. "Guess not!"

She looks between me and Maverick with a glint in her eye, and I have to squash the blush forming in my cheeks when I realize that to her, this probably looks very much like a date. Technically, we're meeting up to discuss plans to stop a crazy woman who wants to use Maverick's memory-erasing ability to kidnap innocent people, but Maverick and I had been together, so I guess it could quite possibly be a date. But I'm still trying to make up my mind about him, so for now, it shouldn't be.

"Well, what can I get you two to drink?" Penny asks.

I order my usual Cherry Coke and Maverick gets water, and when Penny is gone, he opens his menu. "This is my advice: don't get the fries. The deep fryer is a little old, and Tony could never quite figure out that he couldn't just use the preset timer when making them."

I nod in understanding. "That explains a lot."

"The onion rings, on the other hand, aren't too bad when he makes them. But I know you don't like them."

It still feels weird, but of course, he would know that, especially after dating for so long. He knows all of these little details about me, yet in some ways, he still feels like a complete stranger since I don't know anything about him. In another way, however, he feels like the only person who might actually understand me. He knows about my ability, and he even has his own that complicates his life, too. He knows what I've been through when I never thought anyone on the planet would ever be able to understand. How could something like that even happen? I let out a half-laugh, half-sigh at the thought.

Maverick raises an eyebrow at me.

"It's just so weird hearing you say that," I tell him.

He nods thoughtfully. "It's weird for me, too. That you kind of remember me, but only bits and pieces, right?" he says gently, like he's unwrapping a bandage around a wound that might reopen at the slightest amount of pressure.

"I wouldn't exactly call them memories," I say. "They're more like... I don't know. Like watching a TV show about myself where my life is totally different and it doesn't seem real, but I know that it is. Except the screen on the TV only has a picture of the place, no characters. Just a setting and then sound." It's weird to be explaining the echoes to him so casually. With everyone else I'd ever had to explain them to, I felt like I was trying to convince them I wasn't crazy. With Maverick, it's just a simple explanation that he doesn't even question.

"That is weird," he agrees, studying me with a look of fascination that makes my stomach do a little dance. "Can you hear them right now? The—what did you call them?"

"Echoes," I reply. Then, as if on cue, an echo of a baby screaming appears right behind me. "I hear them all the time. Like right now, it was a lot busier in here last year. So there's music playing, people talking, and someone's child just started throwing a fit right there," I point over my shoulder.

Maverick frowns. "That sounds awful. I guess that explains why you never wanted to go places that were very busy while we were dating. And when I did convince you to go, we never stayed long."

I wonder at the thought. That's pretty much how I am with Grace and Leo. "But you still liked me, even though I didn't like doing anything?"

Maverick smiles, a real, genuine smile that shows off a dimple on his left cheek. "I just thought you were above the whole scene. You didn't need to do what everyone else was doing to have fun. You do your own thing. It's one of the many things I like about you."

My cheeks burn red at his switch to the present tense. The corners of his mouth twitch up into another smile, but Penny saves me by setting our drinks down on the table.

"Have you two decided what you'll have?"

"Get the BLT," Maverick tells me. "You'll like it."

I eye him suspiciously. "Guess I'll have that," I tell Penny. After Maverick orders one for himself and Penny walks away, I ask him, "So you think I'll like it because I've already had it before and liked it?"

"No," he replies. He thinks for a second. "I don't think you ever had the BLT. I just genuinely think you'll like it."

"How will I ever know the difference?"

He shrugs. "I guess you'll just have to ask," he replies, smirking. Right here, *this* is the same playful Maverick I remember hearing in the echoes. And with the way he's looking at me right now, no wonder I liked him.

We sit there for a few beats, contemplating. Then I clear my throat. "Speaking of which, I have a few things I want to ask about."

"I guess I have a few things to answer. You go first," he replies, the smirk still plastered on his mouth. I try to ignore it.

"Why haven't you just erased Alice's memories? Couldn't you just… make her forget about being evil, or something?"

Maverick's face spreads into a grin, the dimple making an appearance again. "It doesn't exactly work like that," he laughs.

"What do you mean?" I raise an eyebrow.

"Well, I can't just take away a part of someone's personality." His eyes go serious, his expression following suit. "Just the memories. The things they've experienced."

"So take away the memories that have led her to the choices she's made. Or make her forget about what she's doing. Can't you just do that?"

Maverick fiddles with the straw wrapper in his fingers. "I've tried."

"What do you mean?"

"It doesn't work," he tells me, his yellow eyes flickering back and forth between mine.

"How come?"

"I don't know." He shakes his head. "I've learned how to control my ability well enough. I've done it more times than I'd like to admit. But when I do it to Alice, nothing changes. She still remembers everything perfectly."

My eyes widen. "How is that possible?"

He lets out a breath. "I think she's developed some kind of way to block it. To become immune to it. I'm not sure." I think back to being held captive in Alice's laboratory and having a needle shoved into my arm.

"She gave me this stuff when I was trapped there. It was a shot, and after she gave it to me, I started hearing weird echoes of things just before they happened. It was only temporary, but I wonder if it was some kind of experimental drug."

"She tested things on you?" Maverick's eyebrows inch upward in concern.

"I guess so. Then she took my blood. I don't know why. As far as I know, she doesn't know about my ability."

"Maybe she was trying to use you as a control because she didn't know you're already an anomaly. But for what?"

I shrug.

To my left, the kitchen doors swing open and Penny comes sauntering through with a plate in each hand. She sets them down in front of each of us, tells us to enjoy, then goes back to the kitchen. I reach for the napkins at the edge of the table, and at the same time, Maverick reaches for the silverware next to it. Somewhere along the way, our hands bump into each other.

Instinctively, I jerk my hand away quickly, and in its retreat, it tips Maverick's glass over. Water spills out onto the table, dripping off onto his seat.

"I'm so sorry!" I squeal as he stands, then pulls out a wad of napkins and starts wiping up the mess. I grab another wad of napkins and lay them out across the table, but I'm careful not to get too close to Maverick's hands.

"Don't worry about it," he tells me as he returns to his seat, pushing the sopping wet napkins into a pile at the edge of the table. But he won't meet my eyes, and his lips have formed into a thin line.

"I didn't mean to jump like that. It's just…" I trail off. I don't want to tell him that I'm afraid. That I'm terrified of his ability, of his power. That I'm still afraid of what will happen if I decide that I do trust him.

I don't have to tell him. The look he gives me tells me he already knows. "I understand," he says, an expression that I can't quite read crossing his face.

"I'm sorry," I say again genuinely.

"It's fine," he replies, flashing a hollow smile. Through his eyes I can see him closing in on himself, shutting the doors that were wide open moments ago. I can read the emotion in them clearly now.

Guilt.

CHAPTER 27

AFTER I FINISH EATING my food, I push my plate away from me, resting my elbows on the table. "It's loud in here. We should go somewhere quieter," I say. It feels good to be able to say the words. Words no one else would understand, since it's definitely not loud today.

"Which places are quiet for you?" Maverick asks.

"Cars," I say. "New buildings, since they have no past to echo back to me. Outdoors, too—usually."

Maverick looks through the window at the overcast sky and steady rain falling over the parking lot. "We could sit in the car," he says.

I nod. We stand, and Maverick pays for our food, leaving—I notice—a *very* generous tip. We climb into his Corolla and he cranks the car, turning the heat on.

"So what's the plan? How are we going to stop her?" I ask him.

"First, there are a few things you need to know." He's all business now, the playful, smirking Maverick left behind in the restaurant the moment I'd flinched at his touch. "Alice has a lot of people working for her. She's not someone to be underestimated."

I think of the giant laboratory tucked in the mountains, the guards attempting to halt our escape, the men in the black Suburban who'd kidnapped us. I nod.

"She's powerful. And dangerous. And because of that, we have to be careful about how we do this. You'll need to learn some basic self-defense. And carry a weapon."

A ball of nervousness punches me in the stomach. "A weapon?"

"Yes." His eyes pierce into mine across the center console. "A gun."

I take a gulp of air. I've never touched a gun before, not even for fun. The thought of having one terrifies me, but what scares me even more is the chance that I might have to *use* it. "I don't know… " I breathe.

"You want to get involved. I don't want anything to happen to you. So you need to be able to defend yourself in case we run into her. Consider it a compromise," he says firmly.

"O—okay," I stutter.

"We need to gather more information before we do anything. I want to know what she's capable of, what other things we need to look out for."

"How do we do that?"

"She has a practice here in town. Where she does her... day job, so to speak."

"What can we find there?"

"She keeps patient records. So we might be able to figure out who she's been studying. I'm not sure if there'll be any information about her research and what she's trying to develop, but it's worth a try. It's the safest place to start, I guess."

I nod.

"I'm going to stake out her office for a few days so I can figure out the best time to sneak in. I'll let you know when I've decided on a time, and we can hopefully get some answers."

"Sounds like a good plan," I say. We sit there in the enclosed space of the car, and I wait for him to say something else. But he doesn't. A heavy silence falls around us, threatening to suffocate me.

I'm starting to get the sense that this conversation is over, but I don't want it to be. All I want right now is to sit down and talk to Maverick, to learn more about him, about *us*. But by recoiling at a simple brush of our hands, I fear that I may have snapped the tiny, fragile strings that were attempting to pull us closer to each other. I don't know how to put them back.

"I guess I better get going," I finally break the silence.

Maverick looks at me, but his expression is unreadable. "Stay safe. I'll be in touch soon," he tells me and I nod, stepping out into the rainy parking lot and closing the door of the car behind me.

✳✱✳

SOON TURNS OUT TO BE not soon enough, because after a week goes by, I'm convinced that I'll never get to talk to Maverick again. It disappoints me that he hasn't called yet, but not because I want to know more about Alice and how to stop her. Actually, it's Maverick that I'm interested in, and I can't stop thinking about him. At Louise's, we'd gone from flirting to cold distance in the blink of an eye. I want that other part of him back, the one that was similar to the echoes of his calm, casual charm and his easy understanding. But after I'd basically freaked out at his touch, he just pulled away. I'm sure he still feels guilty about what he did, but hadn't we been on the path to moving past it? I'm sure that someday I'll be able to forgive him, but will he ever be able to forgive himself? I hope so, because now that I know him, all I want is to know more about him, and I can't do that if I never get to speak to him again.

The commotion in the school parking lot on Friday morning is enough to bury my thoughts of Maverick for a while, though.

First I see Grace, trying to sidestep a boy that's blocking her path, saying something to her. Then I see Andy and two of his friends leaning against a car a few feet away, laughing. As I get closer, I start to hear what they're saying.

"Get out of my way before I punch you in the face," Grace says, giving the boy one of her best death glares.

"Before you what? Go psycho and tell my mom on me?" The boy spits at her feet. "Andy was right, you actually are insane," he snarls, then steps to the side to finally let her past. But Grace doesn't move.

"Why don't you tell Andy to come over here and say it to my face, then, huh? Or is he actually so much of a coward that he has to send someone else to do it for him?" Grace fires back, loud enough for Andy—and everyone in the surrounding area—to hear. I watch as heads turn, and a few people nearby pause to see the showdown.

Andy pushes himself off the car, then walks over to Grace, arms crossed, chomping on a piece of gum. He smiles snarkily. "What do you want me to say? That I love you and want you back? Sorry, sweetie, but in case you didn't know, I don't go out with little tattletales."

"I'm not a tattletale," Grace insists. He's a head taller than her, so she has to tilt her head back to look him squarely in the face.

Andy steps closer to her, his finger pointed at her chest. "Listen up, Grace," he keeps moving, forcing her to back away. "If you hadn't gone and run to your little mommy about your stupid problems, she wouldn't have gone to my mom and gotten me in trouble for going to that party, too." Just as Andy finishes the sentence, he reaches for Grace, grabbing her by the shirt.

Grace jolts away, breaking free from his grasp, but in the process, stumbles on a shoelace and falls to the ground. Andy steps closer, grinning.

I start to move, ready to jump in and stand by her side, defending her, but a voice rings out from behind me, stopping me in my tracks.

"Get away from her," Leo demands, rushing to place himself between them, his eyes locked on Andy. He's not as tall as Andy, but he's stockier.

Andy smirks, but I notice he takes a tiny step backward. "Hey look everyone, loverboy has come to rescue her." Andy's friends by the car snicker in response.

Leo ignores them, turning around and holding a hand out to Grace. "Come on, let's get out of here." She takes his hand and he pulls her up. Then she dusts herself off. She looks angry, but also like she's about to break down.

"It's okay, you can have my leftovers. I'm done with her anyway," Andy sneers.

Leo whips around, fire blazing in his eyes. "Your leftovers? What do you call *Dana,* then?"

Andy scowls, but looks confused.

Leo feigns shock. "Oh, you mean you didn't know? That she's cheating on you with Jake? *And* Ben?"

Andy looks taken aback for a moment. He glances over at his friends by the car. One of them—the boy who'd been antagonizing Grace earlier—turns pale and the guy next to him looks down at the ground, avoiding Andy's gaze.

Then, I see everything happening in slow motion. Andy's face flashes into a cold rage, his fist curls up into a ball, and he turns around to face Leo again.

"Watch out!" I shout as Andy draws his arm back. Leo looks at me, questioning, a moment before Andy's fist comes down, crashing into his face.

Everyone starts shouting. Leo stumbles backward, his hand clutching the left side of his face, eyes shut in pain. Grace reaches for him, shouting something at Andy. I step forward to join my friends just as a whistle blows. Everyone falls into silence, turning to face Principal Jackson as she shoves her way toward Andy and Leo.

"Everybody get to class!" she yells, making all of the bystanders spring into action, scattering towards the school buildings. "You three are coming with me. Right now," she says to Grace, Leo, and Andy. She grabs a shocked Leo and a seething Andy in each arm, then marches in the direction of her office. Grace hesitates, watching them go. Her eyes land on me.

"I—"

Before I can finish, she turns and jogs after them.

At lunch, I find her tucked in a corner of the library between book stacks, eating by herself. I need to fix things with her because I need to have at least one constant in my life. One thing I can control.

"We need to talk," I say, and she looks up, startled by my presence. Then she narrows her eyes.

"Oh, so *now* you want to talk?"

"I want us to be friends. What happened this morning wasn't cool, I want to help make it right."

"Make it right? Laura, you've only made things worse. You couldn't be there for me when I *needed* you, and now I'm the laughing stock of the school because of it. And not only that, but when my parents discovered I went to that party, they talked to Andy's parents, and then everyone else's parents, and now *everyone* is in trouble. Because of me. Because of you."

I wince at her words, but then I harden my gaze at her. "Don't pin this on me," I tell her, my voice low.

"You pinned it on yourself, Laura," she spits. She stands, shoving her things into her backpack. "We're done here." She shoves past me, knocking a few books onto the ground. She ignores them, stepping out into the aisle between the book stacks. Then she looks back at me briefly. "What I don't understand is that you told me you were going to come get me. And then you didn't. If you weren't going to show, why did you tell me you were?"

I've tried, many times, to come up with some kind of reasonable explanation, but when I open my mouth, not a single one comes out.

"Thanks. Thanks a lot, Laura." She says my name as if it's some kind of disease. Then she leaves me alone in the library, a section of books scattered on the floor around me. As I'm gathering them up, I feel my phone vibrate in my pocket.

Pulling it out, my focus shifts from Grace back to my previous problem.

It's a text from Maverick.

I have a plan. Meet up after school?

CHAPTER 28

I SIT IN MY CAR in the parking lot, watching my peers walk by. Grace's car hasn't appeared in a few days, meaning her driving privileges are most likely still revoked. Leo's car is here, but he's nowhere to be seen. I wonder if he got detention for fighting, though technically it was Andy who antagonized him and threw the punch.

I'm not sure what to do about Grace. I just want to be able to tell her everything—about Maverick, about Alice, about the echoes. But it seems like such an impossible task. How would anyone believe it all? Anyone except Maverick. He understands it all a little too well.

I've got my face against the steering wheel, trying not to break down when Maverick opens the door to my car, a blast of cold air hitting me.

He slides into the passenger seat, looks at me. "What's wrong?" he asks.

"Nothing," I say, wiping my nose on my sleeve and averting my eyes. It's not very convincing.

"Nothing," Maverick teases, wiping his nose on his sleeve dramatically, making a sad face.

I can't help but laugh, a hollow, choked-up sound. "Shut up," I reply.

He gives me a half-smile, then goes serious, his eyes meeting mine across the center console. "I'm sorry for causing you so much stress."

I let out a long sigh. "It's not that, right now. Mostly just friend drama. It's not important." Not as important as attempting to stop a crazy woman trying to kidnap me, at least.

"Are Grace and Andy having problems again?" he asks casually, as if he's known them his whole life.

I blink in surprise. "You know my friends?" I ask.

He just shrugs. "Once upon a time, we would all hang out together."

"Wow," I say, raising my eyebrows. "Still weird that you know these things."

Maverick looks down at his feet. "I'm sorry."

"It's fine," I respond genuinely. "I'll just have to give you the update, then. Andy and Grace broke up, and then Andy got back with Dana."

Maverick scrunches his nose in disgust. "Seriously?" I nod. "He's a jerk. I never liked him anyway."

"You and me both. And—get this—Leo is, apparently, in love with Grace."

Maverick gives me a sideways glance. "You mean you didn't know that?"

My jaw drops. "What? How did *you* know?" I ask, incredulous.

"You seriously never noticed the way he always sits so close to her? The way he looks her in the eye like she's the only thing he sees? His constant attempts to flirt?" I shake my head as he ticks each item off on his fingers.

"I didn't notice any of those things," I reply, thinking about Leo and Grace's playful banter. Perhaps it could have been flirting, I'd just never put the dots together.

"And they say guys are oblivious," Maverick laughs. I laugh, too, and then silence falls around us.

"Grace is mad at me," I finally say, "because one night she went to this party and got into a bit of a bad situation. She called me, asking me to pick her up, and even though I told her I would be there in a few minutes, I never showed up. Because I got kidnapped by a crazy woman named Alice before I ever made it."

Maverick nods. "So that's why you were heading way out there that night."

Something dawns on me. "You were following me, weren't you? That's how you showed up there. And why you were there the night of the dance."

Maverick nods. "I tried my best to keep tabs on you once I found out Alice was looking for you. I even tried to work for her again so she'd leave you alone. But I was intentionally a little sloppy with my work, hoping she'd get caught. But she didn't, and then she found out what I was doing, hence the kidnapping and everything."

It feels weird knowing that he was out there, watching me, perhaps the whole time I was hearing his echoes and questioning my sanity. I expect to feel some form of violation, but I don't. Instead, the thought calms me. Like I had some kind of guardian angel watching out for me. Protecting me, if only for as much time as he could.

"Thank you," I tell him honestly.

Maverick just stares out the window. "So I've got a plan," he says.

I swallow. "What is it?"

"Alice usually leaves her office around seven. So we'll head there before then, and make sure we see her leave before we go inside."

"How do we get inside? Is it locked?"

"It's in a medical building with a bunch of other offices and practices. The main doors are usually unlocked, so we'll just have to get past the receptionist at the front."

"How do we do that?" I ask him.

He just stares at me for a long moment.

"Oh. Right," I say. Memory erasing abilities. Got it.

He looks away. "Before we go, I want to make sure you know how to use a gun. So you can at least defend yourself in case anything happens."

"What? You don't think I'm capable of taking down a couple of bad guys with my bare hands?" I try to lighten the mood, grinning.

Maverick can't help but break into a smile. "Based on the fact that you still got kidnapped, even *with* my help? No," he says, and then we both laugh.

✳

THE BLUE COROLLA rolls to a stop in front of Maverick's house thirty minutes later. I'd ridden with him and texted my parents to let them know that I was at Grace's for the evening. If they ever figure out what I'm really up to, I'm afraid that I might never leave the house again.

We hop out of the car and step inside, and once again I take in the magnificence of the place. Maverick leads me through a hallway, a few doors, then down a flight of stairs into a basement. The basement is fully furnished, complete with a giant, flat-screen TV mounted on the wall, brown suede couches, a pool table, and a minibar along the backside of the room. Next to it is a wood cabinet that's padlocked shut.

Maverick goes to the cabinet, plucks a key from his keychain, and unlocks it, sliding the dark-stained doors open.

I gasp.

Inside, there are guns. A *lot* of them.

"Dad was a hunter," Maverick tells me. He reaches inside, then pulls out a small handgun, weighing it in his hand for a second. Then he closes the cabinet, sliding the lock back into place. "Come with me."

We go back up the stairs, past a window looking out at the pool in the middle of the house, then through a back door. We step outside onto a wooden deck with floral padded porch furniture and a shiny, stainless steel grill. We go down a few steps and stand in the grass, facing a massive, perfectly manicured lawn edged by a wall of trees.

Maverick turns to face me, the gun in his left hand pointed at the ground. "Rule number one: the gun is always loaded. Never point the barrel at anything you aren't willing to shoot, even if you know it's not loaded. It's a deadly weapon, and should always be treated as such."

I nod. "Okay."

Maverick shows me the safety, how to reload it, and how to chamber a bullet. "Then, you just pull the trigger," he tells me. He gestures for me to back up, and I take three giant steps away from him. He lifts the gun, aiming it at the edge of the woods, then pulls the trigger. The sound of the gunshot leaves my ears ringing.

When it's over, Maverick slides the safety back into place, then holds the gun out to me. "You'll want to use both hands until you get used to the recoil."

I stand there, eyes wide, heart drumming against my ribcage. This is all happening too fast. "You want me to shoot it? Right now?" I choke out.

"Well, you don't want the first time you shoot it to be the time when your life depends on it."

"I—I," I stutter. "I don't *want* to use it."

"I don't want you to, either," he says. "But you need to be ready."

I squash the knot forming in my stomach. "Okay," I try to be brave. "Okay." I reach for the gun. My fingers brush Maverick's as I take its weight from his hands, but I don't flinch like the last time. He meets my eyes, a cautious look on his face, but I look away, turning my focus to the open yard.

I repeat the steps Maverick taught me moments ago, releasing the safety, then cocking the gun. I hold it up with both hands, arms shaking the tiniest bit.

"When you aim, look right there, right above that hole." Maverick points, leaning close. Close enough for me to feel the heat radiating from his body. Then he steps back, the space between us returning to its normal distance. I shiver, but I suspect it's not because of the cold or the fact that I'm holding a deadly weapon in my bare hands.

"Okay," I whisper to myself, staring straight ahead, a tree coming into focus across the barrel of the gun. I take a deep breath, muscles tense. Then I pull the trigger.

A shock courses through my body at the force of the gun's recoil. The sound of the shot permeates the air, rattling my bones. I lower my hands, steadying my breath.

I turn to Maverick, a cold fear piercing through me. I can't imagine pulling that trigger when it's pointed at someone. I can't think about having to do that. I hold the gun out to him. "I think I get the point," I say.

He holds my gaze for a second, then takes it from me, sliding the safety back into place and removing the bullets from the chamber easily. The gun felt out of place and awkward in my hands, but Maverick holds it like it belongs there. "I'm hoping that you won't need it. But I want you to be able to defend yourself."

"Is there any other way for me to protect myself? Preferably a less deadly way?" I ask.

Maverick slides something out of his pocket then tosses it in my direction. I look down at the small container. "Pepper spray?"

"For less life-threatening situations, it works pretty well. Just aim for the eyes."

I nod, pocketing it. "I'll have no problem putting this one to good use."

He lets out a laugh, then starts back toward the house. I trail behind, watching the way he walks, surely and steadily, with purpose.

When we get inside, Maverick leads me into the dining room. The same place where we'd had that difficult conversation, barely two weeks ago. "What would you like for dinner?"

I raise an eyebrow. "Is there a menu?"

"The menu is whatever you want," he replies, serious.

I contemplate his words for a second, realizing that he's probably telling the truth—with all the money he has, he *could* just get whatever he wants. I decide not to test my limits, though. "Honestly, I'm kind of just in the mood for some French fries."

"I can do that. Better than Tony's, too. Come on," he tells me, then starts for a door at the opposite side of the room. I follow him, staring at the sparkling chandelier hanging from the ceiling. The echoes in this house are so quiet; it feels empty. Lonely.

Through the door, there's a restaurant size kitchen. Maverick opens the storage room, pulls out a sack of potatoes, then walks over to one of the many clean counters. He flips a switch on a deep fryer, and I watch as he carefully starts peeling the potatoes, then slides each one through a French fry cutter.

"Don't you have, like, people who cook for you?" I ask him, his back facing me.

He turns his head just enough so he can look at me. "Sometimes, yeah."

I nod. "It must be nice." I watch his shoulders moving under his shirt as he lifts the potatoes into the basket of the deep fryer, admiring his frame. This guy was *my* boyfriend at one point? Grace would have been *so* jealous.

"It's… weird. I prefer to cook on my own, honestly. But the people here, this is their job. They get paid to cook, and clean, and take care of the yard. I don't want to take that from them."

I ponder it. "I guess that is weird."

He nods, sliding the full basket of fries into the deep fryer. He turns to face me, leaning back and resting his elbows on the counter. "Sometimes I feel like I don't belong here. I don't deserve all of this," he waves his hand in the air, gesturing at the room vaguely.

I glance at all of the stainless steel around me, the spotless tile floors. I shrug. "You just got really lucky, I guess."

A half-smile crosses his face, but it looks more sad than happy. "It doesn't feel like that."

I try to imagine Maverick's life. Struggling with his ability. Fighting with his family about it. It all seems too similar to my own experience with the echoes, except Maverick's ability actually caused irreversible damage to his family. And now both of his parents are gone. I can't even imagine having to deal with so much.

The deep fryer beeps, and Maverick turns away, lifting the basket of fries out of the oil. He pulls a plate out of a cabinet, shakes the pile of French fries onto it, then slides it over to me. "All yours."

CHAPTER 29

TWO HOURS LATER, we wait in a parking lot in Maverick's Corolla, watching the doorway of the building. I shiver from the cold. We didn't leave the car on, since we don't want to draw attention to ourselves, and twenty minutes later the bitter cold from outside has already made its way into the car. It's freezing, but the gun burns hot against my hip. Maverick had assured me that I most likely won't need it tonight, but he wanted me to have it just in case.

Twelve minutes after seven, Alice comes walking out of the building. I shiver at the sight of her, dressed in a pantsuit and carrying a briefcase. So normal in appearance. She hops into a shiny white Porsche and peels out of the parking lot. I start to move after it's gone, but Maverick holds his hand up.

"Let's wait a few minutes, just to make sure," he says.

I nod, my breath coming out in clouds of mist. We wait in silence as a few other people dressed in business clothes leave the building. Ten minutes later, Maverick pushes the door open.

We walk into a small waiting room where a receptionist is sitting behind a glass window, typing into her computer. When we get closer to her, she opens the window, looking at us expectantly. "Can I help you?"

Maverick ignores her. He steps past the window, opening a door just to the left of it, and I follow closely behind him. "Excuse me? You need to check in before you can go back there. Your doctor will come and get you when they are ready," the receptionist is saying as we pass through the door. On the other side, a hallway is in front of us and the backside of the receptionist's desk is to our right.

"Hold on, please go back around the other way," she says, standing up from her chair. She steps forward as if to guide us back through the door, but Maverick reaches out and grabs her wrist. I watch as her eyes widen for a half-second, then glaze over. Maverick grabs her other arm, guiding her back into her seat. She sits down, then he turns her forward to face the front door again. When he lets go of her, he goes to the wall behind her, searching for something. He snatches a key chain off a hook, then looks at me.

"Let's go," he says, avoiding my gaze. "She won't remember seeing us." Then he starts down the hallway.

I pause for a long moment, realizing that I've just witnessed Maverick use his ability. The same ability he used on me. I shiver at the thought; it had been so easy. It only took a second. Pushing my fears to the side, I follow him down the hall, taking long strides to keep up with his pace.

Finally, we come to an office, and Maverick uses a key from the keychain he took to unlock the door. It slides open, revealing a homey-looking office with a red sofa across from a desk. It's quiet, probably because it's so late in the evening and even last year no one was here at the time.

My eyes immediately go to the filing cabinet in the corner.

Maverick closes the door and locks it.

"We'll be quick. You start with the filing cabinets," he says as I make my way toward them. "I'll see if I can get into her computer."

I open the first drawer, sifting through folders. I find copies of different types of paperwork: questionnaires, medical history forms, insurance forms. All of them blank. I close the drawer, moving to the second one. This one has more forms, but these ones are filled out. They're in alphabetical order, and I scan a few of them, but there isn't anything that stands out as odd or incriminating.

I'm putting a folder back into the cabinet when I notice a paper lying face down at the bottom of the drawer. I reach in, flipping it over in my hand. It's a photograph.

"This is Dave, that guy that was working for Alice," I say. Next to him in the photo is a woman holding a young child. It's a studio-quality photo, all three of them smiling at the camera and standing in front of a backdrop of a field of flowers.

I hold the photo out to Maverick, still sitting in front of the computer. "I know them," he says, looking at it.

"You do?"

"That's his wife, Amy, and his son, Garrett. They were some of the people Alice had me erase the memories of. They don't remember Dave at all. I didn't know it at the time, but I guess she was using me to get Dave to work for her."

"Does he remember them?" I ask.

Maverick shakes his head. "I had to make him forget them, too."

I look at the photo for a long moment, a sadness creeping into my throat. A beautiful family, torn apart. And they don't even know it.

I fold the photo up and slide it into my back pocket, then go back to the filing cabinet. In the third drawer, I finally find what I'm looking for: patient records. These are in alphabetical order, too, and I pull one out at random. The name on the tab of the folder says "Veronica Starnes."

The top page has basic information: she's nineteen, from Garysburg—a City about twenty minutes away from Shorewick—and has been a patient for four years. There's even a photo of the slender, dark-haired girl. She's beautiful.

I flip the page, taking in the words typed across the second paper in the file:

Veronica Starnes

Anomaly ID#: 52

Status: Contained

Danger: 3

Classification: Involuntary, sporadic

Description: Displays an ability to manipulate emotions. Those in the subject's vicinity are compelled to assume whatever emotional state the subject is in at the time. If the subject is in an emotionally heightened state, the decisions of bystanders can be severely impacted. Ability is unpredictable and uncontrollable.

I flick my eyes across the page, trying to absorb as much information as I can. This is one of the anomalies Maverick had mentioned. But what do all the terms mean? Status? Classification? It seems like Alice has come up with a way of labeling us.

I close the file, then reach into the bin, pulling out another.

This one is of a sixteen-year-old boy named Gabe, from Shorewick.

Gabe Jackson

Anomaly ID#: 41

Status: Contained

Danger: 2

Classification: Involuntary, constant

Description: Subject hears the constant thoughts of everyone around him. This ability causes immense stress to the subject himself because he cannot stop it, though it has no impact on those around him. May be able to use the ability to gather secret information and hurt others with it.

With hungry eyes, I open another.

Gregory Black

Anomaly ID#: 27

Status: Controlled

Danger: 1

Classification: Voluntary

Description: Subject can move small objects without touching them. Can't create high enough velocity or large enough distance to harm another person.

I run my fingers across the edges of the folders. There must be over a hundred of them. One of them catches my eye.

"Maverick, you have to see this." He appears next to me as I open the folder with his name on it. "There are patient files on the anomalies she's dealt with. This one's yours." We both stare at the page intently.

Maverick Schall

Anomaly ID#: 36

Status: Unresolved

Danger: 5

Classification: Voluntary

Description: Subject can permanently erase memories through skin contact with the victim. Victims show no sign of amnesia, but some experience a period of confusion or extreme fatigue after the subject has erased their memories. We cannot detect when this power has been used on someone.

When I finish reading, Maverick is reaching into the cabinet. "There's one on you, too," he says, surprised.

I snatch it out of his hand. "What? How? I thought she didn't know about my ability?"

"I didn't think so, either."

Laura Jones
Anomaly ID#: 124
Status: Unresolved
Danger: 1
Classification: Involuntary, constant
Description: Subject hears sounds from the past.

"Mine is so short," I say.

"She probably doesn't know much. I wonder how she even found out?" Maverick replies.

"I don't know." I scan the folders again, and just as I'm about to look away, I spot one that grabs my interest. "Look," I say, snatching it and sliding it out.

At the top, the name "Alice Wight" is typed in bold script. The folder is darker and worn at the edges more than the rest. I open it.

Alice Wight
Anomaly ID#: 1

I only have time to read the first two lines before the sound of the lock sliding out of place grabs our attention.

We both watch in horror as the door swings open.

Maverick has me under the desk before the light from the hallway touches us. He crouches low next to me, our bodies pressed together from shoulder to hip.

The door swings open and from under the desk, I can see a pair of feet in the doorway. The light flips on and a deep, gruff voice says, "Show yourself."

Maverick's eyes meet mine. "Stay down," he mouths to me, and then he stands up from behind the desk.

"Put your hands where I can see them," the voice says.

Next to me, Maverick's palms go up in front of him. He steps forward, past the desk, and then I can only see his feet, too. Silently, I start to slide the pepper spray out of my pocket.

"Now isn't it convenient that I find you here? Alice will be pleased."

Maverick doesn't respond, but a beat later he moves, rushing at the guy.

Then there's a click: the sound of a gun being loaded. "Stop," the voice says, but Maverick is already frozen. "You come out too."

I wait.

"Right. Now."

Shakily, I stand up, sliding the pepper spray back into my pocket and facing the guy. He's big. Burly. He's wearing long, dark clothes and a pair of black leather gloves. And he has a gun pointed directly at me.

"Two birds, right in the palm of my hand. What a nice surprise," his lips curl into a snarl.

I glance to Maverick, who's staring at the guy, sizing him up.

"I'm going to tell you how this is going to go. You"—he flicks the gun towards Maverick—"are going to walk in front."

The gun goes back to me. "She's next. Any sign either of you is going to run, and I'll shoot."

Maverick and I just stand there, waiting.

"Move," he says, making a little flick with his gun to show us that he's serious. Maverick glances at me then steps forward calmly. As he passes, the guy points the gun directly at him. Then, in one second, Maverick turns on the guy, grabbing his wrist and shoving the gun out of the way. It goes off, the sound punching through the room and startling me, but no one is hit. It topples to the ground.

After recovering from hearing the shot, I spring into action, too, ripping the pepper spray from my back pocket and aiming it at the guy's face. It hits, and he stumbles, gasping, his eyes scrunched up in pain.

Maverick grips my arm. "Let's go."

We turn, exit the room, and race down the hallway. The receptionist from earlier is blocking our path, walking in our direction hesitantly, a concerned expression on her face.

"What is going on—" she starts, but Maverick reaches her before she finishes and touches her arm. She blinks, and he shoves her toward her seat. Then he turns to me and pushes me through the door, glancing behind us as he does.

When we get outside, we tear through the parking lot toward his car. About halfway there, a gunshot rackets through the air. I turn my head, looking back at the building. There's a dark figure in the window of Alice's office.

"Watch out!" Maverick's voice rings out, and just as I'm turning my head to look back at him, he crashes into me, knocking me down onto the ground. At the same moment, a gunshot rings through the air.

We land, a tangle of limbs on the cold pavement. "Stay low. Get to the car," Maverick hisses once we've recovered from the fall. I get back up on my feet, crouched to the ground. I shuffle, squeezing between two cars, edging around them. I look behind me to see Maverick following, but I notice he's moving slower. Clutching his left arm.

"Are you okay?" I ask, reaching for him. My hand touches his sleeved arm, and when I pull it back it's wet.

Blood.

CHAPTER 30

"YOU'VE BEEN SHOT," I say as we sit there, crouched behind a car.

Maverick meets my eyes. "I know." In any other situation, I think he might have rolled his eyes. "We need to leave."

So we do, moving as fast as we can behind cars, past lampposts. When we get to the Corolla, Maverick throws me the keys. "You're gonna need to drive," he says, grimacing.

We climb in and I put the car in gear, tearing out of the parking lot as fast as the engine will let me.

Maverick starts giving me directions. "Where are we going?" I ask.

"My house," he replies.

"You've been shot. You need a doctor."

"No. It's not that bad. We can take care of it ourselves."

I glance over at him as he clutches his arm, face taut. I check my mirrors to make sure no one is following us, then I pull onto the side of the road, shifting the car into park.

"We need to at least stop the bleeding."

I turn to him and reach for his arm. Reluctantly, he lets go, wincing as I touch him. There's a small hole torn through his black, long-sleeved shirt, and blood oozes out, wetting the dark fabric. I can't tell how much blood there is because it blends into his sleeve. "I need to get your sleeve off so I can see the wound."

His eyes flash at me, filled with pain. "There's a knife in there," he lifts his chin towards the glove box. I reach over him, my arm brushing against his knee as I sift through the glove box, then pull out a small pocket knife. I get to work, sawing at the fabric of his shirt just beneath his shoulder. I peel the sleeve back, cutting a line down the length of his arm, trying to be gentle as I pull the fabric away from the wound. He winces but doesn't protest.

Finally, his sleeve is gone, and there's a large patch of skin covered in blood. I reach for his arm, ready to grab it and pull it closer so I can examine it better, but then I stop. Before, I'd been touching his shirt sleeve, so I hadn't been worried about it, but now, staring at his bare skin, I remember how quickly and easily he'd erased the receptionist's memory.

"You don't have to touch me," Maverick croaks out as I sit there, gaping at his arm.

My hand hovers there, above his skin. Certainly he won't try to erase my memory right now if I touch him, I know that. But something about knowing he *can* makes me nervous.

I push the feeling away. Maverick had pushed me out of the bullet's path, even when it meant risking getting shot himself. Without even thinking about it. Without even hesitating. If that doesn't say something about him, then I don't know what will.

"I trust you," I finally say across the darkness of the car. Then, without meeting his eyes, I grab his arm, my hands making contact with his hot, bare skin.

"You do?" he asks as I inspect the wound, noticing that even though there's a lot of blood, the wound isn't too deep.

I tear off my jacket, still avoiding those piercing yellow eyes. "You just took a bullet for me. I'm pretty sure that warrants a little bit of trust."

"Maybe I should have started off by doing that," he tries to laugh, but it comes out breathless.

Shaking my head, I wrap my jacket around the bullet wound, tightening it on his arm despite his sharp intake of breath. "You got lucky. It's not too bad. But it needs to be looked at."

"You're looking at it."

"Someone who knows what they're doing."

"I know what I'm doing. I'll be fine."

I shake my head, turning my attention back to the road in front of us. "Do you think anyone is following us?"

"If they are, we'll know soon enough," he replies.

I nod, then pull the car back onto the road.

TWENTY MINUTES LATER, I come to a screeching stop in the stone circle driveway in front of Maverick's house. I hop out of the car, then walk over to the passenger side and open the door. He looks pale.

"Come on," I grab his right arm, helping him step out of the car.

"I'm okay, honestly."

I look at his left arm skeptically, taking in the blood soaking through my jacket. Then I tug him inside.

We go to the kitchen, where Maverick instructs me to grab the first aid kit from a cabinet. Inside the kit, I find the gauze pads and long white bandages, setting them on the table. Maverick sits down next to the sink. "Should we clean it first? I mean, that's what you do, right?" I ask him.

He nods but doesn't look confident. "Fun fact: this is actually my first bullet wound. But I guess so. There's rubbing alcohol in there."

I grab it, then bring the supplies over to him. Carefully, I untie the knot in my jacket, pulling it away from Maverick's arm. He winces when it gets close to the wound. "I'm sorry," I say, watching as fresh blood slowly seeps out of his skin once the jacket is gone.

"Don't be."

I unscrew the cap of the rubbing alcohol. "Well if I wasn't before, then I am now." I lift his arm over the sink, then carefully pour the liquid over it. His jaw tenses and his other hand grips the edge of the counter, knuckles turning white. When I'm done, he lets out a ragged breath.

"Are you sure you don't want to see a doctor?" I ask him.

He looks down at his arm, touching the skin next to the wound with his finger. It's a small wound, and it looks like the bullet just barely grazed him at an angle, without actually entering his skin. It's bleeding still, but it looks less intimidating under the bright fluorescent lights of Maverick's kitchen.

"I'm sure. Just bandage me up. It's not that bad," he tells me.

So I grab the gauze pads, laying them carefully over the wound, then I take a long white bandage and wrap it several times around his arm tightly.

When I finish, I take a step back. "I guess that should do," I say. I lift my hand to pick up the first aid kit on the table next to him and Maverick catches my wrist, his warm fingers curling around my clammy skin. I don't flinch, I don't try to pull my hand away; there's no point, because when he looks at me, *into* me with those burning amber eyes, it lights a fire inside my chest.

"Laura, I'm so, *so* sorry," he tells me, his voice quavering.

"Why are you sorry? You saved my *life*."

He shakes his head. "If it weren't for me, your life never would have been in danger."

"Maverick, you can't—"

"No, Laura," he tightens his grip on my wrist. "I'm sorry. For everything."

I open my mouth, but he speaks again before I can get any words out.

"What I did to you, it was wrong. I should never have done it. It should never have been an option."

"You did it because you wanted to protect me," I say.

"I did it because I thought I was being selfless. I thought that without me in your life, you'd be safer. You'd be happier." He loosens his grip, letting my hand drop to my side. "But really, I was just being selfish. I should have talked to you. I should have given you that choice."

He's doing that thing again, where his eyes focus on me, never blinking, never moving, like I'm the only thing he sees. I feel my heart in my chest, threatening to beat right out of me.

I ponder his words, trying to imagine being in Maverick's place, faced with a decision as monumental as he had. He thought that I was in danger. He thought that by giving me up, he could save me. He'd done everything in his power to protect me, to keep me out of this, even after he realized his mistake. And now, he'd just taken a literal bullet for me.

Sure, his choice to erase my memories had hurt me, but isn't that the thing about choices? There's no way to guarantee that they'll be the right choice. They can always end up backfiring or hurting someone. And we're here, now, in this strange place between friendship and a relationship, caught up in this terrible mess that we aren't sure how to fix. What happened before has been done, but if it had never happened, we might never have learned about each other's abilities. Our abilities connect us, make us understand each other in a way that no one else can.

I gaze back at him, trying to calm my breathing. "It's okay. I forgive you," I tell him, and I mean it.

He shakes his head. "I don't know if it's that easy."

I shake mine, too. "Even if it's not, I want to try. I want to know you. I want to know how I felt about you before. Which means we both have to get past this."

He blinks a few times. "Are you sure?"

I nod.

He moves to me, then, without warning. He slides off the counter and steps closer. I stumble backward in surprise, but he doesn't let the distance between us grow, stepping forward at the same time until my back hits the edge of the opposite counter.

His hands reach for my neck, curve just under my ears. Ever so slightly, he uses his thumbs to tilt my chin up until my face is aligned with his. His amber eyes flick back and forth between mine, seeming to ask a question: *is this okay?*

In answer, my eyes flutter closed. My heart races in anticipation.

A second later, his lips touch mine, and my stomach responds as if I've just taken a dip on a rollercoaster or jumped out of an airplane. Too soon, they're gone, but he stays close and puts his forehead against mine, his breath mingling with mine. "I'm sorry," he says.

"Don't be," I reply breathlessly.

And he must not be, because a moment later he kisses me again, this time harder, more insistent. Like he's kissed me a thousand times before. *And perhaps he has.*

Just as quickly as he had moved to me, he moves away, leaving all of the places he'd touched me feeling cold and empty. All that's left is a tingling feeling that spreads across my skin. Across my lips. The echoes of his kiss.

I try to steady my breathing as he stands a foot away from me, looking at me with those golden eyes. "You don't know how much I've missed that. Missed *you,*" he tells me.

I don't know what to say, so I just stand there, watching him stare at me. He'd kissed me. I'd let him kiss me. I'd *wanted* him to kiss me. What were the implications of this? I'd just barely started feeling comfortable enough to think of him as a friend. To trust him. And now there's this burning in my heart, in my cheeks that I can't control. I know what we must have been to each other before, but were we on our way to becoming that again? Will it ever be the same, now that I can't remember anything that happened before?

"Come with me," Maverick says before I can come up with something to say. He offers his hand. I take it, and he intertwines our fingers. "There's something I want to show you."

He leads me through the house and up to a pair of wooden double doors. The room contains a large screen and several rows of chairs. A home theater.

"This house never ceases to amaze me," I say.

"I've lived here for months and I'm still not sure I've seen the whole thing," Maverick laughs. He leads me to the front of the room, then lets go of my hand. "Choose a seat."

"This is going to be tough, it's pretty crowded in here," I reply, and he chuckles, nudging me forward. I sit down in the third row and watch as he goes to the back of the room.

"I'll be right back," he says, then goes through a side door. A minute later the screen comes on, displaying a photograph of me standing in front of a chalk sign holding an ice cream cone, smiling at the camera.

Maverick comes back into the room and sits down in the seat next to me. He holds out a small remote and I grab it, examining it in my fingers.

"I can't give you back your memories," Maverick starts, and I meet his eyes, trying to see what's inside them, "but I can give you this."

"What is it?"

"That remote," he points at the screen, "controls that, which has a slideshow of all the photos I have of us."

I gasp. "Are you serious?"

He nods. "This is the first photo I ever took of you. On our first date."

I look at the picture of myself again, realization hitting me. "Oh my gosh," I say. Hastily, I hit the forward button on the remote, and the photo changes to a selfie of us standing in front of an ice cream store. It looks vaguely familiar, like I might have driven past it before. My hair is shorter in this photo—I'd grown it out a little in the past year.

After studying it for a long time, I change the photo again. This one's a candid shot of me sitting at a table in a restaurant, digging my fork into what looks like some kind of pasta dish. I'm smiling, my mouth wide open like I'm laughing at something.

"Second date," Maverick tells me, "Lorenzo's Italian restaurant, downtown. I basically had to beg you to go out with me again."

I shoot him a look. "Seriously?" Then I remember hearing the echo of Maverick cornering me in front of my house before school to question why I was avoiding him. The conversation that ultimately ended with me telling him I liked him.

"You were a tough catch, I'd say," he chuckles. "It took like two months for you to start referring to me as your boyfriend."

I shake my head in disbelief. "I've never dated anyone before. I was probably terrified of you."

He shrugs, "I've never thought of myself as intimidating, but maybe I was a little forward about my feelings."

"Maybe," I reply. Another thought pops into my head, and I start to ignore it before I realize that with Maverick, I don't have to hide certain parts of my life. So I open my mouth instead. "Hearing the echoes always scared me away from relationships. It's kind of hard to juggle all the noise of the past and keep up healthy friendships and relationships without being able to explain why I zone out or don't want to go certain places. I never really thought about dating anyone. I guess until you, that is."

Maverick nods in understanding. "In hindsight, it makes a lot of sense."

I start to flip through the photos again, pausing on a few that stand out to me so that Maverick can explain them. Half of them are candid shots, little moments that Maverick caught of me doing something or laughing at something. The rest are either selfies or had been taken by a third person.

There's me, sitting at a table at Louise's, a fry in my hand, head turned toward the window. Us, standing by my front door, a bowl of Halloween candy on the ground behind us. Selfies of us in front of restaurants, at parks, inside each other's houses. Him and I sitting at the Thanksgiving table with my family and a woman that looks just like Maverick. Us standing under a bunch of mistletoe in ugly Christmas sweaters. The photos are in chronological order, and I watch as the seasons change, the branches bare, and then budding. Our jackets thick, and then gone. Maverick's mansion appears in some of them: me sprawled out across a chair by the pool in sunglasses and a bathing suit, Grace in the chair next to me. The picture I'd seen on the fireplace mantle appears, Maverick kissing my cheek in front of a line of trees. The photos flip by, hitting me with a new wave of feeling at each one.

It's like taking a trip down memory lane, except I have amnesia, so I'm seeing all of the memories for the first time.

The last photo is of just me, staring directly into the camera, smiling. My hair looks windblown, tangled and frizzed out all around my face. My skin is slightly flushed like it's hot outside or I've just run a mile, and there's a blur of greenery behind me. Normally, looking like that, I'd never want someone to take a photo of me. But instead of shying away from the camera, I look confident to be the focus of the photo. I look happy. I barely recognize myself.

"That's the last one I got," Maverick says from beside me. I turn to him, trying to keep my watery eyes from spilling over.

"Thank you," I say. "Thank you for showing me these."

He nods, taking a deep, shaky breath. "I just want you to know that I care about you. I never stopped caring about you."

Even though I only remember knowing him a short while, I know he's telling the truth. "I don't remember how I felt about you," I tell him, "but I want to figure it out. I just need time to get to know you better."

He nods. "As I said before, anything you want to know, just ask. I won't keep any secrets from you ever again. And if you decide you don't want anything to do with me, I'll respect that."

My mouth forms into a small smile. "Thank you, but right now I don't think that's going to be the case."

He smiles back, then he leans close.

His kiss fills all of the cold, empty parts of me with warmth until I'm bursting at the seams.

CHAPTER 31

WITH A START, I PULL away. "What time is it?" I ask. I pull out my phone. Twelve thirty. "Shoot, I was supposed to be home already."

Maverick stands up. "Let's go."

We get in the car, and Maverick has to drive me to the school to get my car that we'd left in the parking lot all those hours ago. It feels more like days, after everything that's happened.

"I'll call you tomorrow, okay? Now that we have more information, we can start figuring out how we're going to take her down," Maverick tells me as we pull up next to my car.

"Sounds good," I say, tugging on the door handle. I look back at him, feeling like there's more that I should say, or do. But I end up just closing the door without another word.

I drive home in the quiet, thinking about everything that happened. The gunshots that hadn't hit me directly, but had felt like they'd punched me in the gut. Maverick's kiss, which had only brought tingles and butterflies. The photos, the memories that Maverick had shared with me. It had been a long day.

When I pull up to my house a little after one, the lights are still on inside. I look at my phone to see what messages my parents must have sent, wondering where I am. There aren't any. I wonder if they are still awake. Certainly, they would have tried to call already if they were. *Right?*

I carry my backpack up the porch steps, holding my key out to unlock the door, but it's already unlocked. Strange. Mom never leaves the door unlocked past dinnertime, even when I'm still out and about.

When I get inside, I drop my backpack on the floor, then sweep the house, looking in every room, thinking maybe my parents had fallen asleep on the couch or something. But no one is downstairs.

My heart starts to race. I run up the stairs, pushing the door to my parents' room open. They're not in bed.

"Mom?" I call out. "Dad?" I go into their bathroom, their closet. I check my own room and the guest room. There's no one here. Pulling out my phone, I dial Mom's number.

After two rings, I hear the chimes of her phone ringing from somewhere inside the house. I follow the sound, racing downstairs into the kitchen. On the counter, her phone is ringing, right next to Dad's phone. Under both of them is a piece of paper.

A note, written in loopy cursive handwriting.

Laura,

Thanks for stopping by my office. Your parents are safe with me, but if you ever want to see them again, you'll need to come by my lab within the next eight hours. Both of you.

Yours truly, Alice

The note flutters to the ground after I've read it. I cover my mouth in my hands, slumping to the floor next to it. My parents. Alice has kidnapped my parents.

Through blurry eyes, I pull out my phone and call Maverick.

"Hello? Laura?"

"Maverick. You—you need to come back," I say between sobs.

"What's wrong? What happened?"

"My parents," I say, then I have to take a moment to breathe. "Alice has my parents."

"I'm coming," Maverick tells me. "Is anyone else there? Are you sure you're alone?"

I look around the house that I'd just searched minutes ago. "I'm alone," I reply.

"Stay there. I'll be there soon," he tells me.

Ten minutes later, he finds me sitting on the kitchen floor, my head on my knees. He squats down next to me, his hand on my back.

"Laura. I'm here. Are you okay?" he asks. I look up at him through teary eyes.

"She left a note," I say, spotting it on the floor and reaching for it. I hand it to him, and I watch as his eyes flick across the page. Then they meet mine. "We have to go," I tell him.

Maverick shakes his head at me. "It's a trap. It's always a trap."

I shake my head back. "But we have to. What is she going to do to them?"

Maverick doesn't answer me. I feel another wave of sobs coming on, and I put my head back down, resting on my knees. Gently, Maverick grabs my arm, pulling me to my feet. Then he wraps his arms around me, and I bury my face into his chest.

When I finally calm down, I look over at the clock on the stove. It's almost two in the morning. When had Alice left the note? She'd written eight hours. What if it had already been eight hours? What if we're too late?

"We need to go. Right now," I tell Maverick.

"She'll be expecting us."

"I don't care. My parents could *die*," I reply.

Maverick just looks at me, his yellow eyes filled with pain. I realize that he understands completely. Both of his parents are gone. Maybe not because of Alice, but still.

"I'm sorry, I—" I start to say suddenly, but Maverick puts his finger to my lips.

"I get it. Let's go get them."

WE ROLL TO A STOP in the small clearing in the woods that Maverick had parked in the last time we were here. We get out and Maverick opens the trunk. He pulls out the handgun that he'd taught me how to use earlier and puts it in my hands.

"Do not be afraid to use this. Especially on Alice," he tells me firmly. Then he pulls out another, similar one for himself.

The plan is to sneak in from a direction Alice won't expect so we can find my parents and get them out. She might have all of the entrances blocked off, but we have to try our best not to get caught anyway. If she finds us, I don't know what she will do.

There's a back door on the building, and we walk through the woods toward it. When we get there, surprisingly, it's unlocked. Inside, it's dark. Maverick's hand finds mine, and we move through the hallways, deeper into the massive, terrible building. Eventually, we reach a door, and we look out through a small window into the main hallway. Bright fluorescent lights shine down on the bare, white linoleum floors. It's empty.

We silently go through the door, then start down the hallway. After about ten steps, the sound of static fills my ears, then Alice's voice rings loud through the building. Maverick and I freeze.

"I'm so glad you could make it. Just in the nick of time, too."

Maverick's eyes flick around the hallway, and both of us spot the camera at the same time. We rush over to it, and Maverick jumps, ripping it off the wall. It falls to the ground and shatters.

Alice is still talking over the intercom calmly. "I'm so grateful for your help, actually. I've never been able to study the parents of an anomaly before, and I've discovered some useful information about the causes of these strange occurrences."

Maverick drags me down the hallway and we enter a side room. He smashes the camera in here, too, before we get into its view.

"I didn't know that you were an anomaly at first, my dear Laura." Chills run through my body at the sound of my name. "But when we took your blood, we realized that it wasn't that of a normal person."

"She knows we're here. I don't know where all the cameras are. I don't think we'll be able to find your parents and slip past her," Maverick whispers to me, urgent.

I pull the gun off my hip, clutching it between my fingers angrily. "Then we'll just have to find *her*."

Maverick reaches out, touches the side of my face with one hand. He rubs his thumb over my cheekbone, giving me a worried look. "Okay," he tells me, "I think I know where her office is."

As we exit the room, she keeps talking over the speakers. "For a long time, we've been hitting a wall with our research. But you, Laura, are special. You've helped us tremendously, and because of you, we've finally had some breakthroughs."

Maverick reaches a solid white metal door. He holds his gun in both hands. "At the first sight of her, we shoot. Are you ready?"

I nod, feeling a drop of sweat drip down my back. I'm ready to face Alice, yes. Ready to *kill* her? No.

Maverick pushes the door open. We rush inside, guns pointed forward. The lights are off except for a small lamp that shines across the desk onto a rolling chair with its back turned to us. We step toward it, guns trained.

"Guns? Now, that's not very nice," Alice's haunting voice rings through the room.

Maverick tenses, then fires his gun at the chair. At the same time, a black figure leaps through the shadows, crashing into him, and they both tumble onto the ground. I take a step back and a hand comes out of nowhere, knocking into my arm. My gun tumbles across the floor as hands grip my arms, then pull them together, handcuffing them behind my back.

Maverick is in a similar situation. He struggles on the ground with his attacker, but soon a second figure appears out of the shadows. Both of them are covered in black clothing from head to toe. *So that he can't use his ability on them.* They grip his arms, handcuff him. The commotion dies down, both of us trapped now. The chair in front of us has a bullet hole in the middle of it.

The bullet must have missed her, though, because Alice spins around in it, smiling. Then the lights flash on, revealing three more men lined along the left wall. There's no way we were ever going to escape this, even with our guns.

"As I was saying before, I just want to thank you for coming," Alice nods to us. She waves a hand in the air, a graceful flick of her wrist. "You can take him away now."

I watch in horror as the guards yank Maverick to his feet, then turn him away from me toward the door. His head whips around. "Laura! No!" he yells.

"Maverick!" I scream back, struggling. Then another guard comes over to help hold me down.

"Don't touch her!" Maverick yells, and then the doors slam shut behind him. I turn my gaze on Alice, a fire of hate burning inside me.

"What do you want from me?" I spit.

Alice taps her perfectly manicured fingers on the desk. "That's what I want to talk about." She gestures to a chair in front of her desk, and the guards release their hold on me. I jerk away roughly. "Have a seat."

CHAPTER 32

I SIT. NOT BECAUSE Alice told me to, but because there are four men in the room that are bigger and stronger than me, and I suspect that even if I resisted, they'd have gotten me into the chair anyway.

"I'm so glad you've decided to join me today," she smiles, her eyes squinting up. She looks both old and young at the same time, with heavy blue eyes that don't miss a thing. She's terrifyingly beautiful.

"What have you done with my parents?"

She sits up straight in her chair, plucking a hair off the top of her gray pantsuit. "Don't worry. They're safe."

"Where?" I demand, leaning closer. I can't slap my hands down on the desk like I want to, but I try to give Alice the same experience with a murderous gaze.

"They're being held downstairs," she replies, unfazed.

I didn't expect her to answer so easily, so I pause, watching her movements carefully. She's impossible to read.

"But your parents aren't what's important right now. Right now I want to talk to you."

"What could you possibly want to talk to me about?"

"I want your help," she says simply, like it's the obvious answer to the question. Then she stands up and walks a few paces along the wall behind her. She turns back to me, a hand on her hip. "Let me explain," she says.

I glance around the room at the men standing at attention. My chances of escape are slim. Probably impossible.

"I'm sorry. Are they making you uncomfortable?" Alice asks, oddly genuine.

I search her eyes, trying to figure out what she's thinking.

"Why don't you guys let us have some privacy, okay?" Alice says to the guards. She waves her hand at them, "Go on."

They don't need any more persuasion. Immediately, they all jump into action, exiting the room swiftly. I watch them go, taking in my gun still lying on the floor behind me. We're alone now. It was dumb of her to make her only defense leave. I might not be able to take down any of them, but Alice can't be much stronger than myself. Maybe this is my chance.

Once the door is closed, Alice sits back down in her chair, folding her hands over the desk. "I don't know what you've been told, so I'll just start from the beginning. I'll give you my side of the story." She pauses, looking me up and down. Then she tilts her head to the side. "Have you ever imagined living a life where you didn't have to hear the noise of the past?"

I clench my jaw. "How do you know about that?"

Alice shakes her head, the corner of her mouth tilting up. "Oh, honey. I know about a lot of things." Then her expression goes serious. "Like how your parents were convinced you were ill your whole life. Like how you can't help but hear the sounds from the past, no matter where you are or what time it is. Like how you've never been able to live a normal life because of it."

I just stare at her, trying to hide the fact that her words are affecting me.

"You see, Laura, you're not the only one. There are hundreds of people just like you."

My curiosity gets the best of me and I blurt a question. "Who hear echoes of the past?"

Alice smiles again, though it's more of a sneer. "No, actually. In fact, you're the only one with that specific ability. Which is why you're special." She puts her hands flat on the table. "But there are hundreds out there similar to you. Anomalies. People who are different, with unique abilities."

I picture the filing cabinet in Alice's office, filled with names and descriptions of those anomalies.

"Each of these abilities creates a problem, a danger to society. My work involves researching them. Looking for ways to stop them."

"So you lock them up here like lab rats so you can study them?" I snarl.

Alice laughs, a light, terrible sound that makes me cringe. "Sometimes, yes. Sometimes we just let them go from this world."

I remember the words on the pages I'd read. Contained. Unresolved. And the third one: controlled. Did that mean she'd killed them?

"The point of it all is that my work is imperative to the survival of humanity as we know it."

"Why would it be?"

"These abilities, some of them are dangerous. Some of them hurt people. You probably already know this, but Maverick is capable of erasing memories." She glances at me as she says the words, judging my reaction. I think I see a hint of surprise when I don't respond. "When he was younger, he accidentally erased someone's memories, causing permanent damage to his life and to his family." I know this, too. I remember Maverick's devastated expression when he told me. "It's not just him," she continues, "It's all of them. All of the anomalies have the power to impact lives, to hurt people. They have to be stopped before they use their abilities against others."

I think about her words for a long moment. Sure, Maverick's ability had hurt people accidentally. But he learned to control it eventually, and now the times he'd hurt others weren't exactly done willingly. But what if someone else had Maverick's ability? Someone like Alice? That could end pretty badly.

But some of the files in the cabinet hadn't seemed that bad. I picture one of them in my mind: someone who could move small objects without touching them. That doesn't sound dangerous.

"Not all of them," I finally tell Alice.

"That, my dear Laura, is where you're wrong."

"The echoes don't hurt anybody," I fire back.

She folds her arms across her chest. "Ah, but can you really say that your parents are unscathed by your peculiar tendency to hear the… echoes, did you call them?"

I don't respond.

"Certainly it was devastating to them when they discovered that their only daughter was never going to be normal." She narrows her eyes. "And are you, yourself, not hurt by the realization that you have to live with this burden, forever?"

I think about her words. I'd spent seventeen years dealing with the echoes, trying to live a normal life despite them. Sure, I'd never felt completely normal, but I dealt with it. I even made friends this year. And then there are all those months I'd spent dating Maverick that I don't remember. Surely I'd felt somewhat normal then. *Right?*

"It doesn't bother me," I tell her.

"Oh, so that's why I found seven years of patient records on you, and your difficulty in living with the situation."

"That's not fair. No one believed it was real," I say.

"But you can tell me, now, that you're honestly fine with accepting the echoes as part of your life, forever?"

It's a tough question because part of me does think it would be nice to not hear them. Part of me wants it to be possible. But then I think about what the echoes have brought me. Fun memories of conversations long forgotten. Things to look back on, like mini time capsules only I can hear. And then there's Maverick. What would have happened if I couldn't hear the echoes? Would Maverick and I have ever ended up knowing each other again?

I decide, then, that I'm fine with the echoes. They're a part of me now, I can truly accept that. "Yes," I say firmly. Finally.

Alice gives me a long, thoughtful look. "So if I had some way to block the echoes, you can honestly say you wouldn't take it?"

"Do you?" I ask instantly. Instinctually.

She smiles again. "That's actually what I want your help with."

I blink at her. "How could *I* help *you*?"

"You could stay here. Help us run tests. To learn more about the anomalies and how they work."

"Something tells me that you're going to keep me here whether I agree to it or not."

Alice nods. "Sure, but it's always better to have someone here willingly. That way, you can describe to us how you're feeling instead of us trying to guess."

"And sit here while you kidnap people and hold them hostage, or just *kill* them? While you study them and destroy their lives? You say that you want to block these abilities to keep people out of danger, but you've been sitting here using Maverick's ability for your own personal gain!" I explode.

Alice slaps her hands down on the table, eyes cold and full of anger. "I've been using his ability for the greater good!"

I shake my head at her. "You're a hypocrite. And you know it."

Alice leans back in her chair, pinching the bridge of her nose like she's got a headache. "So I guess you're not going to help me, then?"

I fix my gaze on her, putting as much rage as I can into my next three words. "No. Absolutely not."

CHAPTER 33

ALICE DOESN'T WASTE any time trying to convince me otherwise. She lifts a phone from her desk, then presses a button on the keypad. When she speaks into it, the sound permeates the entire building. "We've got a Code 2. Please move into phase three."

"What was that for? What did you just do?" I ask, my eyes widening.

"You won't help me, so there will be consequences."

"What do you mean?" I stand from the chair, leaning close to Alice's desk, knocking the desk lamp over in the process.

"Sometimes our choices affect other people. People we love," she sneers.

My panic grows. What was she going to do? Kill my parents? Hurt Maverick? Because I wouldn't help her, even though she was going to force me to anyway? I whip around, spotting the gun on the ground and rushing toward it. I'm not sure how it will help me while my hands are cuffed behind my back, but I do it anyway.

Before I get there, the door swings open and Dave walks into the room. I fall to my knees in front of the gun, but Dave kicks it out of my reach. He grabs my arm, forcing me to stand up.

"Take her downstairs," Alice waves a hand to him, an expression of defeat caked onto her face.

"Wait. No! Stop!" I yell, struggling to break free from Dave's grip. "What did you do?"

Alice just looks at her nails and sighs. Dave starts dragging me towards the door. I can't go. I can't let her hurt my family. Maverick.

"I'll do it, I'll help you!" I scream, desperate.

She meets my eyes, a cold emptiness in them. "Sometimes our choices can't be reversed," she says.

"Please!" I screech. I feel hot tears burning behind my eyes. Alice waves us away, and Dave pulls me closer to the door. "Wait! Dave!" I yell, a thought coming to my mind. "She's been lying to you!"

Dave pauses, only for a tiny moment, but it's enough for me to continue my assault of words.

"You had a wife. A son. Alice took them away from you," I tell him, breathless.

He freezes, his grip on my arm loosening. He glances past me at Alice.

Alice has a good poker face, though. "Come on, Dave. Are you seriously listening to her?"

Dave's gaze hardens, but before he can start pulling me to the door again, I slip away from him, backing up. Behind me, I feel for my pocket, reaching in and pulling out the photograph I'd taken from Alice's office. I spin around, holding it in my cuffed hands out to him.

I expect him to ignore it and continue dragging me out the door, but he plucks the photo from my fingers, turning it over in his hands. I watch his eyebrows burrow in confusion, then raise in shock. "Who are they?" he asks, holding the photo out to Alice.

"Nobody!" she replies, but we all catch the hitch in her voice.

"Where did you get this?" he asks me, serious.

"She had it in a drawer in her office. I found it when we snuck in. Maverick said he erased their memories, and yours. Alice made him do it." The words come out so fast I'm surprised he hears all of them.

He closes his eyes for a second, clutching the photo in his hand. "My wife? My *son?*" His voice cracks.

Alice moves around her desk, crosses the room, and grabs his arm. "Dave, I would never do something like that to you. I love you."

I raise my eyebrows. *Love?* Was Alice even capable of love? Was there something between her and Dave that I'd never picked up on? I'd thought he was just a bodyguard.

Dave lets her hold his arm for a moment, but then he tears it away. Backs up. "Which is exactly why you would do this."

Her eyes widen. "Dave, you don't really believe her, do you?"

He glares at her with dark eyes. "You always get what you want. And you never care about anything that's in your way."

"Dave—"

"Don't!" he roars, silencing her. "Don't lie to me. Who are these people?" he demands, shaking the photo at her.

"No one. It's just a trick. They're no one," Alice says calmly, though I think I can see her hand trembling. She moves toward him, arms stretched out, but then Dave shoves her backward. She stumbles onto the ground, and then Dave raises a gun. Cocks it with his thumb.

Alice freezes. I do, too.

"Tell me. Now," he says.

Alice just shakes her head, speechless.

Dave reaches into his pocket with his free hand and slides out a wallet. Then he pulls something out of it. A photo. "Why did I find a photo with the same exact people inside my wallet the other day? Did you forget to cover up that evidence, too?"

We've caught her. Alice, the cocky, terrifying woman who created this mess, has finally had her crimes catch up to her. And now she's lying on the floor, unable to find a good excuse. She glares at us, but there's nothing else she can do.

Dave closes his eyes, breathing hard. Then, opening them, he pulls the trigger.

I watch in horror as Alice's body jolts from the shock of the bullet going straight into her chest. Her eyes roll backward, and a moment later her head hits the ground.

Two beats pass.

Three.

Four.

Dave lowers the gun. I try not to look at Alice's lifeless body on the ground.

Dave doesn't look, either. He crosses the room to me and grabs my cuffed hands. He unlocks them, freeing me. "Go," he says. He slides something out of his pocket, his head hanging down. He hands it to me. It's his identification card. "They're downstairs. I'm not sure which rooms. There will be guards to stop you," he tells me.

I search for words to say—some way to express my gratitude—but there aren't any. I nod, then cross the room, picking my gun up from the ground. I make sure it's loaded and that the safety is off. Then I leave the room.

Down the hall, I find the staircase Maverick and I had escaped from last time. At the bottom, I peek through the window, spotting a heavily armed guard across the hall. I close my eyes, realizing that the only way to get past him involves shooting this gun. It's not a choice I want to have to make.

Alice's words echo through my mind. *Sometimes our choices affect other people. People we love.* Then, later: *Sometimes our choices can't be reversed.*

Taking a deep breath, I add my own words to the train. *Sometimes we make choices because we love people.*

I fling the door open, holding the gun with both hands, pointed directly at the guard. He starts to move, but I don't hesitate, I just pull the trigger, watching him grip his shoulder, leaning back in pain.

A little further down, there's another guard, but he doesn't have his gun pointed at me. Instead, his hands are in the air, his eyes filled with fear.

"Don't shoot. Please," he calls to me. I don't lower my gun, walking briskly towards him. "He's in that room," he points at a door. "Your parents are in room seventeen. Please just let me go."

"Give me your weapons," I reply. He responds immediately, pulling a handgun off his belt, then sliding the strap of a larger, scarier gun off his back. They drop to the floor. He puts his hands back up.

"Go. Now." I nod my head toward the door to the staircase across the hall. I follow his movements with the barrel of my gun as he walks slowly towards the door, opens it, then starts moving up the stairs. As soon as the door closes, he starts to run, taking them two at a time. When I'm sure he's gone, I walk over to the door he told me Maverick was in.

I hold Dave's ID card up to the gray box next to the door and the light flashes green. I grab the handle and rip it open.

Inside, Maverick is standing against the other wall. He peers at me, bright yellow eyes blinking behind a mask of fear.

I take three breaths in and out, trying to steady myself. He's okay. *He's okay.*

Then, finally, I step forward, ready to close the distance between us, to lose myself in his embrace, to feel all of the feelings I'd been too afraid to let myself feel before.

But I stop, because Maverick flinches, backing into the corner of the room.

"What's wrong?" I ask, putting my hands out to show him that I'm no threat.

He blinks at me, and his next three words send me spiraling into a never-ending circle of cold, unstoppable horror.

"Who are you?"

CHAPTER 34

I STAND THERE, TREMBLING.

Alice has taken Maverick's memories away.

Alice has taken Maverick's memories away.

Alice. Has. Taken. Maverick's. Memories. Away.

My world crashes around me, burning flames and walls caving in on my heart.

Alice must have figured out how to replicate his ability. And now she's used it against him. Against me.

Suddenly, and angrily, I wish that I had been the one holding the gun that had killed her.

Squashing my rage, I turn my attention to Maverick, the terrified boy who has no idea who I am.

"My name is Laura," I tell him shakily. "I'm here to help you."

He blinks at me, doesn't respond.

"Do you know your name?" I ask him. I need to know what he knows. How much Alice has taken from him.

He looks confused, but answers. "Maverick."

I sigh in relief. "Do you know where you are?"

His blinks. "Alice's laboratory."

"You remember Alice?"

He nods but still looks wary. "She's been forcing me to work for her."

"How did you get here?"

"I don't know. One second I was at my house, and now I'm here. I think I was drugged."

A little worse than drugged. "And where is your house?"

"Spruce Lane. Up the mountain. Why are you asking me this?"

He knows where his house is. He knows who he is. Does he know about everything else? "Alice kidnapped you to test her new invention. She found a way to replicate your ability."

I watch him, judging his reaction. He understands. Then his eyes widen. "You mean—"

"She used it on you. She made you forget things."

"What things?" he asks, concern drawing lines across his forehead.

"Me," I tell him. "You don't remember me at all, do you?" I ask.

He stares at me for a long moment. Then he just shakes his head.

I take a deep breath. Alice could have erased his entire memory, made him forget about her, causing him to be easily compliant to all of her demands. But instead, she seems to have only erased *me* from his mind. It's a targeted, specific attack.

She must have had someone with Maverick's ability down here, ready to use it at a moment's notice. Is that what she meant when she said that there would be consequences? Did my decision not to help her cause this to happen? Cause her to make Maverick forget about me?

"Alright," I finally say, burying my growing guilt deep down. "Here's what you need to know: you used to know me. I'm on your side. I'll explain the rest later, but right now, I need to find my parents. And then we need to get out of here."

He nods. Steps toward me hesitantly.

"Follow me."

We race down the hallway and I scan the numbers on the doors, counting down until I get to seventeen. Shakily, I hold Dave's card up to the detector, watching as the light turns green. I'm terrified to find out what she's done to my parents.

When I open the door, I spot them. Mom hunched over, tears streaked across her face. Dad next to her, his hand on her back. They look up at the sound of us.

I wait. They should smile now. They should cross the room and pull me into a hug. Tell me they're so glad to see me, glad I'm safe. But they don't. They just sit there, blinking in fear.

Alice has taken their memories away, too.

The room swirls around me, and I realize I can't do this. I can't take this. I have to get out. But when I turn around, Maverick is standing there, watching me, waiting for me to do something. Mom and Dad give me the same look.

I can't do this, but I have to.

So I open my mouth. "Kara and Jeff. My name is Laura. I'm here to help you," I tell them.

Mom looks at me, hope in her eyes. "Where are we?"

I try to come up with an explanation, but it's a little trickier with my parents. Maverick had known about the anomalies, Alice, and his own power. When I told him that his memories had been erased, he understood because he knew what he was capable of. But my parents know nothing, not about me, not about Alice, not about any of it.

"It doesn't matter, what matters is that we get out," I tell her. Then I look between the three of them. "I need you all to follow me closely and do exactly what I say, okay?"

They all nod in unison.

I start down the hallway, then move up the stairs. We walk in a line: me, Maverick, Mom, then Dad. My gun is in my hands, ready to fire at any moment. I just want to get us out of here. I'll figure out what to do about the rest of this place later. I just need my parents and Maverick to be safe.

When we get upstairs, no one is around. As if everyone decided to run after Alice got shot. Eventually, we have to pass by her office to get to the main doors. I glance inside to see if Dave is still in there.

What I see spikes my adrenaline, and I veer into the room.

Dave is lying on the ground, gasping for air. Alice's body is gone. I rush to Dave, waves of shock coursing through me. He's clutching his chest, blood soaking through his shirt.

"Dave? Where's Alice? What happened to you?" I ask, landing on my knees next to him.

His eyes are wide, staring up but not seeing anything.

I pat his face. "Dave. Please. Are you there?"

Finally, he fixes his gaze on me. "Laura—" he chokes out.

"What happened to you? Where's Alice?" I ask, desperate.

He struggles to breathe. "She's alive," he says, barely above a whisper. "I didn't know."

"Didn't know what? How is she alive?" I shake him, trying to keep him with me.

"She's one of you," he manages. "She's an anomaly."

A flash of the file I'd pulled from her cabinet appears in my mind. *Alice Wight, Anomaly ID#: 1.* "What is her ability?" I ask, afraid I might already know the answer.

"She... she..." Dave starts. He coughs up blood.

And then I watch the life drain from his eyes.

Behind us, laughter fills the air. I whip around, spotting Alice standing in the doorway. There's a hole and dried blood on her shirt where she had been shot. But she seems perfectly fine, displaying no signs of pain.

"What *are* you?" I demand.

She just laughs, almost hysterical. I raise my gun at her, but her laughter only grows louder. "You thought you got the best of me. You thought you won with that little stunt you pulled on Dave, didn't you?"

She's not afraid, not even when I cock the gun. She just shakes her head, staring at me with a combination of malice and pity.

"Sweet thing. How does it feel to not be the only one with missing memories?" she taunts. Maverick and my parents are to my left, but I don't look at them. I keep my gaze solely on Alice.

I grip the gun tighter around my hands, finger curling around the trigger.

"It's too bad things had to end up this way. But I tried to give you the choice."

"Shut up!" I yell.

Alice isn't fazed. She just grins. "This is *all your fault, Laura.*" Then she starts to move, reaching for the door to the room.

In that moment, I hear Grace's voice, accusing me of the same exact thing. She blamed me for getting her in trouble, for ruining her happy little bubble she'd created with Andy. But that wasn't my fault. If she had made better choices, perhaps none of those things would have happened. And now Alice is blaming me for Maverick and my parents' loss of memories. But I didn't do anything. Alice was the one who decided to pull the stunt, and it's not my fault that me not helping her made her angry enough to do it. Sure, Alice is just trying to get in my head, but both she and Grace have successfully made me feel guilty about something that is entirely out of my hands.

And I'm sick of it.

I pull the trigger.

My shot hits Alice in the arm and she staggers back. Blood stains her skin, and her face tightens in pain. Then, almost instantaneously, it relaxes. I stare at her arm as the bleeding stops, the bullet hole shrinks, then closes up. In seconds.

I gasp as Alice wipes the fresh blood off on her shirt. Her skin is smooth. Unscathed.

Her lips curl into a snarl, and suddenly I understand.

Alice can heal. That's her ability. Alice, the woman claiming that anomalies are dangerous, is an anomaly herself. And not only that, but her ability is the least dangerous of all. In fact, it's probably the most useful, if she can come back from a bullet wound that fast.

Maybe she's right about all anomalies being dangerous; even a harmless ability can be dangerous on the wrong person.

"You're going to pay for that," Alice spits at me. Then she turns, rips the door open.

I fire my gun at her as she moves, but I miss. Not that the bullet would stop her anyway.

She steps out of the room, smiles at me for the slightest of seconds, then bolts down the hallway. I race after her, trying my best to keep up, but she's fast. She reaches the end of the hallway several seconds before I do, then exits through a set of double doors that lead outside. Through the glass I see her turn back towards me, placing her hand on an electronic box just outside the door.

Then two giant metal doors come out of the wall in front of me, slowly sliding closed in front of the glass doors, trapping me in the building. Frantically, I quicken my pace, realizing that I might have just enough time to slide between the doors before they fully close. But just before I get to them, I look over my shoulder.

My parents. Maverick. What will happen to them if I leave them in here? What will happen to me if I'm stuck alone outside with Alice?

My steps slow, then come to a stop.

Alice flicks a little wave at me through the small gap between the doors, and then the metal slabs slam together.

We're trapped.

301

CHAPTER 35

A SECOND LATER, A fire alarm screams through the building. Little red lights spin above the doors, flashing white every couple of seconds.

I look back at Maverick and my parents, who are jogging down the hallway towards me. "We need to find a way out. Now."

We race back down the hallway and I throw doors open, looking into side rooms. The first two don't have windows. The third does, but a metal panel has dropped down, preventing us from going through it. Alice must have this place sealed, airtight.

We keep going anyway, but by the time we get to the bend of the L-shaped building, we can smell the smoke. Up ahead of us, an orange glow flashes through a window on one of the doors.

Fire. The building is on fire. And there's no way out.

Maverick's hand touches my shoulder. "There are more people in the building. Downstairs. More anomalies," he tells me.

I remember all of the doors I'd passed by. He's right. There are more. Alice's lab rats. People she kidnapped and had Maverick cover up. We can't leave them in here. That is, if we can even find a way to escape at all. "Let's go get them," I reply.

So we spin around and hurdle down the stairs again. When we get to the bottom, I rush to the first door I see, hold Dave's ID to it, then rip it open. The inside is empty. I go to the next door, finding it empty as well.

The third time's a charm. When I open the door, a thin, dark-haired girl is standing in front of me, like she's been waiting for someone to show up. I recognize her. It's the girl from the file I opened in Alice's office—Veronica.

"Who are you?" she asks, looking over me, then peeking at Maverick and my parents, who are standing by the door to the staircase. A wave of fear rushes into me, more than I'd felt before. I remember something else from her file: *ability to manipulate emotions*.

I try to stifle it. "I'm Laura. I'm here to get you out of here."

The fear coursing through my veins dulls, being replaced by relief. "Okay," she replies.

"I need to get everyone out," I tell her, turning away from the door. "You can wait over there with them," I point at Maverick, Mom, and Dad. She nods, then crosses the hallway.

I go to the next door and inside is another girl, at least a few years younger than myself. I give her the spiel, and then I move on to the next.

Door after door, I release the prisoners. I recognize another one, the boy named Gabe from another of Alice's files. I remember his ability, that he can hear my thoughts, but I have no idea what any of the other anomalies are capable of. I don't know if they really are dangerous, or if each and every one is just another person trying to live a normal life.

Behind one door, there's a young boy in a room that's completely padded in a white rubber-like material. I don't know why, but I just tell him the same thing I've told the rest, and then move on.

They're all fairly young. The oldest looks like he could be at most twenty, and the youngest is a girl somewhere around ten. After opening the very last door, I head back to the group standing by the staircase. All in all, there are thirteen of them, a relatively small group.

"The building is sealed off. We're going to have to break down a door or something," I announce to the group, loud enough that they can hear me over the fire alarms. They all look back and forth at each other, wide-eyed. "And it's on fire, so cover your mouths. Let's try to be quick."

I lead them up the staircase, then into the hall where smoke has created a thick, hazy cloud that's hard to see through. We move toward the back door that Maverick and I had snuck through earlier, but it's blocked by a metal door, too. I walk up to it, put my hands on it. It's thick, unbreakable. Every possible exit is covered in one, metal sheets standing between the captives and their freedom.

I don't know how to get through them. In minutes, the smoke is going to suffocate us, and I don't know what to do.

Then, a finger taps my shoulder. I turn around and a boy is standing behind me, bright blue eyes wide and focused. It's the boy I'd found in the padded room.

"I think I can help us get out," he tells me. He can't be older than thirteen—tall and lanky, but his voice hasn't quite deepened yet.

"How?"

He looks past me at the metal door. "I'll show you." Then he walks up to it. He lifts one finger and a light shoots across the air onto the door. Electricity. A moment later, the door slides up. Then the fire alarms shut off.

I stare in awe. What did he just do? And how? For a moment, I wonder how many other anomalies are out in the world, what kinds of strange things they can do.

He turns around to look at me. "We can leave now."

I nod. I understand why his room was rubberized now. "Let's go," I tell everyone. We slip through the door one by one into the cold night air. Once we're outside, I realize that we have a problem. There's no way all of these people will fit in Maverick's car. And where will we take them?

I pull Maverick aside. "I don't know what to do," I tell him.

"What do you mean?"

"Your Corolla isn't big enough to hold everyone."

"Oh," he replies. He didn't even know his car was here, I realize. He glances around at the group. "A lot of these kids… don't have families anymore," he says. *Because their families don't remember they exist.* "We'll have to take them to my house."

I nod. Maverick definitely has room. "But how do we get them there?"

Maverick doesn't have to respond because someone is pointing. "Look!" a girl says. "We can escape in that!"

I follow her line of sight and there, parked along the edge of the parking lot, is the Suburban. What a convenient reunion.

"Alright. That fixes that. Maverick, your car is parked through the woods, back there," I point. "Take my parents and whoever will fit with you. I'll take the rest in the Suburban. We'll meet at your house."

He nods, then gathers Mom and Dad. The dark-haired girl—Veronica—goes with him, along with two younger boys. The rest of them follow me toward the Suburban. It'll be a tight squeeze, but we'll have to make do.

When I get to it, the boy who had opened the door earlier appears at my hip. "You might need my help with this, too," he tells me. He strides up to the car and touches it. The doors unlock, and the car hums to life.

I stare at him. "What is your name?" I ask him. I think he's someone I want to remember.

"Angelo." He holds out a hand. I hesitate. "Don't worry, I can't hurt *you*," he tells me. So I shake his hand.

Then we all pile into the car and I glance through the rearview mirror at Alice's laboratory, smoking, as I drive us away. She'd locked us inside and sent the entire place up in flames. Her own laboratory, gone just like that. Why would she do that? Was getting rid of me really worth the sacrifice of her entire building? And where is she now?

Wherever she is, we have to find her. And we have to stop her.

Maverick and his group beat us to his house. When we pull up next to the stone fountain, they're already walking inside. I climb out and follow them. Inside the house, Maverick is already talking to Jacob. "Get them all rooms and tell Paula to start some food. Whatever they want, they can have. They've been through a lot."

Jacob nods once, then gets to work, counting the people in the group. Then he takes a young girl and tells her to follow him up the stairs. I wonder if he has questions about who all these kids are and where they came from. But I guess if you get paid enough, you don't really need to ask questions.

"We'll have to explain to them why they're here, once everyone gets settled in," Maverick tells me. "Most of them don't know that their families don't remember them."

"You're right," I reply. That's not going to be an easy task. Then, looking across the room, I spot my parents. Dad looks intense, almost angry, and Mom just looks bewildered. They have no idea where they are, who any of these people are. At least the anomalies know why they were locked up and that they've been rescued. My parents are just blank slates.

What are we going to tell them?

And then, in one moment, I see the answer clearly: we can't tell them anything.

I grab Maverick and pull him into the hallway. "I need to ask a favor," I tell him.

CHAPTER 36

I DRIVE THROUGH THE darkness, the path from Maverick's house to my own almost familiar now. Maverick sits in the passenger seat and my parents are in the back. Dad had questioned me relentlessly about what was going on, why they had been kidnapped, why we weren't going to the police. I told him I was going to explain it all soon, and eventually, he had accepted it. Mom was just quiet, in shock.

Eventually, we reach my house. Maverick gives me a surprised look. "You live near my old house?"

I think of the echo I heard that first night when I originally met Maverick. How that was the moment this whole thing started. "It's how we know each other," I tell him. He looks thoughtful but doesn't reply.

I push the car door open, and Dad stares at me, puzzled. "What does that mean? How do you know where we live?" he asks, and it squeezes my heart.

"I'll explain inside," I reply, knowing that it's a lie. One I wish I didn't have to tell.

When we get inside, I stare at the family photos on the walls. I don't know if we'll ever be that smiling family again.

I turn to Maverick and with all of the courage I can muster, I say, "It's time."

He nods to me, then he walks over to Mom and Dad, who have stopped in the entrance of the kitchen, confused. He places his hands on both of their arms, and I watch as the same look that had appeared in the receptionist's eyes at Alice's office crosses their own.

We lead them upstairs and my parents follow easily, not knowing what's happening, too confused to protest. Maverick maintains his hold on their arms until they're in their room, tucked in bed. He lets go, and they both fall asleep.

When they wake up, they won't remember the past several hours. They won't know I exist.

Alice has already taken away their memories of me. Trying to explain what had happened to them and why—when it had already taken years for me to convince them about my ability to hear the echoes—would be a difficult task. And then what? Would they ever be able to love me the same as they loved the daughter they knew they had raised, the one they remembered? It's impossible to know.

If I just erase myself from their lives, maybe they'll be able to live a happy, normal life. They won't have to bear the weight of all of this craziness, of having a daughter that hears echoes of the past. And maybe they will be safe from Alice, too.

In that moment, I realize that this is probably how Maverick felt when he'd erased my own memories.

It hurts. A lot.

But through the pain, I get to work.

"We have to get rid of everything in the house that shows I exist," I tell Maverick when we're out in the hall.

"I know," he replies. He knows. He's done this before. For Alice. For me, too, though he doesn't remember it.

I go to my room, slide a big box out of the closet. I tear things off the walls, out of drawers. I pack my suitcase, throwing all of my clothes into it in an unorganized, heaping mess. I'm afraid that if I slow down, if I take time to think, I'll lose it.

Maverick helps me, quietly and steadily. He still doesn't know who I am, what we were to each other. I don't know how I'm supposed to explain everything to him when I'm not even sure of it all myself. Before Alice erased his memories, there was barely something developing between us. Now he's been cut out of my life again, and it's impossible to know whether we'll ever be able to rebuild a relationship, or even a friendship.

Within an hour, the house is stripped of me. It's like I never existed here. We'll still have to track down my parents' co-workers, friends, and anyone else who knows about me, but cleaning out the house makes everything feel so final.

I stand in the doorway, holding one last pile of photos I'd torn off the walls. I can't stop the tears now. I can't control them.

"I'm sorry," Maverick's soft voice says from behind me, but he doesn't move closer to hold me like I want him to. Like the

Maverick that knew me would have. I don't face him. I don't want him to see my pain.

"I'm sorry, too," I tell him. "You're just as much of a victim as they are."

"Yeah," he says quietly. "I knew Alice was evil. I didn't know how powerful she was, though."

His words spark a thought in my mind. Alice is powerful because she can heal, making her basically indestructible. Untouchable, even to Maverick, whose ability is powerful enough. I finally turn to look at him, wiping my eyes on my sleeves. "You once told me that you couldn't erase Alice's memories," I say.

He looks exactly like how I felt every time he told me something I didn't remember doing. But he nods. "I can't, it never works on her. I thought it was because she found a way to block it... " His eyes grow wider, filled with a new light of understanding.

"But it's not. It's because she can heal."

"Me erasing her memories is like inflicting little wounds in her brain, but she probably just heals them instantaneously," he adds.

I nod. "And Alice found a way to replicate your ability. Which means—"

"—there must be some way to replicate *her* ability, too."

We stare at each other, trying to figure out what to do with this information.

"If we can figure out how to get it, do you think it will restore my memories? And your parents?" he asks me, bright yellow eyes alive with hope. *And mine*, I add in my mind.

I shrug, but I feel the hope, too. "I think it's definitely possible."

When I walk to the car, a new surge of purpose courses through me. This isn't the end. There's still a way to fix this.

When Maverick gets inside the car, he turns to me, a strange expression crossing his face. "How exactly did we know each other? In what way?" he asks.

I try to squash the sting that comes with his use of the past tense. I ponder the question for a minute because I don't really know the answer myself. "You came over to welcome us to the neighborhood the night we moved here, a little over a year ago. Then we got to know each other. We were… close," I manage.

"Close?" he asks, his eyes boring into me questioningly.

I nod. "We were… together." Is that the right word?

He blinks a few times before responding. "So Alice took my memories away to hurt you. Is that it?"

I'm on the verge of breaking down, but I blink the tears away fiercely. "It's a little more complicated. But essentially, yes," I tell him. And someday, I'm determined to make Alice pay for it.

"Complicated how?"

I don't know where to start. But as I pull the car out of the driveway and as we're driving through the streets, I try my best to explain it to him. How we'd dated for all those months. How once he realized I was in danger, he erased my memories of him. How I hear the echoes, and so I learned of his existence. I tell him about Alice kidnapping us, sneaking into her office, him getting shot, then how we ended up trapped in Alice's laboratory. I leave certain things out—like how angry I'd been at him when I found out he'd taken my memories away, and the searing kiss we'd shared in his kitchen.

When I'm done, I'm breathing hard. As my heart rate calms, I wait for him to respond. Glances over at him tell me he's deep in thought, which makes sense. I remember how I felt when I heard the news. It's difficult to decide how to feel.

When he finally opens his mouth, I expect him to say something about how he understands or he just needs time to process it all. That maybe we can fix all of this if we just figure out where Alice is and how she replicated his ability. But instead, all he does is ask me one, impossible question.

"What do we do now?"

What do we do about Alice? Or what do we do about *us?* Of course, there's no easy answer to either one. But we have to do *something*. Life doesn't ever solve problems for you. You've got to go and solve them yourself.

"We find her. We stop her. We make her fix this," I tell him.

Maverick doesn't look so sure. "I'm not sure if we can. I don't even know where she would be now that her lab's gone."

"We have to try," I reply.

He nods solemnly. "It's weird, that there's this whole part of my life that I don't even remember."

"I understand," I tell him, letting out a short sound somewhere between a laugh and a sigh.

Then, unexpectedly, he asks me another question. "Did I love you?"

The words strangle me. I don't know the answer. I know him better than he knows me right now, but there's no way to know exactly how he felt about me. I know what I want the answer to be.

"I think so," I finally tell him, feeling his yellow eyes boring into me even though I'm staring at the road. It's the best I can do.

He doesn't wait to ask me his next question. He doesn't give me time to think about it. "Did *you* love *me*?"

There's the past tense again. As if he and I aren't sitting in the enclosed space of the car, together, right now. As if everything we had is just stuck somewhere in the echoes, never to be seen in the present again.

Do I love Maverick? Well, we'd dated for eight months. There's definitely got to be some feelings that were lost in those memories. But what about now? We've been through a lot together, but I only remember knowing him for a few weeks. Is that enough time to know if you love someone?

I don't know. All I know is that he had rescued me from danger more times than I could count. I know that when he kissed me, I felt a burning in my heart that was like nothing I'd ever experienced before. And I know that I was devastated when I discovered his memories had been taken away, almost as devastated as when I found my parents in a similar situation.

Is that all it takes to love someone?

I glance over at Maverick, fidgeting with his seat belt. Then I focus my eyes back on the road, my answer coming out firmer, more final than I'd expected it to.

"Yes."

And for the rest of the car ride, neither of us knows what else to say.

* ***** *

WHEN WE GET BACK to the house, the sun is peeking just above the horizon. I roll to a stop in the driveway, forcing myself to accept this new reality.

Inside the house, there are thirteen people who need help. Who need to start a new life or find some way to resume their old ones. Somewhere out in the world, Alice is alive, probably plotting her next scheme, ready to inflict her wrath on someone else. She can't be allowed to do it. She has to be stopped.

I glance over at Maverick as he exits the car. Right now, I want more than anything to be back in my normal life, dealing with only drama between Grace and Leo. I want my parents to remember me. I want Maverick to be there, and I want him to hold me tight, telling me that everything will be okay. I want him to have all the answers like he seemed to have before. I want to live a normal life.

But I can't. All of this mess, with Alice and with Maverick and with my parents—there's no one else who can deal with it.

It's all up to me now.

Read on for a sneak peek at the second installment of the
Echoes Trilogy…

Available Now

))●((

CHAPTER 1

MY KNUCKLES TURN WHITE at the sound of the school bell ringing. This year's bell, last year's bell, and all the bells from the years before layered over each other make me wince.

I used to long for the sound. The same way my peers watched the clock in anticipation of class *ending*, I would count down the minutes until it was time for class to *start*. The bell was a beacon of light in busy hallways and stifling classrooms, signaling the end of the noise: the quieting of both the past and present.

Now, the sound just reminds me of what I am.

As much as I struggled with focusing during class and keeping up with my friends, I still enjoyed going to school. It was the one place where I could pretend to be a little bit normal.

Where I could exist in the world in the same way as other teenagers and feel like maybe I really could pull off a regular life.

But it was just a delusion. A fantasy that I'll never get to live in again.

Not after what Alice did.

We stand near the edge of the parking lot, waiting. The familiar anxiety at what we're about to do washes over me, but this time it's mixed with something else: dread. I know why.

What if I see Grace? Or Leo?

Grace's car is parked at the front of the lot, and Leo's is a few rows behind it, but as the crowds begin to flood out of the school, I pin my gaze to the ground. If I run into either of them, I don't know what I will do. Run away? Ask Maverick to erase their memories of me?

It wouldn't change much if they forgot about me. The last time I spoke with Grace, she made it clear that our friendship was over. I couldn't be there for her when she needed help—because I'd been kidnapped by a crazy psychiatrist who tried to experiment on me, but I couldn't tell her that—and now she blames me for getting grounded and ruining her reputation at school. Leo might have been on my side during all the drama with Grace and Andy, but he was always better friends with Grace (and apparently in love with her), so he wouldn't miss me much.

Beside me, Maverick moves.

"Wait," I say, instinctively reaching to grab his arm, then dropping my hand before it makes contact. He looks back, oblivious to my almost touch. "We should wait until most of the students have left."

I went relatively unnoticed in school, even by some of my teachers, but I don't want to risk the slight chance of running into a classmate I had to do a group project with or sat next to in class. The less everyone from my old life thinks about me, the easier it will be to pull this off.

Maverick nods. "We can go in through the back," he suggests. "It'll take a few minutes to get there, so the hallways should clear out while we walk." Without waiting for an answer, he starts toward the corner of the building where the buses are parked.

I hesitate, glancing back at the parking lot and the staircase connecting it to the school. Students pour down it, happily going home after a long, probably boring day of lectures and tests. What I would give to be among them now.

Ten seconds pass before I shake my head and jog after Maverick. *Stop looking for her. It's over.*

When I catch up, I have the urge to keep jogging until I'm walking next to him, but instead, I trail behind. I want to say something, too—maybe make a joke or ask him a question about his time here at St. Martin High School—but I don't.

Lately, I don't know what to say to him. After his memories of me got erased by Alice, neither of us know how to act around each other. The only thing he knows about me is that we used to be in love before all of this craziness happened, and I'd be lying if I said I knew much more about him. And even though we've spent almost the entire past forty-eight hours together, nothing seems to ease the tense awkwardness that comes with forgetting what we once were.

So we work in silence, and the only thing I can hope for is some way to get his memories—and mine—back so that we can both know how we truly felt about each other before all this happened.

Maverick pauses in front of a door, peers through the window, then tugs it open.

The inside of the school is mostly empty now, with only a few scattered students probably sticking around for an after-school club or making up a test. The past is quiet, too, and we only pass a handful of echoes: footsteps, lockers opening and closing, lingering conversations between friends. Sounds I never thought I'd miss.

Our first stop is Mrs. Andrews's classroom.

I bite the inside of my cheek as we enter, trying hard to swallow the lump in my throat. She's at her desk, typing away at her computer. *Mrs. Andrews.* My bright, always-smiling Chemistry teacher, whose class I'd generally enjoyed. My eyes flick to the desk I'd shared with Grace, but a stab of sorrow hits me and I look away.

Mrs. Andrews glances up, her eyebrows lifting in surprise. Her mouth opens, and she barely has time to utter a curious, "Laura?" before Maverick reaches her, slides his hand across the desk, and touches her wrist.

It always looks so easy. *Too* easy.

I wonder what it feels like, that moment just before the memories drain away. The surprise. The shock. The confusion.

And then… nothing.

She won't remember me. Not the Laura Jones that has been in her class since school started in August nor the Laura Jones standing before her now. She won't remember Maverick or this tiny moment he's spent inside her mind, erasing the image of me from it. Her life will go on, she'll keep teaching classes, and she won't ever think about that girl in her Chemistry class who sat next to Grace Williams and failed the exam she gave last week again.

As if I never even existed.

We make a few more stops at the rest of my teachers' classrooms. Maverick does the job I've asked of him— wordlessly, quickly, thoroughly. Then we have to deal with the office. Erase my name from the records and make sure the school won't call my parents when I don't show up anymore. A few of my peers probably still have vague memories of me, but it's impractical and unnecessary to track down every single one of them. It won't raise too much suspicion if some of them do remember me, anyway. No one knew me well enough to care if I never show up again.

Except for Grace and Leo. I wonder if they'll come looking for me once they notice I'm not coming to school anymore. After the drama that went down the past few weeks, I doubt it. I should probably just have Maverick erase their memories of me, too, but I can't bring myself to ask him just yet. They'd been my only friends, and a small, selfish, probably irrational part of me wants to believe that they still are.

The old Maverick—the one whose memories of me hadn't been erased yet—would have remembered them. He might have insisted that we deal with them, too, so they won't start asking questions that might lead back to my parents and cause a lot of confusion. But the new Maverick has no idea that they exist.

I try to convince myself that that's a good thing.

Outside of the main office, we wait for my guidance counselor, Mr. Aldus, to exit. When he does, Maverick falls into step behind him, reaching up to press a finger to the bare skin on the back of his neck. He falters for a moment, the tiniest hesitation, then continues out the door without looking back.

Sometimes, when Maverick erases people's memories, they become so disoriented that they pass out. It depends on how many memories he has to take, though, so with my teachers and the people I didn't spend a ton of time with, they usually only become confused for a moment before returning to whatever they were doing. With family members and close friends, we have to be more careful about where we are when he takes their memories.

In the office, there are only two workers still at their desks. All it takes Maverick is a quick brush of the arm for them to forget we've even walked past them. We head for Mr. Aldus's office and Maverick sits down at the desk. It takes a few minutes for him to get into St. Martin's online record database—something he's apparently done before, back when he was working for Alice—so while he works, I sift through the filing cabinets. Mr. Aldus is on the brink of retirement, and he's always had a deep mistrust of technology, so he keeps hard copies of all of his records. I pluck mine out, daring to peek inside.

My school photo is paper-clipped to the first page, which has some basic information about me. I'd transferred from my old school a little over a year ago, so the file is relatively slim. It includes class schedules of the past three semesters, a summary of the credits I'd earned, my report cards, and a couple of notes from my bi-annual meetings with Mr. Aldus.

My eyes drift over a note he'd scribbled down during one of our meetings.

Lacks direction for plans after high school. Needs to figure out a possible career path.

My lips pull into a thin line.

For years, I stressed over what to do after high school. College wasn't really a good option, not with the echoes constantly interrupting my life. I'd decided that online schooling was the best route if I wanted to get a higher education, but what would I study? What career path could I possibly take with my ability to hear the past always there to hinder me? A librarian? A programmer? An office assistant? None of them sounded like things I wanted to pursue.

If only I had known that disappearing from existence and setting out to hunt down an evil superhuman was the true path my life would veer onto.

"I think that's it." Maverick's voice cuts through the quiet room, startling me.

I swallow, tucking the files back into the folder and holding it to my chest. "I got the hard copies, too."

He nods, logging out of the computer. "I think we've covered everything that might affect you here."

I run through the mental list of people we've crossed off. We spent yesterday traveling to Drenville to erase my grandparents' memories of me and clear the photos and memorabilia out of their house. Today, we'd stopped by my parents' workplaces to remove my existence from their lives there. Everything from desk photos to computer backgrounds to their co-workers' memories of me was gone now.

When Alice erased my parents' memories of me, I didn't have a lot of options. I could have told them the truth, tried to convince them that I was their daughter and that impossible things—like memory erasing and hearing echoes of the past—really do exist. But I'd spent seventeen years trying to get them to understand the echoes, and I realized it would be easier if I just disappeared from their lives until we find a way to restore their memories.

Easier for them, at least. Not for me.

With each person we take memories from, the knot in my stomach curls tighter. And I hate it. Hate how my life has been ripped from me. Hate how helpless I feel when it comes to fixing it.

"Thanks," I tell Maverick, though the word tastes bitter in my mouth. "I hope we haven't forgotten anything."

"I don't think so," Maverick says, standing. "But if we run into any problems, I can always fix them."

The statement is so matter-of-fact, so simple and terribly accurate. If anyone asks my parents about me, tries to find me, or starts to get suspicious about why I'm no longer around, Maverick can easily deal with the problem. I'd watched him confidently work his way through my parents' workplaces, reaching to shake hands with curious strangers, brushing arms with passersby, draining thoughts and memories from unsuspecting victims. It would be so simple. So easy to erase me from my parents' lives again.

I have to blink away the tears that form in my eyes.

"Good to know," I reply, clutching the folder to my chest as I speed walk out of the office.

When we get outside, a blast of freezing air stings my face, and I welcome the shiver that crawls down my spine. It's a nice distraction from my thoughts.

But soon enough, it's gone, and I'm sitting in the front seat of Maverick's car with hot air blasting through the vents as we head for our next destination. The next person who will forget about me.

We've still got to visit family friends, neighbors, and a storage unit full of photos, my childhood keepsakes, and whatever else we need to get rid of.

Beside me, Maverick is silent. We're so close, his hand resting on the shifter mere inches from my own. I long to reach out, to hold it, to be caught by those golden eyes and that flirtatious smile that had just begun to feel familiar before Alice ruined everything.

But even in this car, even in the nearness, he's still so far away.

ACKNOWLEDGMENTS

FIRST OF ALL, I want to say a huge thanks to you, the person holding this book. However you ended up here, and wherever you are, *thank you.* Books wouldn't do any good without readers, so you're an essential part of the equation.

Secondly, I want to say thanks to my best friend Briana. Your constant support and belief in me all the way from the beginning in my melodramatic high school days has kept me going throughout the years. I couldn't have finished this without you. May you always be the first person I send my stories to, even when they aren't very good yet.

Mom, thanks for instilling a love of reading into me from a very young age, and for driving me to the library every few days while I was growing up to get another stack of books. If you hadn't encouraged that little hobby of mine, I might've never taken on writing.

Thanks to Dad, who passed down the genes I needed to have the brain of a writer, and who always supported me when I told you I was writing. I still remember those "books" I used to write when I was a kid, and your reminders of my desire to be an author even then helped me stay motivated.

Thanks to Michele, whose self-publishing adventure inspired me to take that step myself. When I first learned that you were writing a book, I hadn't written in years, but that night I pulled out my laptop and started scanning through my old stuff. Little did I know I'd find the rough beginning of this book in that pile, and a year later would have a fully completed novel from it.

Thanks to Joe, who actually made time to read (most of) this book when I told you about it, even after you haven't read a book in like 20 years. Also thanks for trying to help me with my grammar, even though almost every time you were completely wrong. It made me laugh.

Shoutout to Michele, Denise, Carole, and Wendy, the wonderful ladies that make up the Southern Scribblers, and whose writing continues to inspire me.

Thanks to Shawna, who helped me take the emotional healing journey I needed to take before I could get this book out there. You've changed my perspective on life in so many ways, and I'm so excited to be doing this self-publishing journey with you!

And last, but certainly not least, thanks to Jacob. Thanks for taking that night job at the hotel, which sparked my sleepless nights and therefore the beginning of this book. Thanks for all of the wonderful ideas you come up with any time I write, even though I don't use most of them. I'm putting them in the quiver for later, I promise.

ABOUT THE AUTHOR

Marissa decided early on that she never wanted to grow up, so she became an author of young adult novels. When she isn't writing her own books or reading everything she can get her hands on, you can usually find her somewhere in the outdoors admiring nature or curled up on the couch playing The Legend of Zelda.

Visit www.MarissaLete.com for updates on her latest writing ventures!

If you enjoyed this book, please consider leaving a review.
Reviews are vital in getting books from independent authors
into the hands of readers.

Some key places you can leave an honest review are:

Amazon
Goodreads
BookBub